HELL WILL RISE
Book 1
The Bloodthirst Mafia Series

Editors
Amy Podejko
Rebecca Swanson

EBOOK ISBN 978-0-9958306-1-5
PAPERBACK ISBN 978-0-9958306-2-2

Printed in the USA.

Cover Design and Interior Format
© THE KILLION GROUP INC

HELL WILL RISE

SKYLA MURPHY

My name is hunter garciez.
But I see we've already met.
Your eyes are reading my demons.
Through the print of my alphabet.
I summon you to my misery.
I welcome you to my regret.
I invite you to know my story.
And all the tears I've bled.
But before you flip my pages.
I feel I must advise.
When wicked comes at dawn break…

HELL WILL FUCKING RISE.

CHAPTER INDEX

"Hell is empty.
All the devils are here."

W. Shakespeare

THE HAND OF THE SYNDICATE

HUNTER GARCIEZ

Friday. 9:30 P.M.

I SLID INTO THE FRONT SEAT of the murderer's car, shutting a door as black as night behind me. The other men had already climbed into the bench seat in the rear, joking around like we were on our way to paradise. None of their bodies were conveying any indication of anxiety. Mine, on the other hand, hadn't stopped twitching for weeks now.

A dark energy lofted from the Mexican bigot next to me. Pity, grief, and shame were three concepts that a radical like him just couldn't come to grips with. His soul had been contaminated at birth by a demonic hate for everything, everyone, and even their little dogs too. The mouths that danced on the streets of Cali liked to refer to him as Grimsaw Santiago. For those of us who knew him personally, we referred to him as mentally unstable instead.

He was a great felon. Before faking American citizenship, he'd spent years practicing criminalities in the heat and heart of Mexico. He knew any gun you could list. Despite being psychotically deranged, the lunatic had managed to make it to the age of thirty without ever getting caught. This said enough in itself.

Currently, the only thing I had going for myself was that I sat perched on his team. By entering his car, I was fastening my eternity. I was sealing the consequences of my choices; the choices I had made to protect my little sister; the choices I had made after burying my parents just weeks ago; the choices I now had to live with.

Grimsaw's eyes began to dilate with excitement. With one look at him, I could see the blood he'd thieved during his days of being faithful to the mafia. I wasn't yet certain of the abhorrence I had linked myself to, but there was no time for me to mull it over now. I had already taken a seat beside him.

He pushed his boot against the gas pedal. Since he was mentally wrecked, it seemed fitting that his driving was no less. He swerved his old Chevelle in and out of traffic, speeding through tightly knitted convoys along the Southern Freeway, and I knew I wouldn't like where we were headed. I'd only known the front-runner for a month now, but it had taken me merely seconds to understand his stigma. Grimsaw wasn't someone you wanted to piss off. If you valued your life at all, you obliged and did everything he requested of you instead.

"I become very irritable when people disobey me," he threatened, aiming his warning in my direction. "I don't just get angry, Garciez. I always get even. If you're a smart man, you'll remember that."

The guys in the car exploded with laughter. The sound echoed off the roof like nails on a chalkboard, penetrating my ear canals like a colony of red ants. There wasn't another word spoken until Grimsaw set the manual transmission into neutral.

As he jerked upward on the emergency break, I stared at the storage unit ahead of us; the one sitting with a cockeyed, orange door. He hurriedly slid out of the driver's seat while feeding me a venomous glare. I knew this implied I should follow him, but to hell if any part of me wanted to.

"This place looks old as shit, *brah*," Antonio spoke to me from behind. "I doubt this storage block has any cameras. I don't know about you, but I'd like to avoid the pen if possible."

"Mistaken belief, *brah*," I clipped back, hating the way they all spoke. "Getting thrown into lockdown wouldn't be the worst thing to happen to any of us."

"Then what would be?"

"Sitting on your mom's doorstep in the morning beside her

subscription to the *San Francisco Chronicles*, laying chopped to bits in a garbage bag," I answered blandly, giving a dry smirk to match.

"Get out of the fucking car," Raphael instructed, dropping a slap against the back of my head.

Every part of me wanted to break his dark hand for touching me, but his fingers were too fat to crush. Aside from that, Raph was Grimsaw's main bitch. I had to watch what lines I crossed.

I mimicked Grimsaw and climbed out, internally wishing I could be anywhere else. I tugged the lever to tilt the passenger seat forward, allowing the three guys in the back of the car to exit in sequence. Having no real voice in the matter, we all followed our leader toward the storage cube.

There were two things that Grimsaw hated the most about me. Firstly, I was a half-breed. In his racist mind, being half Caucasian did nothing but weaken me down. He viewed anything less than fully Mexican skin as useless paper that should be shredded.

Secondly, being born and raised in California like I had been, he saw me as beach slew. It didn't matter that my dad had been involved with the mob before death had tracked him down. It didn't matter that I had been raised by a criminal. Grimsaw had labeled me as a cautiously cradled American softie, and I couldn't deny this accusation either. Compared to him, a softie was exactly what I was.

Unless you had previously hustled drugs for the worst cartel of Coahuila, Grimsaw would say you didn't belong in his violent tribe. Unless you had rivaled the military in the region of Tamaulipas, you had no backbone or sense of civilian pride. Unless you had once sold a fistful of *chicas* down in the heart of Sonora, you were as weak as Christ on the cross. Unless you had earned the price of homicide in Guerrero, you weren't much more than smeared shit on the sidewalk.

"I'd ask you to look away while I punch in the code, but I'm sure you already know it..." Grimsaw's gaze flew into mine, and I knew exactly what he meant. "You ready to see what's lurking behind the orange, ése?"

While he began to type the passcode in, I didn't watch his fingers work against the buttons. Like he figured, I already knew the digits.

I stared at the chipped paint decorating the metal door, sensing

I wasn't fully prepared for the brutality I was about to lunge into. The orange gate began to slide open with a creak. Each of us stared upward, waiting until the gate had finished scrolling to the end of the pulley system before walking beneath the deathtrap.

Inside the unit, a black tarp covered a high pile. The contents weren't suggestive in shape, but I didn't need a warning label to tell me that I wasn't standing in a chocolate factory. Nothing sweet would be found here.

"*Cierre la puerta!*" Grimsaw ordered for someone to shut the door.

"I'm on it," Antonio obeyed his command. Tony and I were the youngest of the group, making us the weakest too.

"This is where the fun begins, Garciez," Grimsaw smiled at me. "I ain't gonna demand too much from you. This task shouldn't take you and Tony more than a few hours to complete. I hope you brought an extra t-shirt, though… it's gonna get a little messy."

As the psychopath removed the polyethylene covering, the oxygen in the room vacuumed to the lowest space of my lungs. The smell of sweat and blood began to permeate the air around me, layering the room with the coldness of death. If it weren't for the goosebumps pursuing my body like a poisonous fungus, I might have sworn the past month had been nothing more than a nightmare.

The dead bodies before me were… *misshapen*. Their faces were contorted, as if they had died in mid-scream. I could imagine the pain they had endured with just one look. Their arms were laying bent, legs snapped beyond repair, eyes open and lifeless. Their faces were relaxed, but nothing was peaceful about any of it.

I tried to keep the sludge in my stomach down. It wasn't in my best interest to show emotion around these crooks, but I couldn't silence the demands of my body. As I vomited on the cement flooring by my feet, flashes of my old life began to pang against the back of my closed eyelids; visions of a life I had once loved; visions of a happy existence; a life I could have made something with; a life that was nothing more than a vague memory now.

Now, I was a mafia man.

That was all I would ever be.

I knew it would be my job to clean up Grimsaw's hurricane. It would be job to get rid of the bloodstains and dispose of the remnants; the remnants of men who'd had families; families who would never know what had happened to their fathers, brothers, or husbands; families that would never get a reprieve from the haunting unknown; families that would never be alleviated from the what-ifs.

One wrong move…

This could be me.

"Tough sight to see?" Grimsaw asked me. "I know you're used to seeing numbers everywhere you look, but I sense murder isn't a common protocol in your life. That'll be an easy fix, though. You'll become desensitized soon enough. This is how I take a soldier and turn him into something of value. You're rolling on my crew now."

If eyes were the windows of the soul, it was clear that Grimsaw had been born drenched with malicious intent. What I felt in this moment was conflicting. Obeying him was the only way I knew how to protect my little sister, but I had never destroyed lives like I was about to. I didn't want to be *this* person; the person who made bodies disappear.

I clenched my jaw tightly, aiming to limit what words I spoke aloud. Alongside the monsters these guys were, I may as well have been a six-year-old with the bad habit of chewing on my fingernails. I felt queasy, but Grimsaw's expression was steadfast. After all, this was what I had asked him for; a life owned by the syndicate. I had signed myself up for this hell to protect one person; my little sister. If I hadn't needed help when it came to adopting her, I wouldn't be staring at a pile of carcasses right now.

With Grimsaw, my main bargaining chip had been the forfeit of my freedom. To protect the blood of my sister, he was about to force me to clean up the red of many others. A yellow chainsaw sat in the corner of the cube, waiting to fulfill its duties.

"Raph will come back for you in a few hours," Grimsaw grinned cruelly. Behind his smile, there was a soul who lived for violence. "Skin and disjoin their bodies. Separate their bones from flesh. Grind their teeth into powder. There better not be a drop of DNA left after you two are done cleaning this herd up. I won't be happy if I gotta send in somebody else to fix up your failures. Do you little monkeys understand me?"

"Got it, boss," Tony answered for the both of us.

I was thankful when he did, because no part of me had been

planning to. At this point, there was little I could say. My strings were snapping on the inside, and I couldn't ignore the moans coming from the stacked pile of bodies next to me. It was apparent that some of the victims were still alive.

"Sounds like I left you a few squealers," Grimsaw laughed, evil shading the brown in his eyes. "I enjoy the act of punishing, but I don't care to see if their pulses are still kicking when I'm done with them. That's what I got you maggots for. Don't let me down, Garciez."

With that, he and his two sidekicks left the storage facility through a two-foot-wide crack beneath the bottom panel of the door. Once they had shut the metal behind themselves, Tony turned to give me a light tap on the back.

"Your first ten bodies will be the worst, but all we're doing is putting the injured out of their misery. Even the ones who are still alive in the pile are wishing they weren't. One way or another, they're all going to die. We may as well bring an end to their suffering sooner rather than later."

"They had families."

Three words were all I could manage. I had grown accustomed to routine nausea over the past month, but I didn't think anybody could familiarize themselves with the smell of carnage and slaughter.

"They probably did," Tony agreed grimly, staring at the pile with the same repulsion I was. "But you've got to disengage yourself from humanity. You can't act weak in front of Grimsaw. Torturing is in his nature. You're either on his side or against him. Do you want to be laying in his next load of slayed bodies?"

I shook my head. "No."

"Then create a switch in your mind. From here on out, you're two people. Garciez #1 is the normal you. Garciez #2 is the psychotic you. Segregate them from one another. You can't allow your personalities to tango."

He stalked across the room to open a red duffel bag. After pulling out two plastic suits, he passed me one while surveying my face. I accepted what he offered, watching as he slipped into his own plastic suit, conforming when he nodded for me to do the same.

"When I first met Grimsaw, my mom was a hundred grand in debt," Tony continued. "She's got a bad case of pancreatic cancer.

That's the only reason I'm here. You and I aren't all that different, Garciez. We each got a sad story, but that doesn't matter to a guy like Grim."

The way Tony was talking was rare for his character. He'd refrained from using the word '*brah*' since Grimsaw and his boys had left us alone in the bloody unit. Come to think of it, he'd dropped his moronic front entirely.

I had a list of questions for him, but only one managed to reach the tip of my bitten tongue. A question I really needed the answer to. I had only just joined their gang a month ago, but it terrified me to think of who I might be after a few years of involvement in their illegal operations.

"How do you live with yourself?" I asked.

A sadness washed over his features, features as young as mine, but he reflexively brushed it aside just as fast. While giving a shrug of his shoulders, he threw a pair of latex gloves at my chest.

"I chew pills like they're candy," he confessed. "Narcotics help me to contort what's real and what's not. At the very least, they help me to suppress the truth. I create a stupid version of myself intentionally. The smarter Grimsaw knows you are, the more he'll begin to expect from you. He already knows you can see numbers through our pupils. Do you think it's wise for you to add to that?"

"There wasn't anything I could do to keep the truth from him," I frowned. "He knew about my dad's mental condition. He knew I had inherited it. Why do you think he let me join the gang in the first place? It wasn't my looks that landed me here."

If you were to research the definition of *psychometry*, you would find something similar to the following; an extrasensory perception that becomes kindled upon the touching of an object. It is the ability to steal information about someone by holding one of their possessions.

Me, I was born a different case. I didn't need to touch anything. My abilities didn't rest in my hands. To see someone's personal information, all I had to do was stare into their pupils. One deep glimpse was all it took for me to rob an identity. Grimsaw knew this.

The science of math played a heavier role in my upbringing than it did in most. It came naturally to me at a young age, more than it had to the lady sitting beside you in the coffee shop or on the train. Numbers have designed me, constructing me since I was a child. From a young age, I had been calculating the answers to far more sophisticated equations than I should have been. With a photographic memory, I had been slated to end up a hacker. I had graduated high school as the Valedictorian of my class just last month, but I'd never been meant to go very far.

My abilities were comparable to the way a cop could run a criminal record check at the drop of a dime. Whenever a Fed typed a name into the government's search engine, all information regarding their person of interest popped up without hesitation. Much like that, a digitalized hologram presented itself to me willingly upon visual contact with another individual.

I could see their phone numbers, driver's license digits, stock holdings, bank figures, pin numbers, home security passwords, their website data, even their vehicle entry codes. I could see everything they'd ever needed to know in numerical format; *everything they wouldn't want me to.* As strange as this seemed to everybody else, it couldn't be any more normal to me.

"It doesn't matter how Grimsaw found out about your abilities. What's important here is that he knows," Tony brought me back from my thoughts. "Anyone connected to this side of the mafia has heard about you and your old man. Your visual powers make you feared, but they also make you a flashing neon target on the streets. Everyone wants to see what you can do. On one hand, this could keep you alive longer. On the other, it might put you in a grave faster."

"What the fuck was I supposed to do?" My words glided out harshly, flaming with misdirected aggression. "I'm a spitting image of my dad. With one look at me, Grimsaw knew exactly who I was."

"You knew how highly respected Emiliano Garciez was in this business. You should have done something to alter your appearance before you came to ask Grimsaw for a job. You should have done something to shield your genetics. Instead, you left your freakish talents on display for everyone to see. You better hope that wasn't a lethal falter on your part. You stand out too much. In the sea of the mafia, that isn't what you want."

"My dad didn't hold back when telling people what his eyes could do. He hacked and piloted for the mafia for years before he died," I argued, fighting a battle that wasn't even worth the war. "It might work to my advantage too."

"Your dad was sold to the Mexican underground at the age of ten by drug-addicted parents. You're eighteen and only just entering this life. Are you really comparing yourself to him?"

"Everything I know, I know it because of him."

"True." An amused smirk began to dance on Tony's upper lip. "People have been talking about you since the day you stepped foot in the warehouse. You're the kid who can see everything about us by glancing in our eyes. You're the kid who was receiving military training to become a helicopter pilot. You received a full scholarship to aviation school. Rather than taking it, once your parents were murdered, you became involved with the gang to save your little sister from foster care instead. You're the kid who had a future and fucked it all up. I fucked up mine too, but most of these guys never even had one. Your dad sure didn't. Right from the age of ten, this life was all he knew. He was bound to die through mafia entanglement. The same faction will claim our lives too. By joining the brotherhood, we've committed to a premature death. We've signed our names beside eternal damnation."

"I couldn't let my sister wind up at a creepy shack in the woods with a couple who was only looking for a monthly paycheck." I stared at my feet, diverting my gaze from his. "You chose this life to pay for your mom's medical bills. How is that any different than what I'm doing for my sister?"

"Because I'm a nobody. I don't have the legendary name you do. When I walk into the warehouse, half of those guys don't even know my name. I can fly under the radar without much issue. As Emiliano Garciez's only son, you'll never be able to. When you walk in, everybody goes stiff; even Grimsaw. He might not show it, but you terrify him. You've got a dangerous fame attached to you. If you aren't cautious, that fame will get your throat slit. Keep your friends close and your enemies closer."

"I'd rather have those guys scared of me versus the opposite," I shrugged, seeing my oddities as a positive attribute instead of a negative. "You make it sound like I'm the only one with problems here, but you're a pill popper."

"What else could keep me sane? A woman?" Tony scoffed at the thought. "The pills keep me from testing out suicide. They are my only love. As the hand of time continues to click forward, prepare for them to become yours too."

"I'm not a druggie."

"Not yet, but nobody makes it through this shit sober. Take a good look around you." Tony held up his hand, motioning toward the mound of bleeding men. "Think about what you're about to become. Not who... *what*. You don't get a white picket fence and a hot wife anymore. Moving forward, all you'll be concerned with is staying alive. I had a good girl when I locked myself into this mess. You got one?"

"I fuck without commitment."

"With a pretty boy face like that, I figured as much," he chuckled. "But it won't be long before you forget what it's like to feel altogether. Your soul will begin to bleed black. After that, you won't care about slamming pussy. You won't even feel worthy of a woman's touch."

"I somehow doubt that," I muttered.

I didn't want to believe him, but maybe Tony was right. After all, what kind of girl would want to sleep with a guy who deconstructed corpses for a living? What kind of girl would want to get a monster off in her bed?

"You're better off alone," Tony claimed. "You've officially been tainted by the hand of the syndicate. You've positioned yourself in the pathway of Grimsaw's destruction. In the final explosions of it all, there ain't no two ways about it. From here on out, everyone you love will die."

Ominous shudders crept down my spine. I stared at his shorter stance, keeping cautious when asking, "What happened to your girl? You took a split from her?"

"You could say that," he nodded, raising his sorrowful vision to meet mine. "What we're doing here is easy. We don't know these men. We might lose a piece of our soul with every body we slice apart, but initiations are the truly challenging aspect of mafia life. Initiations are when what *you* love gets taken from you. Grimsaw made me choose between killing my girl and my mom."

"And...?" I cringed.

"And I've always been a mama's boy."

THREE YEARS LATER

"Give me my Romeo;
And, when he shall die,
Take him and cut him out in little stars.
And he will make the face of heaven so fine,
That all the world will be in love with night."

Juliet Capulet

1
THE ANTAGONIST OF MY REALITY

SHAYLA STONE

Wednesday. 5:00 P.M.

I CARVED THE NEXT X INTO the concrete wall of my cell, stashed away in the depths of somewhere much like hell. If my tallies were accurate, it was Wednesday again today; my twenty-first day of captivity.

Dried blood was splattered on the concrete flooring of my new home. Some of the red was undoubtedly mine, but many other droplets were evidence of prior struggles. The dried handprints along the walls were telling me the stories of many other slaves before me. All in a row, our bloody prints depicted a painting of a morbid reality. My handprint was the last in line.

Three weeks had passed since I'd tasted more than blood and saltine crackers. Three weeks had passed since I'd showered, turned eighteen, and had then said goodbye to my freedom forever. Three weeks had passed since the thugs had given me my first tattoo. And now, whether I managed to escape from this prison or not, a barcode would mark me indefinitely.

My identification number was 40347. I had memorized the digits within moments of staring at the unwanted code on my right wrist. I had memorized everything right down to the dirty needle. My barcode had become infected now, just like I'd anticipated it would, leaving me certain of one detail; whoever chose to abuse me would consequently become infected with whatever diseases I had. For participating in such a masochistic scheme, it would serve the motherfucker(s) right.

My friends had been with me that night during spring break. We'd been out celebrating my eighteenth birthday on the grass down by the marina. Since most of us were attending different colleges come fall, inevitably vanishing from each other's lives one by one, we'd made a pact to make good use of the time we had left together. Little did any of us know, when I had insisted I was fine to make the short walk home alone that night, it would be the last time they would ever see me.

I pressed my ear to the cell door. A slab of closed steel was blocking my only exit, making it difficult to hear the voices chattering in the distance. It wasn't until the men footed closer that I managed to make their words out. Once I could, I wished I couldn't.

"Rows of whores…" The voice sounded like the man I had woken up to on my first day of captivity. "But it's that blonde bitch who caught my eye. Once Garciez finds out who she is, the white girl will be dead within hours."

I stared at the mats in my blonde hair, suddenly wishing I'd been born a brunette. This week had been the absolute worst so far. My hallucinations had kicked into overdrive, a cause of low blood sugar and dehydration. But in this moment, I was aware of my fever. Another few days, maybe even just hours, I wasn't confident my sanity would still prevail.

I wanted to believe this was just a nightmare. I hoped I was in a parallel universe, in a hospital bed, maybe even in a coma. I prayed this was just a sick plot my unconscious had stirred up. That all seemed better than this reality; the reality where an ice-cold floor was my new home.

I didn't have much to compare being locked in captivity to, but I'd seen movies of this type of thing. In Hollywood, the lead female always gets rescued. A timidly sweet girl generally plays the role, perfect in all the right areas. Unlike her, I was far from timid and even further from perfect. I carried a chip on my shoulder; a chip that only came from nearly dying of cancer.

My world had been semi-normal before this. My mother had passed away when I was twelve from breast cancer, but I can still remember her clearly. Just after her death, I had been diagnosed with a different variety. Unlike her, I had managed to triumph in my war against Leukemia.

My father had raised me up until this point, and I had just been accepted into Berkeley University to obtain my lifelong dream of a Psychiatry degree. I'd initially had my sights set on Harvard, but my dad had nearly dropped dead upon my mention of it. Harvard was on the opposite side of the country, making his fears relatable, but it didn't matter now. University was the least of my concerns.

I wished the cells had bars. The steel door made it impossible to match faces to any of the voices, though there was a positive to this obstruction too. If I couldn't see them, they couldn't see me. With any luck, the criminals might just forget about me. This thought occurred to me...

Until my door began to slide open.

Three men appeared on the opposite side of the threshold. Grimsaw Santiago stood in the middle; the scariest thug of all. The sadistic smile staining his face did anything but make me feel at ease.

I slithered along the concrete floor, tucking my body deeper into the corner of my container. As they licked their lips like wild wolves, their eyes shamelessly scanned over my trembling form. If they were the savage beasts, my weakened body was merely one thing; raw steak.

One of them was tall, bald, and overweight. I'd learned his name to be Raphael. He had dark skin and eyes, a mean face, bad teeth, and his chunky gut was trying to break free from a pair of blue coveralls. As far as I could tell, Raphael was the only member of the gang who wasn't Mexican.

In the center of Raphael and a dirty man I didn't recognize, Grimsaw's head was shaven to a light buzz. The goatee on his face had been groomed with precision. A black t-shirt was slung over his bulky torso, while an expensive pair of jeans hid his legs below. He had dark brown eyes; eyes that would smile while killing you. He was dressed clean, but I knew he was far from hygienic. Disgusting would be a more suitable adjective.

"Guess how much I just made off your fine ass, *chica*?" Grimsaw asked, as if this was a carnival ride I had willingly placed myself onto. I was half expecting him to make me guess his weight next. Sad to say, if a capful of water were to be my winning prize, that'd be one game I might play with the creep.

"Ten thousand?"

They laughed in synchronization, indicating I was nowhere close to guessing my worth. Their faces warned me that my life was about to be enveloped by a blackness; a territory I had no choice but to enter. What Grimsaw wanted, he would get. This fact lofted from the mobster.

"An old man picked you out of the pamphlet specifically. He even paid for rushed delivery," Grimsaw explained in his accent. "Trust me when I say this, Barbie. It'll all be much easier if you just take what's coming to you silently. He owns you now, so you may as well get used to it."

I shook. I didn't want to hear that I was being exhibited in a demented magazine for the rich to swipe through while enjoying their morning coffee. In this secret world, the wealthy got to decide whose life would be ruined next. As it turned out, today was my day to step into fire.

"She's gonna go wasted," Raphael frowned. "You should let one of us touch her before Garciez gets his hands on her. All he's gonna do is kill her."

"*La niña es una virgen,*" Grimsaw told his friend that my value was connected to my virginity. "Besides, Raph, you wouldn't even know what to do with her. You're so fat, I bet you can't even see your own dick when you piss."

Grimsaw refocused my way. The leader didn't suspect a girl like me could understand the Spanish language, especially not as well as I did. My skin didn't show any trace of it, but my father had been born and raised in the slums of Mexico.

Since I was doomed to die regardless, I figured I may as well give the crooks some attitude on my way to hell. Smiling sweetly like they wanted me to, in their choice of language, I announced, "*Ninguno de ustedes son dignos de amor.*"

They all stared at me incredulously as I declared none of them were worthy of love. With tightened eyebrows, it was Grimsaw who chose to speak first.

"We don't want love, bitch. We want fat stacks of cash, and you just brought that in for us. No matter what happens to you now, whether you die or not, I've made my money off you."

His sneer held a vicious undertone. It was an undertone that told me I would never see my father again. After being kidnapped like I was, taken on a night that should have held good memories, I knew my dad would be searching for me. His life would be filled with sleepless nights and endless phone calls. He would be tracking the gang down. He would be lining something up with the cops. He wouldn't allow me to disappear without a fight.

"Why are you doing this?" I forced the words from my mouth. My throat felt like sandpaper, but it wasn't enough to silence me. "How heartless you must be."

"Heartless people do things without reasoning. Me, I always have a reason." Grimsaw placed his hand over his begrimed heart. "I'm not heartless; I'm *cruel*. Every villain has a background, Barbie. Every psychopath has a motive. Even if a serial killer only slays for enjoyment, that still counts as purpose in his mind. There's a reason antagonists do what they do. That's exactly what I am to you; the antagonist of your reality."

"Antagonist is a big word for a gangster," I ruffled his feathers. "I knew the Mexican cartel hustled drugs. I knew you liked to push cocaine and guns, but I didn't think human slavery was a typical trait."

"Now you know better."

As I took a hard look at his face, I noticed how hooked his nose was. I could just imagine the amount of people who'd broken down and punched the wolf. In the end, they had most likely died for the maneuver. Foolishly, this thought didn't keep my tongue from lashing, "Was it daddy issues that turned you so callous?"

"That's something you and the rest of America will never know," Grimsaw sustained his cold smirk. "The who's and the what's aren't gonna come out just yet. If I gave you the details this fast, it would ruin the fun of my little game. You'll learn what I want you to learn, only when I want you to learn it. As of right now, I will allow you to know that you were worth two and a half million dollars. The bidding war got intense."

On that note, he threw a red dress at me. The skimpy outfit smacked me in the face, seeming to be missing half its fabric. Just the sight of it made me want to burn it. I didn't need Einstein to tell me what he wanted me to do with it.

"I'm not wearing—"

"Garciez will like it."

"Is that who bought me?" I rolled my eyes, masking my fear like a professional. "You can dress me up like your little Barbie. You can try to present the illusion that I'm a prim and proper bombshell, but I'll still spit in his face like a classless whore when I meet him. After all, a whore is what you've sold me to be."

All three of them laughed, as if they genuinely got a rise out of me. It was difficult to read where any of their emotions sat. Even while grins were impacting their lips, they still came across as hollow and empty inside.

"G would never spend money on a bitch like you," Grimsaw answered. "He flicks broads away from him like bugs. I've watched him turn down models from Paris, even slutty ones from Hollywood. You, California beach slew, ain't nothing more than the test I have for him."

"Explain the test."

"My boy's been making some sly jokes behind my back. I can't understand it, because I gave him everything he needed when he was forced to adopt his baby sister. Unfortunately for you, Garciez doesn't seem to remember that. As the General of this operation, sometimes I gotta throw on the witch's hat and remind everyone who the fuck they're dealing with."

"What do I have to do with him?" I kept my palms pressed to the ground, prepared to kick my feet if they approached any closer. "I don't even know this guy."

"You might not, but G's parents were murdered three years ago. Wanna take a stab at who killed them? I'll give you a hint; it was somebody close to you."

"The only person I'm close to is my father," I gave a haughty laugh, but Grimsaw's face told me I wasn't far off with my guess. "That's impossible. My dad isn't like you. He isn't a murderer. I don't believe a word you're saying."

As far as I knew, my dad was the second in command to the CEO of a popular marketing agency in downtown San Francisco. Marketing brought in wealth, making the prodigious level in his bank account seem normal. I knew he had connections to people in suits, but I strongly doubted he associated with the mafia.

"No sweat off my back," Grimsaw chuckled, enjoying the way he could generate misery. "Garciez doesn't know who killed his parents. When he drives your ass to Vegas, you'll have six hundred miles to decide if you're gonna tell him or not. G is the least vio-

lent of us all, because he is the youngest, but even he might make
you disappear. Once he learns the ties you hold to his family, there
ain't no telling what he'll do. He's wanted revenge for three years,
never quite sure where to find it. In the game we're gonna play
tomorrow, blonde revenge will be seated beside him in the passenger seat."

While the lead thug cracked his neck from side to side, I scurried mentally like a lab rat. If my father had killed Garciez's parents,
which was as farfetched as an idea could come, retribution could
easily be gained by killing me. Even though I didn't buy into
Grimsaw's words, I knew I held no chance at freedom. I had long
come to accept this, but keeping my life at all seemed improbable
now too. I had predicted something worse than captivity would
inevitably come my way. I had been anticipating this very moment,
but there was no way I could have properly prepared for it.

"You're pathetic. You sell girls for paychecks," I slandered, knowing it wasn't productive on my behalf. "I mean, how old are you?
Like thirty? What if I was your family? Could you live with yourself then?"

"You won't get in my head with that shit, *Shayla Stone*," Grimsaw
scorned, proving he knew my full name. "Ridiculing me won't get
you very far. I'm not after money in this transaction. I just wanna
know my boy can kill when necessary. If all goes my way, Garciez will leave you dead and dumped by sunrise. We all have our
snapping points as humans, Barbie. Some of us are just viler than
others. It's up to you what you tell G, but the truth will always
come out in the end. If not from your lips, from mine."

"If what you're saying is true, there must be a reason my dad
hurt his parents," I said, swallowing the blood in my throat. "He
wouldn't do something like that without a damn good motive. In
fact, I don't believe my dad would do it at all."

"Six years ago, Garciez stole a briefcase when he was fifteen.
Inside this briefcase was a hard drive. This was the same year you
were diagnosed with Leukemia. How old would that have made
you? Twelve…?"

I stayed dead silent, because he was right.

Grimsaw unrolled a cigarette pack from the sleeve of his black
t-shirt. He pulled an orange-filtered stick from the cardboard box,
tucking it between his cracked lips. After removing a lighter from

the front pocket of his jeans, he lit the end without shying his dim eyes away from mine.

"It's all very simple, Barbie. After you were diagnosed, your pops stole something special from the government. He stole files with many recipes that could have cured you from Leukemia within hours. The problem? Someone else paid Garciez to intercept. Once word broke out there were cures for cancer, everybody wanted to get their hands on them. In the end, Garciez was the one who walked away with the chip your dad stole from the government. Not your old man, not nobody else; a fifteen-year-old kid. My boy has a way of snaking through streams nobody else can. I normally like the punk, but in this moment... I hate the slimy maggot."

"There is no automatic cure for cancer, you fool," I contended, baffled by his stupidity. "Nothing can heal you within hours. It doesn't work that way."

"You're wrong," he smiled slyly. "Three years after Garciez stole the chip, when you were about to die in the hospital after conventional medicine had seemed to fail you, your dad retaliated against Garciez by attacking his family. You lucked out and beat cancer without the cure, but it was a brutal three-year battle for you, *correcto*? I know everything there is to know about you."

"What makes you think my father won't track you down?" I challenged, silently praying he was still alive. "If he murders people like you say, I'm sure he won't have a problem offing a piece of shit like you."

Grimsaw's face began to glow with fury. I knew he wanted to break every bone in my body, but I seemed to be worth more alive than dead. I didn't comprehend his motives fully, but there was a reason I was still breathing. After the things I had said to him over the past few weeks, if the leader was planning to kill me, I would be long dead already.

"You don't really think you're Diego Alvaro's kid, do you?" He took another draw from his stick of chemicals. "You look nothing like him. Your dead mother was as white as Michael Jackson in his later years, but your pops is fully Mexican like me. You've got cream colored skin and blue eyes, Barbie. Diego's too brown to create white trash like you. I'd say you were adopted."

As they all howled, Grimsaw threw his cigarette at me before thundering my cell door closed. With a deep sigh, I brushed the flame from my lap and stood to stomp it out with a bare foot.

I turned to stare at the marks tallied into the wall of my cell. I didn't believe a word Grimsaw was saying. Not only was my father a kind man, cancer wasn't something that could be magically reversed. Miracles could happen, but the idea of a guaranteed cure was nonsense. After the damage Leukemia had done to me…

I would know.

2
THE COST OF TREASON

HUNTER GARCIEZ

Wednesday. 5:30 P.M.

"**D**ID YOU OPEN THE BOX?" *Grimsaw asked.*
I stared at the wooden crate, uneager to learn what it contained. Nothing concealed was ever good. If I couldn't make out the contents, I probably didn't want to know their existence.

"No. I was waiting for your instructions."

"You've been doing good, amigo." He clutched his filthy hands around each of my shoulders. "I didn't think you had what it took at first, but you've been doing well since the initial shock of it all. I've grown to like you."

Since I didn't share the same like for him, I didn't respond. Rather than propelling the conversation with the crazy fuck forward, I stared at the wooden box before me instead.

"From here on out, I wanna use your visual capabilities," he added. "We should be robbing banks, compañero. With your ability to see the personal codes of everyone you meet, we could rob thousands of accounts without ever being held responsible. If you want it, I offer you progression within the hierarchy. I think you're worth more than a maggot to me."

"Sounds good," I agreed, because anything would be better than what I'd been doing for the past six months with Antonio. I hated removing limbs. I hated the blood and the gore. At this point, a bank heist sounded great in comparison.

"I applaud the loyalty you have for your sister, G. I'll never have a rela-

tionship like that with any of my siblings. None of them would ever take a bullet for me. I wouldn't think of taking one for any of them either..." A humanizing expression molded over his face, lasting longer than I'd ever witnessed before. *"What you're gonna find in this box ain't personal, amigo. It's just business. I caught him saying some shit he shouldn't have been. He got cocky. I was taking care of his mamá's medical bills, all while he was trying to sneak away from my brotherhood. This is the cost of treason. This is the price of betrayal."*

"You didn't," I whispered.

"Disloyalty is infidelity; infidelity is punishable by means of murder. Tony knew this, but he got arrogant. His dying mother can have what's left of him now. I want you to make her a necklace. Make it with her son's fingers, toes, and teeth."

"You didn't have to kill him," I snarled, aggravated that he would take the life of the one I liked most in the gang; the one who had shown me mercy when I'd first become involved in this world.

I knew Tony had been digging some deep ditches. He'd said he was going to make a move against Grimsaw soon. He'd said that dying would be no worse than what soldiers like us had to do on the daily. As I stared at the leaking box, aware of the torture Tony would have suffered while being decapitated alive, I doubted he would have stood by those words in his final moments.

"Loose lips can't be given the chance to speak," Grimsaw shrugged unremorsefully. *"You're part of the mafia, ése. You ain't working at Chucky Cheese. Don't make a big deal out of this. Like I said, shit wasn't personal. It just had to be done."*

"You didn't have to kill him," I repeated. *"Antonio hadn't even lived yet. He was too preoccupied trying to save his mom from pancreatic cancer. I wanted to blend the cure for her. You wouldn't let me. He was the only thing that motivated his mom to fight for her life. You could have taught him a lesson, but you didn't have to do this."*

"Love gets men like us killed, so let this be the real lesson. I don't care how young or old a person is. I always follow through when I make a deal. The problem is, not everybody shares that same etiquette. Those people must be eliminated from my circle."

"You didn't have to kill him!" Every part of me wanted to deck the son of a bitch, but I knew my position well. My words were already enough to get my throat slit. *"You're a real piece of shit."*

His fist came soaring at my left eye, colliding with an impressive blast *that threw me back multiple feet. It wasn't long before my shedding blood caused double vision to take over my eyes. As for the pain, it never did come.*

That's when I realized...

I was living in the past again.

3
FAMOUS LAST WORDS

HUNTER GARCIEZ

Wednesday. 6:00 P.M.

SOMETHING WAS PUSHING AGAINST MY lungs. I could have sworn I was dying. I could have sworn Grimsaw had finally completed the task. I could have sworn I was on my way to a better place…

Until my face was met with a hard slap.

As my eyes fluttered awake, I caught sight of the caveman standing next to me. Russ Delaney had been my best friend since elementary school, but there was no disputing our differences. The brown of my short hair wasn't in greasy dreadlocks like the shoulder-length black of his. I didn't have a mangy beard, piercings on my face, or tattoos clothing my arms down to my knuckles. The ink I did have was easily hidden beneath a t-shirt, and the only piercings I had were two black studs through my earlobes. Nonetheless, throughout everything, Russ was the only friend I had kept after joining the gang. This was because he'd refused to let me ditch him.

"I don't need mouth to mouth resuscitation," I grumbled, swatting him away from me like a mosquito. "Get the fuck out of my space."

"Sorry," he smirked, doing as I requested by taking a step back. "But I don't like hearing you call out for a guy named Antonio while you sleep. It makes me think you might be playing for the wrong field. I see the way you look at me sometimes…"

I glanced down as he snickered, finding my guitar still resting across my blue jeans. I couldn't even remember falling asleep.

Pure *Zolpidem* was what I swore by to knock me out. It had a working span of two hours, but I was lucky if four of the crystalized pills put me out for even half that. I was trying to wean off the narcotics, subsequently vibrating like a victim of hypothermia. My lips felt cold, but I was sweating at the same time. My mind was flashing over everything I had done; everything I had *seen*.

"You look like the walking dead," Russ inspected my face with a squint. "Sleep deprivation can severely gnarl a person. You should go see a Shaman or something."

It might have been the pills that had turned me this way. It might have been my insomnia. It might have been the things I had done over the past three years. In the end, I couldn't decipher which demon had officially claimed sovereignty over my soul. All I knew was that one had.

This was the point where I consistently caved during detox. There was still a bottle of pills up in my room, because I could never bring myself to throw them all away. When my body began to hurt like it was, it was easy for the darkness to lure me back in.

Because I was a weak man.

Because this was my cycle.

Because my life was no longer mine.

"I can't fucking take it anymore," I cursed, running my hand over my jawline. "I've slept six hours this week. No matter what I do, the dreams don't stop. Grimsaw has me pulling all-nighters down at the warehouse, and Tessa is a fulltime job by herself. I can't keep up with everything. It's becoming impossible."

"Start smoking weed," Russ suggested like a hippy. "The bush is all natural. It's much better than the pharmaceuticals you choke down. This whole zombie look isn't doing anything good for you."

"I don't live in a house with no mirrors," I retorted, conscious of the dark bags around my green eyes. I knew my face was always drained. It wasn't like I hadn't noticed these things, but the blood on my hands had tainted the nerves in my mind. Nothing was medicating enough to purge me of the memories. Dying was the only thing that could. For me, death would be a soothing experience.

When all the pain subsided.

If my father were still around, he would know what I should do. He had been a damaged man, but he'd known how to keep everything aligned. He'd never allowed his involvement with illegalities to follow him home to the kitchen table at night. As for me, I hadn't figured out how to do the same.

Three years had gone by since the night of my parent's deaths. I hadn't been home on the night of flames, but I'd arrived back just in time to save my younger sister from the fire. Summertime in the upstairs of our old house had been suffocating, so Tessa had often slept on the couch in the first level living room instead.

I had seen the smoke roaring from a mile away, bustling from our chimney in thick puffs. My mother had been upstairs as I'd stepped onto our grass, slamming her hands against the windowpanes in her bedroom. The thing was, she hadn't been banging for help. Her fingers had been pointing downstairs toward Tessa instead.

A gunshot rang out in our backyard at the same moment, but there had been no time to scope out the creator. There had been no time to see who had triggered the bullet; the bullet that had ripped through my father's forehead.

Fiery boards had been falling around my sister's unconscious body. A black vapor had been swallowing the entire house, devouring it like an expert of homicide. I had known I wouldn't make it to her without being burned myself, but this thought hadn't stopped me.

In an instant, I had entered the blaze. I had chosen to ignore the ringing bullet, praying that someone had heard the gunshot and called an ambulance. I had chosen to retrieve Tessa, because I couldn't have saved them all. I'd been forced to decide who would die that night. Everyone but my sister had lost out.

The house had exploded while I was carrying her away from the embers. The gust of pressure had sent us both flying. The flames melted the skin on my back, but they hadn't touched Tessa's face. This was something I would always be thankful for.

Adopting my sister after just graduating high school had been more than just life altering. It had been hard to explain that our parents were in heaven, especially when it wasn't a concept I fully believed in myself. Becoming her sole guardian was the most challenging thing I'd ever done, but I hadn't been willing to sail her off into the system of orphanage. That was when I'd decided to personally introduce myself to Grimsaw Santiago. Instead of allowing Tessa's life to be flushed down the shitter, I'd chosen to ruin my own.

When I'd first tagged up with the gang, I had needed proof of employment for the adoption agencies. By falsely employing me as a mechanic at his auto shop, Grimsaw had managed to engineer this for me. I had needed money, a stable job, and even a new house for Tessa to live in. Becoming the dream team with him had given me each of these things. Joining the syndicate had kept her by my side.

Tessa would have been shipped off to who knows where if I hadn't, but nobody could take her from me now. I was her brother, but Tessa was like my kid. I'd been forcing her to school for three years. I'd been paying her tuition and providing her heat. How I chose to accomplish these things didn't exactly define lawful, but that didn't negate how much she meant to me.

I watched Russ retrieve a beer from my fridge. Tessa and I had lived in our new house for three years now, but neither of us had cared enough to spruce the place up. No trinkets were laid out for our rare visitors to drop while inspecting. No pictures lined the walls. Decorating was a mom's job. Since we no longer had one of those, everything remained bare.

Trying to keep my mind away from the pills, I tugged my guitar back into my lap. Idle hands were the devil's work, but I found the guitar helped to ease my fidgets. If I told myself I didn't need the pharmaceuticals, *maybe this time…*

"I could go pick up some sluts to make you feel better," Russ smiled, cracking the lid from his beer in the kitchen. Sad to say, even my best friend didn't seem to think I could give up my drug addiction.

"If I make one wrong move, it'll be Tessa's head on a post beside mine. Trying to detach from the mafia is suicide. You know what to do if I die, right? You know how to protect Tessa?"

"What the fuck are you talking about?" Russ ran to take a seat on the couch across from me, his face holding a look of alarm. "You're thinking of bouncing soon?"

"After tomorrow's robbery," I decided with a nod. "I can't live like this anymore. I'm only twenty-one, but I've already met my grave. I should be out flying helicopters. Like an idiot, I'm addicted to painkillers instead."

"I'm coming with you," he staked himself as a tagalong in my life. We'd been friends for so long, I wasn't sure if either of us could function without the other. "Look, you aren't an idiot. If anything, you're too smart for your own good. Having superpowers has dropped you where you sit in life. Nothing else."

"It's *psychometry*," I groaned.

"Call it what you will, but regular people can't do the shit you can. Nobody gets away with robbing as many banks as you have. You're notorious, Garciez. You've managed to divert the pigs away from you for years."

"Don't glamorize what I do. It's only a matter of time before I get caught doing it. Once that happens, the media will finally have a face to put beneath their headlines. I'll go to jail for life, while you'll get at least five years for slinging words with me. Consider yourself an accomplice by association."

I thought back to the things Russ had seen me go through. With my knack for numbers, it hadn't been overly difficult to learn how to hack computers on an elementary scale. I had used my digitalized capabilities as a way to mess around with some of the teachers I hadn't overly liked growing up. I had broken into the school's syllabus nearly blindfolded for Russ, but that had all been adolescent bullshit.

During my fifteenth year was when I'd really managed to push shit through the fan. Long story short, some men had offered me a hefty bundle of cash to snatch a briefcase for them. Being young and naive, I had agreed.

There had been nothing but a hard drive on the inside of the briefcase. It had taken me a few days to translate the encryptions. After realizing what I possessed, everything changed. Once I understood I had the cures for cancer, I never did deliver the case to the men who'd wanted it. I never did collect any money. I had kept the contents for myself instead.

Very few people could recite the cures to the world's deadliest diseases, but I had them memorized. I had spent weeks reviewing every transcription on that hard drive. I had made sure I knew how to heal everything imaginable before destroying the physical copy.

"You sure you don't want me to round up a few girls?" Russ asked, trying to be a decent friend in his own unhealthy sort of way. "I know a few who've been eyeing you up."

"Tell them I died."

"It's been weeks since you've had sex," he reminded me, as if I didn't already know. "For the sake of your dick, I hope you find the chick you're destined to be with soon."

"I don't want to talk about that," I rejected the topic. "I don't care about anything, including the time it takes to feed a girl meaningless bullshit in hopes of seeing her naked. I'd rather jack myself off than listen to another girl talk about her shoes. I'm not suggesting a female shouldn't speak, but she should at least make it interesting when she does. They're all the same in different forms."

"Maybe, but tugging your own dick is going to get old real fast," Russ said, knowing I wouldn't hold firm to my state of celibacy for long. "Besides, what if you met *the one*? What if you could stare into a girl's pupils without seeing any numbers looking back at you? What if her eyes didn't tell you every time she changed her phone password? What if things were different with her? Wouldn't you want to know her?"

This all stemmed from my dad's theory that there was a girl out there for me; a girl who I was destined to be with; a girl who my supernatural abilities wouldn't work on. My dad hadn't been able to see my mom's numbers through her eyes. In theory, I wouldn't be able to see this girl's either. Russ loved the concept, but it was only because my dad had established it. Emiliano Garciez was a man that everyone had respected upon meeting. Subliminally, his demeanor had demanded for it.

"The odds of meeting her are slim," I said, plucking the strings in my lap. "Even if I did, why would she want me in her life? Like you said, I look strung right out. I'm involved with some of California's worst minds. Romeo and Juliet were all sorts of fucked up. Love isn't worth death."

"Haven't you heard, Garciez?" Russ' expression grew determined. I cringed as he leaned forward to rest his elbows against his knees. "Love makes people do crazy shit. You might be a badass now, but you won't be nearly as stealthy once you fall in love."

"I don't need to worry about that," I gave him a confident smile. There was a hopeless romantic hidden in Russ, but I didn't share his viewpoint on the matter. "I only roll my dice when necessary."

"You never know," he shrugged, laughing as he flicked on the TV above my fireplace with a remote. "Those might end up being your famous last words."

4
THE CONSEQUENCE OF MY BEHAVIOR

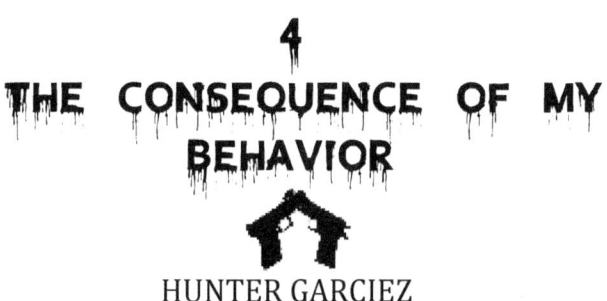

HUNTER GARCIEZ

Thursday. 4:00 P.M.

I MADE MY WAY DOWN THE streets of suburbia, popping out along the harbor on the west edge of the city. I had made this walk so many times before, directly past the many scattered ships, but something about tonight's robbery didn't feel right.

For being such a large city, San Francisco's security was a little on the shady side. I had played a key role in seven bank robberies in the area so far, none of which had I been caught for. If all went well, tonight would be the eighth and final. After it was over, Tessa and I would need to flee in the upcoming weeks. We had to leave San Francisco behind; the city we'd always called home. The time had arrived to sneak myself away from the gang, but it had to be done just flawlessly.

I had debated moving to Texas, but Tessa wasn't a fan of alligators. I had considered New York, but it was a little too crowded for either of our tastes. California was where we wanted to be. The thought of leaving here was bitter. I hadn't found the sweet part just yet.

I didn't enjoy the thought of taking Tessa away from her friends, but I was also desperate at this point. Now that I was tangled in this mess, I wasn't leaving simply. It would only be a matter of time before Grimsaw caught wind of the crooked comment I had made a few weeks prior; a comment that had implied I would leave the syndicate to go hack for the government if the Feds offered me enough cash. It had only been a joke. I had more than enough money to live my life twelve times over, but Grimsaw probably wouldn't see it as the hilarious knee-slapper the rest of the coffee room had.

The Mexican mafia was like a puppy mill. It bred as many dogs as it could in the shortest timeframe possible. The more disobedient the dog, the lower the chance it had of survival. A chain of command aligned the syndicate. Orders were given out based upon the triangle of affiliation. The lower your standing, the more dirt you collected beneath your fingernails. The more dirt you got under your nails, the higher the position you achieved. I held a respectable ranking in the gang now. I even had my own office in the back of the warehouse. In other words, my hands were filmed with disease.

I pulled open the warehouse door and climbed into the fake auto shop situated behind it. Grimsaw dealt his business out of here. This way, if any authorities were to check in on him, he had a valid business establishment to keep them from snatching at his tail. I was sure he didn't mind the tax breaks either.

I made my way through the vehicles needing repairs. Some were on lifts and towering above my head, while some were without wheels and down on the floor. Grimsaw had crowds of employees turning wrenches around his warehouse, all fitted in the same blue coveralls.

The Bloodthirst Mafia.

"Garciez, my man, I was wondering when you were gonna show up. I told you to be here at four…" Grimsaw glanced at the gold watch on his left wrist, lecturing me in a thick Spanish accent. "But I see it's a quarter after."

"I ran into some issues."

I avoided telling him that it was my twelve-year-old sister who had wound up my time. I'd sworn to take her to a movie tonight. Since Grimsaw had called, I'd broken another promise to her instead.

"I hear you've been looking for a government job?" Grimsaw asked it like a question, but I knew there was no good answer. Once he identified betrayal, there was no playing reverse psychology on him.

He tapped a gray pistol in his palm, warning me that nothing good was about to come my way. Everything he did came with a price tag. He didn't offer favors. He did things to claim ownership over people instead. He thirsted for power, and he had a damn lot of it too. After crossing him like I just had, you didn't breathe the next day. Your fingers were shipped out to your family. That was the end of that.

"I'm flattered you're so frightened to lose me. I didn't think you would cause a ruckus over something so fatuous," I smiled, taking a casual glance around the warehouse. It took seconds to realize that most of his grease monkeys had formed a threatening circle behind him. There were at least fifteen men in blue coveralls, all ready to take me down if I made one wrong move. "I thought we were robbing—"

"Don't play dumb with me. That was my way of leading you down here. You know what this is." He spun his finger around the garage, glaring at me ruthlessly. "So, what is it?"

"Another initiation?" I guessed.

These guys were the worst thugs known to the west coast. They were great allies to have on my side, but that wasn't where they stood now. I had already completed my fair share of initiations over the past three years. I had done things I would never speak of, but this was Grimsaw's way of testing my loyalty now.

"This is the consequence of your behavior. I gave you everything you needed during your darkest of times, and this is how you repay me? By being a pussy?"

"If I was a pussy, you wouldn't be so upset right now," I countered, welcoming the devil on my shoulder to stand himself tall. "I've already done a lot of messed up shit to prove myself to you. I won't like it if you try to run me through hoops another time, Grim."

"Then you shouldn't have chomped down on the hand that feeds you." Flames of fury sparked in his eyes. "Once we ride, we die side by side. There are two types of people in this world; the good and the evil. I shouldn't have to remind you which side you chose to leap onto."

He kicked at the metal pail by his feet, as if the thud would somehow convince me to put my head on straight. It didn't, so I watched the pail roll away unproductively instead.

"I consider you a pal, Garciez," he carried on. "But we're not homies right now. You've been the brains behind the operations for a while, but I draw the line at disloyalty. None of your talents will help you out in this moment. I got no problem lining the streets with your half-breed blood. I've got years on you, monkey."

I watched his fists tighten and decompress in an unnervingly steady rhythm. Everything about him reeked of temper. After knowing him for a few years, I could always tell when Grimsaw had met his breaking level. He wasn't there quite yet, but I was sure pushing him close.

"You wouldn't know how to rob a lemonade stand without me." I probably should have let him domineer, but I chose the alternative instead. "You could kill me like you did Antonio, but you would never make this kind of coin again. I taught you how to rob a bank. It wasn't the other way around. You know death doesn't scare me."

As I met his dark scrutiny, my smile was cocky.

Grimsaw had turned me into his own brand of robot. He had desensitized me over the past three years. In return, he'd managed to make me numb. This numbness brought a lack of fear, because I knew Grimsaw didn't want to kill me. He would try every possible tactic before allowing things to reach that head. If he were to lose me, he would lose his ease of acquiring money too. As it stood, I was the one quenching most of his thirst for wealth.

"You might not fear death..." Grimsaw arched his eyebrows vindictively. The dislodged look on his face caused my guts to wrench like bar rags. "The thing with disloyalty, *amigo*? I'm better at it than you are."

Only one face entered my mind.

Tessa's.

5
THE STING OF A SCORPION

HUNTER GARCIEZ

Thursday. 4:30 P.M.

I LUNGED AT GRIMSAW. I DIDN'T care that he was holding a gun in his hand. The ramifications didn't even enter my thought processes until I'd already physically decided on the maneuver. I managed to get in a good throw against his face, but it wasn't long before nine of his guys were detaching my weight from him. They used their boots to beat my ribs. I received a few knees to the head next. Someone even had a baseball bat, but the pain didn't hurt like I thought it might... like it probably should have.

"Let him go!" Grimsaw demanded.

I knew he was less than amused by my recent stunt, but he deserved more than just the slam I had managed to strike him with. For everything I'd seen him do, he deserved to die an agonizing death.

As the punches to my head lessened, I looked up from the floor where I laid. Blood dripped to the concrete surrounding me, but I ignored it and met my fate in the eye. "You kidnapped my little sister over a fucking joke? She's twelve years old." I spat blood onto his shoes. "Where the fuck is she?"

"I'm probably not gonna tell you," he smiled, eyes pitch as black. "You dug this grave with your own two hands. Of all people, you should've known better than to betray me."

"Why not just kill me?" I offered myself over.

I couldn't allow my sister to get hurt because of my choices. I had done some unfortunate things, but getting Tessa kidnapped was by far my greatest life failure so far.

"What would be the fun in that?" He drilled his heel against my chest. I hadn't been looking to achieve the status of a collapsed lung today, but you never could be too certain of where a day might take you. "Besides, I don't plan to hurt your sister. It's you that's gonna hurt someone." Grimsaw turned toward his minions and requested, "Bring out the blonde."

A wide, steel gate on the far side of the warehouse began to slide open with a buzz. Raphael pulled a gagged female through it by her ashy, blonde hair.

Although Raph was the same height as me, our masses differed greatly. He wasn't just overweight. With one movement, he could crush the blonde into dust beneath his steel-toed boot. He was also the only dark-skinned guy in the gang. The rest were brought in mainly from Mexico, but Grimsaw often welcomed the Portuguese too. Raphael was accepted because he did anything Grimsaw told him to. He probably even sucked his dick.

Once I had peeled myself into a standing position, Raph threw the girl at my feet. Thick wire was chaining her wrists together. Blood lined the rivets with evident infection, while mine continued to paint the concrete beside her. She stared at the pool of red, frowning as her vision slid up to my face.

Taking in her dirty features, she was beautiful. Her complexion was soft. Her pale hair was dangling over her shoulders, greasy with grit and grime. Her cheekbones were angled and her eyelashes long. She was attractive, but it was disturbing to see how thin she was.

Raphael grabbed her forcefully. He began to drag her away from me, scraping her body against the dirty floor like she was a mop. She tried to fight him off, but she may as well have been rebelling against a gorilla in the wild. He raised her four feet into the air, preparing to make her bones crumble. I heard her cadaverous body ricochet from an antique truck, but I didn't look to see if her skull had left a dent in the front fender.

"Is that really necessary?" I shook my head. "It isn't like she doesn't understand who has the upper hand around here. Since when do we hurt females?"

"I do a lot of shit that you don't know about," Grimsaw snarled back. "You haven't been introduced to the extents of my morbidity, but that's about to change. At the end of all this, you'll understand my reasoning. You'll wanna kill this blonde just as much as I do."

The girl moaned lightly, curving into a fetal position on the filthy floor. I could feel her concentration still glued to me, but I couldn't bring myself to meet her blue eyes for a round two. I left my gaze on Grimsaw's face, keeping the expression on mine dead like stone. Since he'd kidnapped Tessa, I knew he was willing to get as morbid as he deemed fit.

"Did you pull her out of a club?" I referred to the red silk decorating the blonde's body. The constricting dress was flaunting her ribcage, leaving me to wonder if they'd even fed her.

I didn't get much time to dwell on it. I found myself stumbling as Grimsaw's knuckles split open another inch of my flesh. Even though the whole left side of my head was beginning to throb like a dick on a lonely Saturday night, I refused to back down. I had been through too much shit to bend over and be Grimsaw's puppet now.

"I dressed the Barbie up for you. I thought you might wanna take a ride on the bicycle before she goes pro..." He licked his canine teeth. "Don't be so tender, G. In our line of business, you can't have feelings like you do. Weakness doesn't blend well with the color of your Mexican skin."

"This girl means fuck all to me," I said the words harshly, listening to her snatch furiously for air. The gag in her mouth was making it impossible to retrieve. "But I don't understand why you're cutting off her breathing supply."

"Who gives a fuck if she's not getting any air?" Grimsaw slammed his palm against an arrangement of toolboxes, unimpressed by my concern. "That right there proves my point. You don't have the balls for this business."

"I don't get off by watching her suffer, but that doesn't make my balls any smaller than yours," I defended myself, masking just how repulsive I found his decadence to be. "Like I said, the broad means nothing to me. I just think it's fucked up how you choose to go about your business."

Grimsaw's eyes began to twinkle with something noticeably perverted. He made his way over toward the female in question, but she didn't jitter upon his arrival. As he snaked his hand around her neck, she kept her vision adhered to mine.

"What do you want me to do with her?" I tried to snag his attention back my way, hoping he might leave her alone. Once his tongue began to ascend her throat, it was apparent I wasn't successful. "Where's she going?"

"I know a guy who's dying to get his hands on her. Ray Barnes is an old friend of your dad's. Your job is to have this girl in Vegas by dawn. I'm gonna give you an address. Once you drop this bitch off, Barnes will have directions to your sister." I stayed silent as Grimsaw tilted the girl's face and forced her to meet his cold eyes. While his hand took a stroll up her thigh, he asked, "Do you like that, Barbie?"

Without a hint of hesitance, the girl impulsively head-butted him. Their foreheads clashed together in a blood-drawing collision. Grimsaw's palm connected against her cheek with an icy slap as payback, but all it did was make her laugh.

"And if I refuse to comply?" I braved.

"Tessa will pay the price for your stupidity. Both girls don't walk away unharmed, so don't even think about stewing up some heroic plan to save each of them. I'm not the type of man to pass out second chances," Grimsaw cautioned me, evil in his malevolent eyes. "Not like I'm willing to pass out common street whores like this one."

"But why *this* girl?" I questioned, curious of his motives. Grimsaw never did anything without reasoning, but his reasons were never simple to figure out.

"Because she's just like you, G."

"How do you figure that?"

"She's lippy when she ain't got no right to be." He strangled her throat, squeezing until she was close to passing out. I wanted to intervene, but doing so would only derive more discomfort for her. Grimsaw wouldn't take lightly to having me protect her. I knew this, but I also hated hearing the strains of her esophagus as she began to lose consciousness.

"Some would argue that being insubordinate is better than being spineless. I'll take your last remark to be a compliment. You could have compared me to worse women than her."

"You think she's a looker too, *eh amigo*?" Grimsaw gave a laugh, but his eyes didn't lose their rage. "This leads me to my next concern. Since the bitch is basically you with a set of tits, I worry you two might get along a little too well for my liking."

Grimsaw dipped into the front pocket of his jeans. After uttering a few threats in Spanish, he hauled the blonde back over to me. He flung a key at my chest, pointing toward the supercharged Camaro parked behind me. It was jet black with smoked out windows, just begging to be noticed by a group of bored cops.

"You couldn't have been a little less heat-bag?" I criticized his judgement with a laugh. "Why would you give me a car with tinted windows? Does it have aftermarket exhaust strapped to it too? Are you trying to ensure the Feds catch me?"

"I'm sorry," he faked an apology, his hand over the space where his heart should have biologically been stationed. "Would you have preferred a 1986 Corolla?"

"I would have blended in that way."

"I had the boys install NOS in the Camaro. That dragster will beat any police unit on any street. You should be grateful that I'm giving you a hope to get away from the pigs at all."

"Why are you?"

"Because I don't really want you to wind up in jail. I just want you to learn a lesson." He closed our distance, untangling his hand from the blonde's hair to do so. "You're quick with your thinking, Garciez. I've seen you crack codes that some of my best boys can't dip their fingers into, but don't think about detouring the direction of my plans. Drop this Barbie off and save your sister. Keep it clean and stay on my side. You know the price you'll pay if you don't."

My tongue toyed at the back of my teeth as I absorbed the situation around me. Uncertainty shredded through my throat with waves of relentless bile. I thought of lunging at him again, but I knew it wouldn't change anything. Twenty of his guys had accumulated now, but there was still only one of me.

Numbers weren't on my side today.

"I just sold this broad for two and half million," he praised himself, spitting on the floor of his warehouse. "When dawn breaks, if this little white bitch ain't where she's supposed to be, hell will rise. Do you understand me, monkey?"

Grimsaw lifted the steel of his pistol to my forehead, cocking the trigger with an eager readiness. A gun had been pressed against my skull so many times, it didn't even faze me anymore. With the memories I had of cheating death, I was left wishing someone would pull the fucking trigger already.

Ignoring the pistol aimed my way, I leaned over and tugged the girl to her bare feet. Using a rough edge for show, I tossed her into the passenger seat of the car. I shut the door before any of them could say any last words to her, but Grimsaw had a different idea in mind.

He yanked it back open, pushing me out of his way with a determined shove. Being reminded of the angry posse behind him, their knuckles already mangled past the point of healing, I knew I had no choice but to let him.

"You ready for your ride to hell, 40347? I know we've been spending a lot of time together lately. I'm sure it saddens you to say goodbye to me."

Grimsaw removed the tight gag from the slave's mouth, revealing rings around her flushed cheeks. As if on cue, she immediately spat saliva into his face.

"Go fuck yourself." Her voice was hoarse from dehydration. "If you ask me, the world would be a better place without the disgrace you're trying to pass off as a soul."

As I winced at her lack of respect, she did nothing but politely smile. Although she was equipped with a voice as sweet as honey, her words held the sting of a scorpion. Even with blood staining her teeth, her smile was pretty. It was an ungodly thing for me to think, but the sick side of me could understand why someone would pay a couple million to have her around all the time.

Grimsaw wiped at the saliva stringing from the bridge of his crooked nose. After delivering another lash against her already swollen face, he cocked his pistol against her bruised throat. I wanted to strip him of his front teeth, but Grimsaw was no punk. If I tried to act like a superhero in this moment, it wouldn't get myself or the blonde very far.

"You better not be a starfish in the sack," Grimsaw tried to inject her with fear, but it didn't seem to work on a girl like her. Rather than quivering, she kept her expression schooled like a wise felon. "Barnes will expect you to follow his every command, Barbie. If he wants his dick sucked, it'll be your job to do it."

"Each of you will die alone," she took a verbal stab at the rest of us now. "Unless it's forced, none of you will get the chance to experience love. Isn't that why you sell girls? Because no sane woman would ever date any of you willingly?"

Grimsaw pressed the gun deeper into her throat, making her cough with every centimeter he dug. As salt pixelated her eyes, I sent her a glare that told her to keep silent if she wanted to live. The girl was arguably in one of the worst situations she ever could be, but it didn't slow down her word agility in the slightest.

"One girl lives. One girl dies. Garciez must decide whose soul will cry," Grimsaw gave her a cold wink as he tossed me a sheet of crumpled paper. After positioning the gag back into her mouth, he slammed the door shut on her just as fast.

I unfolded the paper.

RAY BARNES
CAESARS PALACE

69TH FLOOR

RAINMAN SUITE
VEGAS, BITCH.

I forced my eyes into his, disregarding the many other bodies surrounding us. Against my better judgement, I slammed him against the passenger door of the Camaro. Grimsaw's men instinctively began to swarm me, but a wave of his hand settled them quickly.

"I'll gut you like a pig if anybody lays a finger on Tessa," I warned him, keeping my forearm locked across his throat. "I will floss my teeth with your tendons. I've learned how to torture from the very best, Grim."

He pushed me away, knowing I was referring to everything he had taught me. He dug into the back pocket of his jeans, taking his time to pull out an oversized bottle of pills. Like a fiend, my spine stiffened as he threw the unlabeled container my way. I caught it, curious of what it might contain. I functioned by eating pills, but like hell if Grimsaw knew that.

Antonio had introduced me to the chalky tablets. He'd shown me a way to escape it all. My cravings weren't something I spoke about to Grim. Having an addiction wasn't allowed in the syndicate. In his eyes, pills would make me a liability in my tall ranking; a weakness he couldn't afford.

"What are these?" I sent him a tentative glance, unscrewing the cap. "Why are you giving me pills?"

"Because every good movie has a climax." He gestured toward the girl, but I doubted she could hear us through the smoky windows. "When I reveal the twist, you'll want to kill that bitch. Since I know you won't be able to stomach cutting out her tonsils, I've decided to make this easy on you. If you drop a fistful of those down her throat, Barbie won't ever speak again."

6
MY ONLY HOPE

SHAYLA STONE

Thursday. 5:30 P.M.

WE HAD BEEN DRIVING FOR at least twenty minutes now. There was something sexy about a man who could slap a stick shift around, but Garciez's ability to manhandle a lever didn't make him any less cryptic.

Something dark radiated from him, smothering me as I tried to work out what type of person he was. The beat of my heart was the only noise to be heard. My fingers were tapping at the skin on my left thigh, but the connection wasn't enough to disturb the peace. Garciez had pulled the gag from my mouth as soon as we'd left Grimsaw's warehouse, but I hadn't spoken yet. As if he couldn't face me, he hadn't asked me anything either.

The silence was nearly deafening.

He swiftly changed gears from fourth to sixth on the interstate. I watched the tendons in his forearm rustle beneath the golden hue of his skin. The chocolate hair on his head was kept short, groomed around the edges, and I could tell he was older than me. I also knew he was Mexican, being that his last name was Garciez and he rolled his R's, but the natural tan glazing over his skin would have been a solid indicator too.

Swirls of blood decorated his face like a Christmas craft had gone wrong. Because of this, his emerald eyes stood out all too well. Silver lined his pupils in an eerie sort of way. Bruising had begun to settle in along the structure of his chiseled jawline, cloaking him with a sunset violet. Not only was his eyebrow sliced wide open, his cheek held a gouge that was leaking a red river.

I pulled down the hem of my dress, knowing there was no extra fabric to be found. Needing a distraction, I leaned forward to peck the radio to life. A song began to fly from the speakers; a mix between techno and rap. I hurriedly changed the channel and settled on a rock station instead, but it wasn't long before Garciez clicked it off.

He went back to tapping his fingers against the steering wheel, much like mine were doing against my leg. Dark clouds were casting over his face while he mentally slayed his thoughts, but I didn't understand it. His options seemed rather direct to me. If he handed me over, he would get his sister back. I certainly didn't expect him to choose me over his own blood. I was blonde, but I wasn't a complete idiot.

"You don't like *Black Sabbath?*" I broke the silence, watching him flinch as I did. The raise of his eyebrow drew more blood to fall onto his cheek, but it didn't seem to affect him.

I assumed he wouldn't reply to me, and he didn't challenge my low expectations. Rather than repeating my question, I rolled down the passenger window and stole a deep breath of ocean air. It was hot as sin out, as it generally was in Cali, causing my skin to melt into the leather seat beneath me. Sharp wiring continued to slice through my wrists, coloring me with blood every time the Camaro hit a bump. As Garciez took a sudden swerve to the right, making a detour into the east side of San Francisco, it didn't help.

He slowed the transmission down with forceful shifts, staring at my wrists instead of at the road. Although I didn't mingle my eyes with his, I could feel his green gaze on me as he whispered, "You're dripping a lot of blood."

"You look worse than I do. I've never seen anybody try to take on twenty guys alone before. I mean… what did you think was going to happen? You got your ass kicked," I replied, staring at a strand of multicolored houses in the distance. The thing I loved most about San Francisco was the city's passive nature when it came to creativity.

"Hardly," he disputed.

"You really did."

"I got my ass kicked *a little*," he shrugged, as if he genuinely believed the crap spilling from his lips. "I've had my ass handed to me thirty times worse than that."

I studied him with caution, wondering how anyone could become used to being beaten with a baseball bat. By the lift of his broad shoulders, I knew he was the alpha type who thought he couldn't be brought down.

"Are you okay?" I asked.

Emotion broke over his face at the sound of my question. Like an android with only three functions, he seemed to be programed with nothing more than confusion, rage, and sadness. All three settings were visibly cycling around his face, but none were holding steady for more than ten seconds.

"We should avoid conversation," he decided, speaking in a flat tone. Part of me wanted to poke him, just to see if the robot would feel the effects. "You don't want to know me."

"Are you really so awful?" I asked the question, but he was right; I didn't want to know him. "Are you the same as your friends?"

"They aren't my friends."

"What are they then?"

"Business associates."

"Do they feed you whatever drugs you're hooked to?" I tested my limits. I could tell he was on something by the way his body jittered. "Maybe I can help you somehow?"

I knew the offer sounded strange coming from my lips; the slave. Even as the words were leaving my mouth, the sound of them made me shudder to myself. I didn't know how to act in this situation, but I figured trying to get on the thug's good side would be better than the alternative.

"Help me?" The look he bestowed my way was all too vacant. An emptiness was haunting him, and he didn't try to hide it. "I'm about to destroy your life. In trade for my sister, I have no other alternative. I can't do anything to save you from that fate. There's fuck all you can do to adjust mine either. Don't waste your time trying."

"You speak in paragraph form too?" I faked surprise, despite the impact of his brutal wording. "I was beginning to think you only knew how to engrave symbols into cave walls. You've said as little as possible so far."

"I'm not a Neanderthal."

"What are you then?"

"Quiet," he answered.

Like a bat out of hell, he crossed over multiple lanes of traffic. He flung the car into the parking lot of the nearest convenience store, proving he understood the definition of a California lane change.

He tapped the transmission into neutral, his knuckles white like ocean foam as he grabbed a handful of tissues from the box tucked between us. I watched him attempt to clean off his damaged face, but it was unmanageable without water. Once he realized this, he stepped out of the vehicle and locked the doors. In my next blink, he was gone.

I thought of making a bolt for it, but nothing budged when I hit the electronic buttons on the side panels. It was as if the doors couldn't be opened from the inside while locked. Judging by the excessive number of digital gauges lining the dash, the car was rigged with aftermarket supplies; designed specifically for kidnapping.

It was roughly ten minutes later that Garciez reappeared from the summer shack. He climbed back behind the steering wheel, setting two plastic bags between my feet. Taking a deep breath in, he knelt across my body and began to search for something specific. Once he'd retrieved a pair of garden snippers, he curled the blades around the wire on my wrists and clipped.

I pulled my arms apart and tossed the bloody cable into the backseat. Grimsaw's face floated through my mind as I did; memories of when I'd insisted the wiring was too tight; memories of him mercilessly making me hurt.

Garciez watched me cry with an emotionless face. He was nothing more than another monster bred by Grimsaw; a robot who did nothing but obey; a desensitized maniac with no morals; a cold-blooded killer with a drug addiction. Worse than all those things, when it came to surviving...

He was my only hope.

7
THE GRIM REAPER'S SCYTHE

SHAYLA STONE

Thursday. 6:00 P.M.

GARCIEZ MADE NO MOVEMENT TO drive away from the storefront. He inspected me while I twisted my unlatched wrists, but a man like him didn't really care what happened to a girl like me. He would care even less once he found out what my father had supposedly done to his family.

"Thank you," I whispered.

I schooled myself to evade his searing regard. His vision was digging through my skin, but the last thing I wanted was to look vulnerable in front of him. To pretend I wasn't crying, I turned my head to the side. I looked at the mountains in the scenic backdrop, silently issuing a final goodbye to California instead.

"I can see why Grimsaw didn't bother to feed you much," Garciez spoke his mind. "After listening to the way your mouth goes rampant, it's clear you lack street smarts. Your tongue will get you killed. Worse than that, your tongue could get *me* killed too."

"Death is far from my worst option," I laughed at him, though the truth was closer to sad than it was to funny. "Besides, you're in no position to be giving me a lecture on the boundaries of over-confidence. I heard you tell Grimsaw you would gut him like a pig if anything happened to your little sister."

"I can get away with slack-jawing the way I do. I've built that respect for myself. Grimsaw would love to kill you, but he won't take my life. I have something he needs."

"What is it?"

"If I told you that, you'd want it too," he shot down my attempt to investigate. "Back to your death wish. What were you thinking when spitting in Grimsaw's face?"

"*Thou know'st 'tis common; all that lives must die.* Expectations of immortality are unfeasible. Nobody can avert the grim reaper's scythe forever. Since I'm bound to die regardless, why would I go down quietly? I plan to give each of you a run for your money; including you."

"How? By quoting *Hamlet*?" Garciez seemed to be teasing me, but I couldn't be certain. There was a constant blanket of vagueness draping his face. "That'll sure teach me a lesson."

"Leave the sarcasm to me," I mumbled, tendering a rude glare in his direction. "I'm amazed you know poetry at all. I figured you could list off drug slang, but *Shakespeare*?" I added sweetness to my snotty smile. I half expected him to hit me for it, but a mishandling never did arise.

"Act 1, Scene 2; *Seek for thy noble father in the dust. Though know'st 'tis common; all that lives must die, passing through nature to eternity,*" he sent me a cocky wink. "Did you assume I was an idiot?"

"Definitely," I admitted.

"Only silly girls make assumptions. You don't want to be a silly girl, do you?"

I could tell there was a threat lurking beneath his words, but I couldn't quite place the seeding. All I knew… I did not want to be the girl he was referring to.

I shook my head. "No."

"Well, since you've already labelled me as stupid, I'm going to take a guess about you now," he warned me. "Before you were abducted, I bet your life was absolutely flawless. I doubt hardship is something a girl like you is familiar with."

"You're wrong," I gave him an icy scowl, offended by his judgements. "Much like the looks of you, sleep is a rare commodity for me too. I've been through things you couldn't even imagine."

"Right. I'm sure you've had it real rough as a privileged white girl." He lifted his arm from the center console and leaned away from me. After properly positioning himself back into his seat, he changed the topic by instructing, "Eat something."

My fingers willingly began to rifle through the grocery bags in a hurry. The food was excessive; two Kit-Kat bars, two peanut butter cups, two bags of different flavored chips, an ice cream bar, three sandwiches, two bottles of juice, and five bottles of water to top it all off.

"I would hug you for bringing me this, but not only do I want nothing to do with you, my veins might circulate AIDS now," I paused after speaking the horrid words, allowing the truth to excavate deeper into the subterranean of my bones. "In case you haven't noticed, we're both bleeding. Just like I don't want to be a silly girl, I doubt you want to be contaminated."

He glanced at my barcode tattoo and pieced it together with a grimace. As something illegible glazed over his face, he burned out of the parking lot faster than I could have swallowed. His erratic driving ignited a layer of dust to thicken the air upon the spin of the rear tires.

Although Garciez was young, something about him was still unnerving. After all, why was he feeding me? All gangsters had ulterior motives. Hollywood had taught me that.

I cracked one of the many plastic casings open, choosing to dive into an egg-salad sandwich first. Since no part of me cared how much of a pig I looked like in front of the crook, I devoured the sandwich in just over thirty seconds flat.

"After three weeks, that was amazing," I appreciated, thankful for the momentary hush of my tyrannical appetite. "I would have settled for dinner from a dumpster, but that was much better."

"Three weeks?" Garciez ran his fingers down his face. For a few moments, he refrained from asking anything else. When he did decide to speak again, his words came out in a thorny tone. "What did they do to you? Did they *touch* you?"

Still lowering in my shoulders, I prayed to be graced by the power of invisibility. I would have loved for the snap of my fingers to hold something of value at a time like this, but nothing happened when I flicked them.

"They beat me every few days, but they didn't touch me sexually. Grimsaw said he had to keep me alert. He said he couldn't allow my heartrate to fall in my condition. That's why he smacked me around, but raping me would have ruined my worth."

The look on his face made it clear he understood me.

"You're a virgin, aren't you?"

"Yes," I confessed, embarrassed by the truth.

It wasn't like I wanted to be a virgin at the age of eighteen. It wasn't like I was proud of it, but I had never met a guy who had tempted me enough. Many members of the opposite sex had tried to sneak down my pants, but it had never felt right to go all the way. For that reason, I never had.

As Garciez's face grew primitive, the vein in his forehead began to convulse with what seemed to be the hankering to kill. It didn't take more than a second before his eyes began to glint with a green venom, and I knew all too well what was zapping through his mind like fireflies; *her first experience with sex is going to hurt like hell.*

"How many times did Grimsaw hit you?"

I debated how to answer. I couldn't trust Garciez much further than I could throw him. I couldn't be certain that he wasn't just another one of Grimsaw's guinea pigs. For all I knew, anything I said would be translated back to the ringleader through Garciez's teeth.

"I don't want to talk about it."

"I don't give a shit what you want, blondie. You've already pissed off more than your fair share of gang members. I advise you not to add my name to that list next."

"Why does it matter to you?" I met his pervasive stare. "Do you want to beat me more than Grimsaw did? Is that a sick game you guys play with each other?"

He ran his hand along his jawline. I got the sense he was only doing it so he wouldn't backhand me. I knew I deserved a good lashing too. Garciez wasn't wrong. My mouth did go rampant, but it was a habit I'd always had.

"I won't lay a hand on you unless you step out of line," he said, eyes in slits. "If you don't piss me off, I'll take you to a hospital instead."

"Right," I laughed, hating him immediately for dangling such a thing in my face. "You and I both know a hospital isn't scratched into your agenda for tonight. My health doesn't even matter anymore. Just take me to Vegas."

"What the fuck is wrong with you? Do you think it'll be some sort of vacation in the sex trade? I didn't think you would need a reminder, but the guy who bought you plans to use you as his sex toy. Being as young as you are, forever is a long time."

"I wouldn't go that far," I rolled my blue eyes. "I'm sure he'll swap me out for a younger version of myself eventually. Do you know what'll happen to me then? Will he kill me? Will I be thrown into the middle of the ocean? Will I just rot in a basement somewhere? Worse; will he force me to have his children?"

I watched my words drive into the gangster's core. He winced like I'd splashed acid on his skin, but he never did give me an answer.

Instead, he asked, "What's your name?"

"Penelope," I lied.

His presence gave off an alluring sense of security. He didn't seem as bad as his acquaintances, but that didn't mean I trusted him any more than I had the last gorilla. I trusted all of them like I trusted the devil; *not a whole hell of a lot.*

"You're trying to bullshit a professional con-artist," he glowered at me with murky eyes. "I can see through your lies. What's your real name?"

"You first," I challenged.

"Hunter Garciez."

He was undoubtedly American born, but he identified himself with a Spanish finesse. I was struck infatuated by the way the syllables left his tongue.

"Hunter?" I laughed to myself. "I thought your first name would be more Mexican. I had you pegged for a Ricardo. Maybe a Pedro."

In an instant, a paralyzing kind of magic happened. He showed off his perfectly arranged teeth in a full-blown grin. It was the kind of smile that made a female's blood freeze over with lust, even though she knew the man displaying it would bring nothing but catastrophe her way.

"My real name is Cazador. It means Hunter in Spanish. It's just easier to go by Hunter. White people can pronounce my name properly this way. White people like *you.*"

Nothing could beat a name like Cazador Garciez, but he was jumping to assumptions much too quickly. My skin didn't advertise it physically, but I was a half-breed just like him. At least... I was *fairly* sure I was.

Withering in humiliation, because I hated the thought of following a strong name like his with the feebleness of mine, I
introduced myself next as, "Shayla Stone."

8
CHILD'S PLAY

HUNTER GARCIEZ

Thursday. 10:00 P.M.

T HIS POSITION FELT ALL TOO familiar; choosing whose life
would get to play out. I didn't like it, but I knew the scenario
well. Three years ago, I had chosen Tessa instead of my parents.
Tonight, I would choose Tessa over the blonde.

It had been hours since I'd last spoken to the slave. Not only was
there nothing I could say to make her feel better, there was nothing I could do to change the hand she'd been dealt. The kindest
gesture I could think of offering her was a shower. Compared to
what she'd been through, such a miniscule effort seemed pathetic
when balanced on the scales.

Nonetheless, I took a quick sweep off the Westside Parkway near
the interchange. I slammed on the breaks after arriving at the first
roadside hotel in Bakersfield, bringing the Camaro to a halt with
a screech in the manual transmission.

"What are you doing?" she asked, alerted by the hotel before us.

She probably assumed the worst, like I was going to forcibly
touch her or something. She didn't know I had her best interests
in mind. She didn't know I wasn't like Grimsaw. Then again, aside
from a shell for an insomniac to dwell in, I didn't know who I was
anymore either.

"You need a shower."

"That's kind of you to say," she scowled at me. "You must be single, huh? I doubt any girl could handle the compliments you toss out so freely."

"I'm the guardian of a twelve-year-old," I stared out the front windshield, allured by her steady flow of sarcasm. "Raising a pre-teen who tells you to get fucked every time she turns around is a bit of a life trial. Not many girls my age could deal with my sister."

"You assume."

It was getting dark out, soon to be the dead of night, but Shayla's blue jewels were still clearly visible. Her eyes stuck out under the illumination of the neon hotel sign, glistening with a story of a life I was being expected to destroy.

"Does your boyfriend have a kid or something?"

"I don't date," she claimed.

Bullshit. A girl like her couldn't manage to stay single for a week, let alone always. I was sure she had a search team of men trying to find her by now, but I headed toward the front lobby to pay for a room rather than dwelling on it.

The scent of patchouli filled my senses upon entry. A blonde rose to greet me from the chair she'd been leaning in, catching up on the newest episode of *Days of Our Lives*. I couldn't figure out how the show was still managing to score routine airtime. It had to be on its ninetieth fucking season by now.

The attendant sent me her best smile. Her regard trailed down to my gory t-shirt, checking me out with blatant interest. After the beatdown I had just received, I knew I wasn't looking my freshest.

"Are you looking for a room?"

She didn't miss a thing.

"I am," I kept pleasant.

"How many beds do you need?"

The attendant brushed her bangs behind her ears, inspecting my face as she did. The strands of her hair were much duller than the near white of Shayla's blonde, while the blue in her eyes wasn't nearly as captivating either.

Attempting to snag her attention away from my lacerations, I tapped my palm against the chipped counter, and replied, "The smallest room you have will do fine."

The female began to peck at the keyboard before her. She had pink fingernails that were much too long to stroke the keyboard accurately. I watched her press the backspace key six times before finally asking for my method of payment.

Regardless of her hooker nails, it didn't take long before I was back out at the Camaro. Upon my arrival, something wasn't right. The passenger door was wide open, warning me that Shayla would be nowhere in sight.

I began to trace the hotel on foot. After about fifteen minutes of constant circling, I finally found her. Her body was crouched against a tree, her eyes crystallized with fear.

"I understand I've brought you to a hotel, but my intentions aren't malicious," I said, approaching her like she was poisonous. "I'm just trying to clean you up."

"It isn't for my benefit," she cut me with her words, shaking like a battered dog. "You just want me to look good for the man in Vegas. If my hair is too greasy, he might not hand your sister back to you. All you're doing is prettying me up for a demented pervert. Who are you trying to kid? Me or yourself?"

She stared at me with glossy eyes, tossing buckets of fuel on me with her tongue. I wanted to lose my mind, but she didn't need any more hostility to pollute the air around her. Whatever Grimsaw had put her through, it wasn't something she would get over without a battle. I didn't want to add to that. I couldn't save her, but I also didn't want to be the same as him.

I knelt and raised her to her feet. She clung her arms around my neck, wincing as I forced her to rise from the grassy earth. She wasn't a weak girl. I knew she'd fought like hell to survive through Grimsaw's keeping, but she would never be capable of physically restraining me. And I couldn't release her back into freedom. She was all that would bring me to Tessa.

I forfeited a helpless shake of my head and began to stalk back toward the hotel, listening to her feet as they cracked twigs behind me. My guilty conscience told me I shouldn't be making the slave walk at all. She was bruised and injured, unable to keep up.

I cranked around and brought her to a dead halt. Within a breath, before she could try to resist my strength, I had her cradled in my arms. It was hot outside, despite the now dimming sky, but her body was still freezing with fear. A hot shower was exactly what she needed.

I wished I could offer her more. I wanted to give her the keys to the Camaro. I wanted to tell her I could figure out another plan for Tessa, but Grimsaw had hit me good this time. I was right where he wanted me to be. Not only was I on a time restriction, I was already breaking the rules too.

I stood in place for a moment, shutting my eyes with a deep sigh. I thought I might forget the situation drowning us if I looked away from her face, but the opposite ended up happening instead. Eliminating my sense of vision did nothing but enhance my sense of touch, allowing the quiver of her body to split my heart apart.

She was someone's daughter.

She could be someone's sister.

Grimsaw was right. I was too weak for this business. The thought of ruining an innocent girl's life wasn't something I did for enjoyment. It wasn't a pastime I called fun. It should have been, but I called most of my own shots around the warehouse. I didn't do things I didn't want to anymore. Since Grimsaw was scared to lose me like he'd lost my father, he generally didn't force things like this upon me either.

It was no secret that I had my own mind. Most of the other guys in the crew hated that I wasn't required to do the same things they did, but I was a rare case. I had special gifts, and I had paid my dues. I had spent months chopping Grimsaw's victims into small pieces. I had spent months making bodies disappear. Three years later, I now sat behind a keyboard and did what I did best; I hacked.

I did not sell slaves.

I walked to the second floor of the hotel using the outdoor stairwell, wincing as the air grazed the edges of my facial cuts. After setting the blonde back to her bare feet, I slid the card into the pass box and gestured for her to enter through the threshold first.

The room was what you would expect to find at a small hotel on a highway in California. Crooked and dusty pictures were coloring the walls. The bedspread was decorated with an ugly print of orange flowers. There was a small desk in the corner, banged up and potentially moldy. At its very best, the room was basic.

"It's old," I noted.

"I haven't showered in weeks. It's perfect."

"I guess," I frowned, trying to ignore the images I had of Grimsaw striking her face with his palm. "I want you to know that I don't condone what Grimsaw is doing to you. I'm not as sick as he is, but I also don't want you to get it tangled. My morals aren't fantastic either."

"You've never stuck a pistol to my jaw, so I doubt you're as bad as he is." She stared down at the carpet, leaving her bangs to conceal most of the tribulation sheeting her face. "I don't understand how you're still breathing. You should have been killed for attacking Grimsaw the way you did at the warehouse. Why did he let what you did slide?"

I scratched at the back of my head. I didn't want to admit that I was a hacker. I didn't want to admit to a lot of things, but I could tell this girl was like a lobster hovering over boiling water; definitely the type to pry.

"I'm good with technology," I stayed vague.

"What does that mean?"

The creases on her forehead made me smile inside, but I found myself wishing I could hate her instead. Ruining her life would be easier that way… *somehow.*

"What kind of clothes do you normally wear?" I transferred topics, diverting her attention away from my line of work. "I'll go get a few things while you take a shower. You're constantly pulling that dress down, so I know you didn't pick it out for yourself. I also know you're uncomfortable around me, but I won't hurt you."

"We'll see about that," she whispered distrustfully, and I didn't blame her for being so cautious. "I normally wear casual attire, like beach dresses and cardigans. I surf too, so you can't go wrong with board shorts."

As I stood clothed in a bloody t-shirt and fraying blue jeans, it was obvious I wasn't a big fan of fashion.

"What's a cardigan? Like a sweater or something?"

"Yes," she nodded, staring at me with intent. I could tell she was on the verge of saying something I wasn't going to like. "I don't know when this whole nice act of yours will be letting up. I'm sure you have your boundaries, but I could use something else too…"

"What do you need?"

"Female products."

I tried to figure out if she was kidding. I wasn't a total newbie when it came to chick problems. My sister had been an early bloomer, leaving me all too familiar with the subject, but the blonde was stepping over some questionable lines with me now.

"I don't even know you, but you're asking me to buy you tampons?" I vaulted my right eyebrow. "Since you just tried to escape from me, don't you think that request might be a little too audacious?"

"I don't even need them yet," she sighed, allowing her cheeks to fill with air. "But I want to be prepared. What if I have no way of getting them in a week? I doubt the man in Vegas will buy me any. I don't know how human slavery works exactly, but I assume my needs won't be placed at top priority."

Despite how badly I wanted to, I didn't take a step toward her. I hardly even breathed. I wanted to tell her that everything would be okay, but the sad truth recited the exact opposite. Nothing would ever be okay... not for either of us.

I knew she was on the verge of crying. I could see the fluid building up in her eyes, but she didn't allow the river to break free. This was fortunate, because I didn't do well with a crying woman. I didn't do well with anything other than fucking them, but the sight of the fingerprints bruised into this girl's collar had me right twisted. I knew why too.

Because this could be Tessa.

This could be my sister.

"I'll think about it," I nodded, overrun by guilt as the emotion sank through my skin. "Do you realize how stupid it is of me to walk out this door? You're all that stands in the way of my sister. I don't know you from a hole in the ground, but she's very important to me. If you run, I will hunt you down. If that happens, things won't be good for you. I advise you to stay here."

"Even if I did try to escape, I can't make it very far."

She didn't look at me, and I knew it was because she didn't trust me. She had every right to question my character, especially given the people I associated with, but I was growing determined to find her a way out. With a little time, I would think of something to save her alongside my sister. I had to. There was no other option.

"You're not a bag of luggage," I stated.

"Grimsaw is trying to sell me like I am."

"Trying to sell you and actually doing it are two different things. I don't permit sex trafficking. I won't let this go down the way he wants it to. Your life isn't over yet."

"How can I believe you?"

"Have a little hope."

As she tugged the red dress down for the fifteenth time, her blue eyes flashed back to the crimson carpet beneath her feet. I doubted she believed my confession, but I had just made up my mind. I couldn't live with myself if I didn't help her. I couldn't be a duplicate of Grimsaw.

"You seem nothing like those other guys," she alleged softly, wiping away a strip of hair that was stuck to her wet eyelashes. "You shouldn't be involved with them."

"You don't know anything about me," I denied her faith in me. "I don't have a soul anymore. Nothing hurts or makes me happy. All I do is exist. Under Grimsaw's watch, that's all I'm allowed to do. I haven't always been so highly respected by him. I've had to do a lot of sick shit to achieve my standing; things that would terrify a girl like you."

"I can handle more than you think," she refuted, her bruised condition a physical exemplification of her statement. "Why do you assume these things would terrify me?"

"Because they have destroyed me," I answered with a twitch. "You probably think I've never tried to detox before. You probably think the pills I swallow are killing me, but you'd be wrong if so. In truth, the pills are what have kept me alive this long. The skeletons I have buried in my closet would make my narcotic addiction look like child's play. If it weren't for the drugs and my sister, I would have killed myself months ago."

After speaking the most I had yet to her, I disappeared from the dirty room. I shut the door with a clang, entering the heat to make my way back toward the car. With every step the length of my feet marched forth, I prayed I wasn't making the worst mistake of my life by leaving her here alone.

WELCOME TO MY PARTY

HUNTER GARCIEZ

Thursday. 10:30 P.M.

ONCE I REACHED THE CAMARO, I threw three of the pills Grimsaw had given me into my mouth. I didn't know what they were, nor did it really matter. I needed something stronger than I was used to. If a handful would end Shayla's life, I figured the concoction might alleviate at least a fraction of my stress.

Shutting my eyes, I pushed them down my throat with nothing but saliva. I had just pulled away from the hotel when a call chimed through on my cellphone. My screen illuminated with the name I didn't want to see most; Grimsaw Santiago.

He couldn't know I wasn't with his slave. He couldn't know I had left her alone, but screening his call wasn't an option either. He had my sister, which was a life I wasn't willing to gamble with.

Succumbing to reality, I linked the stereo's Bluetooth to my cellphone. Seconds later, his thick accent filled the speakers in the car.

"Garciez, how's the ride been treating you?"

"You're a piece of shit," I snarled, losing grips with sanity. "This wasn't how I wanted to spend my day. When you promoted me, I was supposed to be done acting like your little monkey."

"The way I see it, you've got it good. I gave you a blonde bombshell. Rather than feeding her, why don't you try fucking her instead?"

My brain froze as I realized the car had been tapped with a

microphone this entire time. I had known to assume there was a GPS stuck to the dragster, but a mic wasn't something I'd had time to consider.

"Rape isn't my style."

"So I've learned," Grimsaw chuckled. "Look, let's not fairy step around here. I know you're on route. I know you're sitting in Bakersfield, but I don't like the direction some of your conversations have been headed with the whore."

I began to squire around in search for the recording device, but I found nothing. I ran my fingers over the visors and dash, then alongside the leather seats, again finding nothing. It wasn't until I reached my hand into the very back of the glovebox that I finally struck gold.

"I'm doing what you requested of me, but that doesn't mean I have to like it," I said, twirling the wires for the installed mic in my hand. "You've put me in a contorted position. You know that already, because you wouldn't have wasted your time doing it otherwise. It's no surprise that I'm far from accepting of this shit."

"True," Grimsaw agreed, his teeth grinding together even louder than mine. "Just don't get your head warped. The blonde might be a looker, but she's been lying to you this whole time. She knows why she's sitting beside you. It's you who doesn't."

"Lying to me about what?" I asked, distracted by my need to arrange an immediate plan. I knew I had to drop the Camaro now, leaving it in some parking lot for the Feds to find, but I wasn't sure how I was going to get my hands on a new vehicle just yet.

As Grimsaw's following words plunged through me like a wad of explosives, my mental searching came to a direct halt.

"Her dad killed your parents, G."

In the moment that followed, I didn't breathe. On the exterior, my body showed no signs of panic. On the inside, a quiet rage began to consume my mind; a rage so subtle, it was destined to turn fatal.

"Bullshit," I growled, trying to convince myself he was lying. The thing was, Grimsaw didn't lie. No matter who the truth hurt, he was always savagely honest instead.

Up until this point, I hadn't known who had killed my parents. All I knew, whoever it was had been familiar with my father. It was the only thing that made sense. Aside from my dad's mafia entanglement, our family had been quite normal. He had been involved with a lot of shit he shouldn't have been, just like me, but my mom had owned a flower shop. My mom hadn't deserved to die like she did. Aside from choosing my father as a spouse, she had done everything right in her life.

It was because of my parent's story that I swore I would never fall in love myself. I didn't want to be the reason an innocent girl took her final breath. In the end, it was my dad's fault that my mom had burned alive. He had allowed her to stay by his side, knowing he was no good for anyone. He'd willingly brought her into his circus. He'd done the opposite of what he should have, which was leave her after realizing she was falling for him. As a mafia man, he knew he destroyed everything he touched. The problem was, he'd been too blinded by love to care.

And look where that got them.

"It's the truth, bro," Grimsaw professed. "The little bitch knew it too. I told her she could tell you, but I guess she thought better of it. Kill the blonde if you wanna, but you'll owe Ray Barnes a few million for her. It's a small price to get revenge on the man who ended the lives of your folks, though, ain't it? Her dad took your blood, so you take his? I figured it was rightfully suiting."

If the slave's father really had killed my parents, which was an idea I wasn't fully sold on yet, she and I had just morphed into sworn enemies. If what Grimsaw was saying was true, remorse wasn't something I would feel while my fingers were wrapped around her father's throat. Even if Shayla was begging for me to stop, I wouldn't. I didn't owe her anything. Her dad, however...

He owed me everything.

"I bet you want to take a ride on that pony now, *eh amigo?*" Grimsaw enjoyed the plot. "You should have never made a wisecrack about leaving the gang. If you hadn't, you wouldn't be back down to maggot status right now."

Grimsaw was mistaken. I didn't want to touch the slave sexually. I wasn't a total freak like he was, but I did gain the sudden desire to murder her father. Torturing the man who had killed my parents was a pleasing thought; one I couldn't control.

I even considered harming the blonde for what her dad had apparently done, but I didn't think it would help my problems any. It wasn't her I wanted to kill. It was her father.

An abnormal tingle began to stir in my limbs. It suddenly became clear why she was the girl seated beside me. Grimsaw always had a motive, and now I knew exactly what it was. I had spent three years trying to conclude why my parents had died, always coming up emptyhanded. Whoever had killed them seemed to be a professional when it came to concealing their tracks. I didn't know who Shayla's dad was personally, but it was clear he was no idiot.

The information hit me like a goddamn Bugatti, but the worst of it all... *she* had known. While I had been mentally devising a plan to protect her, Shayla had been filtering lies my way through her teeth.

"I would dare you to run away from it all, but it'd be pointless," Grimsaw's tone was cancerous, but I hardly listened to his words. "No matter where you go, no matter where you attempt to secure yourself safety, I will always find you. You might be a genius, but I'm a fucking lunatic." Even the simplicity of his oxygen inhalations sounded pitiless. "Welcome to my party, G. You might wanna buckle up for this one. It's gonna be a long and bumpy ride."

With that, the line went dead.

As dead as my parents were.

10
THE WORST KIND OF FRIEND

SHAYLA STONE

Thursday. 11:30 P.M.

I COULD HANDLE CANCER, BUT I was battling thugs now. Of all the monsters under my bed, the mafia was the very worst. When it came to the thought of nearly dying from Leukemia versus dying from abuse in the sex trade, I couldn't decide which would be worse.

I sat in a white towel on the ugly bedspread. I had thrown Grimsaw's red dress directly into the trash. Since I had no other outfits with me, a towel was my only clothing option until Hunter returned. Until then, there was nothing for me to do but fidget. For all I knew, rather than exiting to buy me clothes, he could have gone to buy the supplies necessary to clean up the scene of my soon-to-be murder.

Speak of the devil.

The door to the room began to creak open slowly. I stopped clicking through the channels on the television, turning away from the small screen to meet his heavy gaze. He'd changed into a pair of tan jeans. His torso was sporting a black t-shirt with a logo across the front, while his head held a dark baseball cap that dimmed his features. His face was cleaner than it had been before. Without the blood, it was almost too clear now. I hated to admit it, but the sight of him wasn't totally repulsive.

I counted the six bags he was holding in his large hands; hands that might just kill me. The straps were digging into his wrists with their hefty weight. I wondered if he had remembered my tampons, but the question didn't seem important as I took note of the evil on his face. I had thought he would be happy to find me still sitting at the hotel. I had obeyed him, but something was wrong.

As he set the bags onto the bed beside me, glaring at me like I'd just shot his puppy in the head, he ordered, "Go get changed. Do it fast."

When I was younger, back when my mom had still been alive, she'd had her favorite sayings to use on me. '*Because I'm your mother*' was her most beloved of all. Rightfully so, after hearing it so damn much, I'd grown to hate it the most. '*Don't talk with a full mouth*' was second on that list. Lastly, a slogan of hers that had stayed with me the most since her death, she used to say, '*Don't speak unless your voice can improve the silence*'.

Listening to her advice from beyond the grave, I decided to keep my mouth pursed with muteness. After clutching onto the bags, I obligingly headed for the washroom.

Upon shutting the door behind myself, I pulled out the blue maxi dress that had caught my eye first. The fabric was polyester, decorated with silver poinsettias, and the navy was long and concealing; a comfort I didn't deserve to have Hunter supply me with.

Along with numerous amounts of clothing options, which even included a few pairs of panties, none of which were thongs, he had also bought me a toothbrush and paste. There was perfume, body lotion, black sandals that looked to be my size, and even medicating salve. He hadn't forgotten my tampons either. Ironically enough, there was a box of fine chocolates in the bag too.

If Hunter had any knowledge about what my father had done to his parents, he wouldn't have bought me anything. He would have never stood in the tampon aisle trying to decide which brand would be best for me. As I stared at a box of plastic applicators instead of cardboard, I knew the guy wasn't a complete amateur when it came to the needs of a female.

Although Hunter seemed sympathetic, compassion only went so far. It wouldn't hold up in the court of betrayal. It wouldn't hold up against what my father had supposedly done to his family. It wouldn't hold up against the treachery I was committing by not telling Hunter the truth. Even if he was tamer than his acquaintances, if he ever found out I had been keeping what I knew from him, I would die one hell of a painful death.

Feeling a price tag stab at the skin on my back, I reached under the dress and ripped it from the fabric. I wondered how much all of this had cost him. The poinsettia dress didn't look cheap. Neither did the other six. Being as late as it was, I imagined there was a limited number of stores with open signs still hanging in their front windows.

My guts tangled as I stared at the small chunk of paper in my hand. *$349.00 for one dress.* I forced myself to take a seat beside the corroded sink, wondering why Hunter had so much money to spare. It didn't take long before I remembered he worked for Grimsaw.

Lifting the front of the navy dress, my fingers began to outline my midsection. Tears had just begun to slide down my cheeks as I stared at myself, but an abrupt knock on the door caused me to brush the salt away. Hunter entered the restroom before I could argue, scoping my thin body with eerie eyes. I dropped the fabric in a rush, not wanting him to see my protruding ribs, but his frown told me I had been seconds too late.

"Just be thankful you're still alive," he said.

There was something off in his voice; something I couldn't place. As for the melancholy on his face, that was something even the blind would notice. I got the feeling it wasn't just the thin looks of me that was causing his current glare.

I brushed my cheek against my shoulder, attempting to avoid his scrutiny. I knew my situation wasn't one where the handsome prince would stride in on his white horse and save the day. Men like Hunter didn't protect the damsel in distress. Instead, once Grimsaw told him the apparent truth about my dad, Hunter would probably kill me himself. I would never end up like one of those rescued girls in Hollywood. Me, I would end up six feet under instead. The faster I came to terms with this, the better off I would be.

"I know things could be worse," I answered.

"Like if I found out you were a liar?"

As shivers crept down my neck, he turned toward the sink. I watched him scrub his inflamed knuckles, as if he thought the action might clean him of the muddy situation surrounding us too.

Once he had deemed himself clean, he retrieved the tube of salve from one of the bags and gave me a questioning look; a look that asked if I was going to hit him if he tried to disinfect me.

Taking his chances, he began to rub gentle circles over the lacerations on my wrists. I tried to pay attention to the swirling salve, but the crease denting the space between his lightning green eyes was making it a challenge. I got the impression that he was waiting for me to strike up conversation, but I had very little to say. The way I saw it, I couldn't incriminate myself if I didn't speak.

Once Hunter was done painting my wrists, I streaked a glob of the ointment onto the end of my pointer finger next. Lifting my hand, I asked, "Can I do the same to you?"

He nodded and lowered his face, aiding in my ability to reach the gash on his left cheek. His following words, however, weren't nearly as welcoming.

"You're a good actress, blondie."

"I don't know what you mean."

I chewed on the inside of my cheek, continuing to coat him with salve. I shied away from his smoldering stare, but I knew the rattle in my voice hadn't passed by as subtle.

I focused heavily on the depth of his incisions. He needed stitches, but I perceived he wasn't the type of guy who cared about things like that. As I stood close to him, only inches separating us, I could see other scars already engraved into his flesh. Every scar told a hidden story; a story part of me wanted to read.

"I thought we were becoming pals," he whispered, taking the swipes of my forefinger like a champion. "But if so, you're the worst kind of friend to have."

That was all it took for me to understand.

He knew about my father.

My hand dropped as my eyes met his. We stared one another down, resembling two beasts about to mangle each other with their horns. I was half expecting him to swipe his feet on the linoleum flooring, but he did nothing but glower instead.

"I knew there was a reason Grimsaw placed *you* beside me. He could have tested me in many other ways, but he had specific motives by involving you. You've known your relevance to my family this whole time, haven't you?"

As Hunter took a menacing step toward me, eliminating the final space in our already scarce distance, I said nothing. The looming scent of him smothered me, causing my words to fail as our chests rubbed together. The faintest layer of cologne was wafting from his body.

"Answer me!"

He sealed his hands around my hips, trying to force me to speak by shaking me. When I refused to comply, he pushed me up against the wall and held me in a secure position with the compact build of his body. The bitter haze in his eyes rendered me motionless. Although vulnerability was bleeding from me, the anger in his face didn't falter at all.

"Has this been fun for you?" He gave my body another jangle. "Have you been laughing at me while I've been scrambling to get you showered and fed? I must look like a fucking idiot to you."

My back hit the wall a second time, but the force wasn't enough to break me. His fingers continued to grapple with my boney hips, bristling me with their suffocating touch. A seething glare maintained position in his deadly eyes, but I didn't allow myself to look weak beneath it.

For what my father had allegedly done, I knew a slice of Hunter wanted to kill me right here and now. I could see the smoke bellowing from his ears, poisoning the air I breathed. I tried to push him away from me, but I was no contender for his weight. He knew he could crush me. He was using it to his advantage too.

"¿Qué habrías hecho?" I fired back, asking him what he would have done if placed in my position. I knew what I had done was wrong, but there were reasons for my deceit. "Firstly, I don't believe my dad did it. Secondly, if you were lined up to become a slave, would you be so willing to risk your last shot at freedom by speaking a lethal truth like that one? I didn't want you to start shoveling my grave yourself."

"You speak Spanish?" He leaned away, allowing my fear to decompress slightly. "Is there anything else I should know about you? Or should I just assume everything you say is a lie?"

The grief on his face was burdensome, and I hated that I had conjured the arising. No words could fix what I had done. In his eyes, I was a liar now; nothing less, nothing more.

I had just ruined my chance at survival.

"Just listen—" I tried.

"I should have known you'd be the same as every other girl; manipulative and fucking selfish. For a second there, I thought you might be different." No words could properly detail the hatred masking his face. "Consider this my dismissal of whatever comradery might have been forming between us. Don't bother looking my way for sympathy. Now that I know what your father did, I no longer have a reason to feel any for you."

11
MASOCHISTIC

SHAYLA STONE

Friday. 12:00 A.M.

I KEPT MY MOUTH SHUT WHILE we exited from the rented room. As I followed Hunter into the parking lot, it wasn't long before we stood beside a new mode of transportation. A shiny, red truck sat in the stall ahead of us, done up with bushwhacker flares and a macho lift kit. Hunter looked at it like it was his, and a nod of his head suggested I should climb into it.

"Fuel efficient," I mumbled, glancing at the emblem broadcasting the type of motor beneath the hood. "I would ask if you'll go broke paying for the diesel to fill the tank, but I've already learned you aren't hurting for a dollar. You seem to spend racks like they're going out of style. I wouldn't be wearing a three-hundred-dollar dress if you weren't frivolous."

"While I'm in the middle of a war, costs aren't a predominant factor in my thought processes." His eyes shot green daggers at me. "Besides, what's a girl like you know about a truck like this?"

"It looks brand spanking new," I smiled like a ditz, playing the role of a mindless Barbie. Having blonde hair had always benefited me when it came to acting stupid, because stupid was what people naturally anticipated me to be. "It has big tires too."

"No shit," Hunter shot me a mocking stare, fueling me to do what I was about to. Little did he know, I knew more than I was letting on.

My lifelong friend, Bree, had a boyfriend who was a few years older than us. That boyfriend of hers owned his own auto shop. Unlike Grimsaw's, Rylan's warehouse was legitimate. On the weekends, her boyfriend did up old muscle cars and took them to the dragging strips. Since Bree had never been interested in speed, Rylan treated me like his apprentice instead.

"It's a 2500 Big Horn Diesel," I said, gearing my body toward the truck. "It has a Cummins 6.7-liter turbodiesel inline-six motor, which is an upgraded feature from the 5.7 and 6.4-liter HEMIs. The engine has about 370 horsepower and 900 pound-feet of torque. It doesn't look all that after-marketed, so I suspect no mods have been made to the engine other than the original upgrade of the motor. Stock, the truck will tow just under 9,000 kilograms if you want it to. It gets 14 MPG on a good day, making it a moronic vehicle to drive around unless you're hauling something." I coiled a strand of my hair around my forefinger, just to emphasize how much I disliked his impetuous judgments of me. "I don't know much about a truck like this, but I bet it goes vroom real fast."

"Point taken," he shrugged, seeming to dislike me even more now. "The Camaro was laced with a microphone and a GPS. I had to ditch and swap it. This truck was the first vehicle I could acquire."

I thought about the words we'd exchanged in the Camaro. Grimsaw wouldn't have been pleased to hear any of them.

While Hunter tossed the bags into the backseat, I situated myself up front. I didn't want to know how he'd gotten his hands on the truck so fast. I didn't know of too many dealerships open at this hour, leaving me with one dreadful assumption; he'd stolen it.

I shot him an inquisitive look as he entered the truck's cabin. I knew better than to poke the bear, but I picked up the stick and took a stab at him anyway.

"Can I assume you're good at hotwiring an engine?"

"I'm good at anything that involves working with my hands," he replied, offering a glare of sexual temptation my way. "Put your seatbelt on."

I did as he requested and strapped the restriction over my chest, wondering what reason there was to keep myself safe at all anymore. As far as I was concerned, flying through the windshield would be nothing more than a blessing in disguise at this point.

"Eat as much as you can," he instructed, reeling his neck as he shifted through various lanes of late-night traffic. "I'm no fan of yours, but I also refuse to starve you. It's clear you need the calories."

A pizza box sat sweltering on the center console between us. The smell was worth a million bucks at a time like this. Although I was cautious of him, I didn't need to be told twice. I dove into the luxury of Italian cuisine with two hands. If Hunter wanted to watch me eat, I would star in a very unladylike scene of hunger just for him.

Unlike I'd been expecting, the brute in the driver's seat didn't head out of Bakersfield. He didn't hop onto the 58-E like he should have. He ignored every green sign that signaled for him to go left to Vegas instead of right.

"You're going the wrong way to Nevada," I noted with a swallow. "You either have an unbearable sense of direction, or you're intentionally burrowing us deeper into Bakersfield. Which is it?"

"You need to see a doctor."

"You were serious about that?"

"Of course," he frowned. "My ducks are right fucking scattered. They're nowhere close to in a row, but I will find a way to repair the hand you've been dealt. You can take me for face value. I always mean what I say."

"You said those things before you found out who my dad was," I whispered shamefully, a new layer of filth dirtying my soul. "Even if I don't believe my dad did what Grimsaw claims, you do."

"Grimsaw wouldn't make it up, but it doesn't matter in this moment. I'll never like you, but I understand your reasons for not telling me. I'm trying to put myself in your shoes, because I can see you've been through a lot."

Hunter might have been trying to understand my reasons for lying to him, but the doleful expression canvasing his face was still unfortunate to see. He wasn't a stupid boy. Being a gang member, it was obvious he did some stupid things. An addiction to narcotics seemed to fog his judgement, but he wasn't a useless bag of rocks in the mental department.

He didn't seem to concern himself with law and regulation. Rather, I sensed he liked to create his own. The drugs had visibly done damage to him. The man sitting in the driver's seat wasn't portraying the best version of himself, and the wannabe psychiatrist in me longed to help him… but a guy like him didn't accept assistance willingly.

I knew I would be better off not knowing a damn thing about him. Not only did he have bad habits, his boundaries between right and wrong were much vaster than mine. He had a lost end that seemed totally daunting to find. Yet, something about that enamored me.

And there was a word to define people like me; people who enjoyed inflicting pain onto themselves; people who reached for unobtainable things; people who kept faith when they had no reason to…

Masochistic.

12
HEPATITIS A, B, AND C

SHAYLA STONE

Friday. 12:30 A.M.

WE PULLED INTO THE PARKING lot of a hospital a few minutes later. I had managed to pork down five pieces of Hawaiian pizza along the way, which had to be a personal best of mine. Since food still felt foreign to me, no surprise came when the overindulgence caused my guts to churn.

Hunter exited the truck and made his way around to the passenger side. After opening the door for me, he offered his hand to assist me down from the elevated height. I tried to think of a way to thank him for bringing me to medical aid, but my feet hit pavement before anything of value came to mind.

"They're going to make us wait for hours." I pointed toward the emergency clinic. "It isn't like either of us have a dismembered limb. We're going to stay at low priority."

"You said this truck goes vroom real fast, right?" He shot me a dubious look, nodding toward the red vehicle as he locked the doors. "If I drive with a lead foot, we should make it to Vegas in no time. But if we get pulled over along the way, you'll have to start sucking my dick. It'd be the only logical thing for you to do."

"How do you figure that?" I contended, reciprocating his dubious gaze. I did my best to conceal the red-hot blush that wanted to brighten my face.

"Because a male cop would relate to my erratic driving that way.

A pretty girl like you… shit. Once he saw who was slurping me down, he'd probably just let me slide with a tip of his hat. *Have a good evening...*"

I smiled at his unorthodox compliment, finding something so strange about him. I intentionally hid my shredded wrists by wrapping a black cardigan around my body, but Hunter's gory face was no less discreet. As we walked through the electric doors of the facility, our shoulders nearly touching, all eyes in the lobby bombarded our way.

"Take a seat and wait," Hunter directed me, acting like he was used to stirring up static. Before walking toward the service area to work his charming magic, he lowered his head to add, "If you try to pull any fancy shit on me in here, I won't hesitate to slit your throat. We clear, blondie?"

I bobbed in recognition. "Crystal."

Glancing to the right of the white room, rows of chairs were filling the vast wing. The hospital seemed to be home for an eighth of Bakersfield. Since I'd been sheltered in a cell for nearly a month, I wondered if there was a virus epidemic on the rise that I didn't know about.

A Latino boy was sitting on the floor, staring at me. Plastic building blocks were scattered around his small body, and his brown eyes lit up once he realized I was watching him back.

Eagerly, he asked, "Do you want to play too?"

Deciding that I wasn't too old to play with *Legos*, I made my way over to him and took a seat on the floor. I veered my head toward his mother who sat protectively in a close chair.

"Do you mind?"

A warm look confirmed that she didn't. I knew she was assuming I was anorexic, or something along those lines, but she kept her thoughts to herself and encouraged me instead.

"He would love a new friend."

"I don't have friends," the boy said, slamming a yellow brick into a red one. "My mom takes me to the park, but I like to play alone. Do you play with *Legos* a lot?"

"I wish," I giggled, sloping my head in fascination; a fascination his mother noticed. "Playing would be much more fun than doing adult things."

"Like having a bath?"

"Just like having a bath," I agreed, helping the boy construct an off-kilter house. For whatever reason, he seemed to like the smaller blocks. He had a routine going too. Only yellow and red bricks were allowed.

Feeling a precarious heat on my back, I jerked my neck to find Hunter seated a few rows behind me. He sent me a warm smile, cocking his eyebrow like it surprised him to see me sitting on a hospital floor. I sent him a shrug before turning back toward the young boy.

"He hates the tub," the child's mother laughed. As she pushed her dark hair away from her face, I decided she couldn't be any older than twenty-three herself. "I tell him it's a part of life. I say he needs to get used to it if he wants to get married one day. I tell him girls don't like smelly boys."

"Girls are gross," he grunted, laughing as his mom poked him in the guts. "But I have soldiers. They keep watch for me while I'm in the tub. I have pirates and ships too. The pirates are the bad guys. The soldiers are always the good. The soldiers keep everybody safe."

I stared at the kid, lost in my own state of mind. If only it were so simple to decipher who fit into which category in real life; the pirates and the soldiers; the peacemakers and the villains; the good versus the bad.

"Penelope Stone?" A nurse called out, distracting me from the plastic architecture. I had to keep myself from laughing at the name she sought.

"Here," Hunter answered.

"That's me," I told the boy.

"I'm Carlos," he introduced himself.

I smiled at him, ignoring his mother's obvious speculation of how I had managed to get my name called so quickly. Even I didn't know what Hunter had done to pull that one off. I probably didn't want to either.

"It was great to meet you." I gave his dark hair a quick ruffle, causing his shaggy bangs to fall in front of his brown eyes. "You be good for your mom, okay? When she forces you to take a bath, it's only because she loves you more than life itself."

"I'll think about it."

I sent Carlos a final look before raising myself from the linoleum flooring. The nurse began to grow agitated by my slow movements, but Hunter didn't try to speed me along. The boy's mother said a quick goodbye to me, sending me a smile halfway between sympathetic and worried, but I disappeared before she could ask any questions.

As we followed the angry nurse down the white corridor, I nudged Hunter in the arm and asked, "How did you get me in so fast?"

"Money talks."

"How much did this cost you?"

"More than I'll admit."

"What if I have AIDS?" I feared.

"You don't."

"But what if I do?"

"I'll brew the cure for you."

"There is no cure for AIDS."

"There is a cure for every disease," he whispered, shaking his head like I was a pain in his ass. "The world is a sick place. Do you think the government wants you to know the things they do? Fuck no. It would cause an uproar."

"Is that a conspiracy theory of yours?"

"No. It's pure fact." There was no doubt in his hushed tone. "If the authorities were to cure every sick body dying in a hospital bed, which they can do, the earth would become overrun. Depopulation needs to occur somehow. Darwinism just isn't enough. Society is led to believe these cures don't exist, but they do."

As his words trickled through me, something like maggots began to crawl over my skin. A vision entered my mind. Only one thing sat before me; a briefcase full of magical cures; recipes that my dad had thieved from the government; recipes that Hunter had then stolen from my dad.

If the cures existed, which I now had reason to believe they did, everything Grimsaw had said about my father could be true. For all I knew, the man who had raised me was a coldblooded killer. For all I knew, I could have been cured from Leukemia years before I had been. For all I knew, it was Hunter's interception of the cures that had kept me from entering remission sooner.

I would never forget what it was like to battle Leukemia. I would never forget the pungent taste of the medication or the vomiting.

I would never forget the needles or the scalpels. I would never forget the Chemotherapy or the baldness. I would never forget the stem cell transplants. Most of all, while I'd been begging to be put out of my misery, I would never forget the fear in my father's eyes.

If my dad had known there was a cure, it made all too much sense that he would have gone after it for me. If it was true, I was the reason that my dad had murdered Hunter's parents. I was the reason people had died. The timing lined up. Three years ago, I had been on the verge of dying in a cancerous way. Three years ago, Hunter's parents had been killed. Although I didn't believe much in coincidence, in this moment, I was sure as hell trying to.

I jerked at Hunter's hand, forcing his body to face mine. Both of our feet abandoned motion, irritating the nurse ahead of us just a little more. "Why are you helping me?"

"I think hope is for cowards who need a fake backbone to survive." He speared me with a look that held a thousand words. "But after all you've been through, despite who your father is, the least I can do is pretend to think otherwise."

***

Along with multiple stitches on my wrists, I had gotten four vials of blood drawn. The doctor had unavoidably noticed my tattoo, but he hadn't asked about the cause of infection. Hunter had remained in the room for the entirety, making it difficult for the health practitioner to speak of his curiosity. The man's expressions, however, had made his interest evident. His brown eyes had been silky with the desire to meddle.

"What is your role in the gang?" I asked Hunter, nervously ripping my fingernails off one by one. As my test results were being deciphered, he and I had been given a few moments alone. I planned to make good use of them.

"It doesn't matter," he brushed me off, pacing around the room faster than I was. "Whatever I do is illegal and immoral. That's all you need to know about me."

"What if I want to know more?" I remarked, immediately regretting the way I had said it. "I mean, you've been helping me. What if I want to help you in some way too?"

His pacing came to an instant halt as his body shifted my way.

His eyes began to analyze me, but he wasn't quick with his reply. When his lips finally parted, only one sentence fluttered through them.

"Then you would be a very stupid girl."

I opened my mouth to continue harassing him, but the doctor re-entered the room and cut my opportunity short.

"Your test results are back. What did you think you might have?"

"Hepatitis A, B, and C?" I guessed, quivering at the many possibilities.

Hunter glowered at me, unenthused by my response.

"Do you mind giving me a minute alone with Penelope?" The doctor asked Hunter, a sly hint of something in his eyes. "You could use a set of stitches yourself. My assistant will get you cleaned up."

"In a second," Hunter decided, perceiving my angst as I began to hyperventilate. He cupped my chin with his palm, forcing me to meet his frosty gaze. "*Por favor, confía en mí?*"

Hunter was asking me to trust him. I knew this, but the doctor looked confused as he attempted to break the language apart. By the way his face crinkled, it was obvious he couldn't comprehend Spanish dialect.

After I had nodded, Hunter made his exit from the room. Oddly enough, as I watched his bulky body leave through the door, I had to command myself not to follow. I despised the feeling immediately; the feeling of being an abused pet who shadowed their caretaker.

"Is there something I should know about?" The specialist fixated on me. Beneath his orange hair, a new rumple appeared in his sweaty forehead. "Anything at all?"

I stared at the crow's feet near his eyes. In this moment, I knew I was being given my way out. I was being offered a safety net from Grimsaw's games; a chance at freedom, which was all I had wanted for weeks. Yet… it didn't feel right to take it.

"I appreciate your worry," I replied, cautioning him with my eyes to back off. It wasn't in his best interest to know anything. The fact that he'd seen my face was already enough to put him in grave danger. I grabbed my test results from his slender hands, shaking them. With the fattest of all frogs in my throat, I asked, "Am I totally diseased?"

"No." Although the doctor was giving me good news, sorrow

still painted his face. "Did he put those marks on your body?" He pointed toward my mangled wrists, hoping I might crack under the pressure. "I know you didn't try to cut your own wrists. Judging by your tattoo, I think there's more to the story. I can't say anything without receiving your consent. If you give me that, I can have that man arrested in just ten minutes. The police—"

"No police," I interjected.

Maybe the doctor could save me, but could he save Hunter's little sister too? There was no way in hell, and that wasn't a burden I wanted on my conscience. I already had enough guilt weighing me down. I couldn't knowingly allow a twelve-year-old to get swept up in all of this too.

I wanted to run away. I wanted to take the easy route toward guaranteed safety. I wanted to sneak myself into the witness protection program. I wanted to go anywhere instead of where I was fated to wind up, but Hunter had gone out on a limb for me. He had fed me. He had trusted me to be left alone to shower when I had given him no reason to. I wouldn't be sitting in the hospital right now if some part of him didn't want to help me. Because of all these things, I needed to do the same for his sister.

"He wasn't the one who did this to me," I finalized, meeting the doctor in the eye. "Not only did this guy feed me, he is the only one who can save me now too. If I thought you could do anything to help me, I would have already told you so. You'll be bringing death to many innocent people by magnifying my visit here today." I rose from the bed and made my way toward the door. While placing my hand on the steel knob to depart from the sterile room, I pleaded, "I'm asking you to forget what you've seen. You'll be helping me the most if you'll do just that."

"I can save you if you are in danger. The marks along your skin…" Pain struck his already worried face. He reached to hand me a bundle of gauze and antiseptic wipes, as if he thought I might be needing them in the upcoming hours. "We haven't even gone over your results yet. You don't know the outcomes."

"Will I be pleased?"

"I believe so." He calmed me with a nod of his head, but his face continued to sacrifice a beseeching stare. As I accepted the bandages, he guessed, "Your name isn't really Penelope, is it?"

Evidently, his anxiety hadn't banished. This fact was transparent, but I had no time to ease his tension. I had enough problems of my own to sort through. At this point, all I could do was pray that the rules of doctor/patient confidentiality were legally secured with an iron fist.

"Take care of yourself," he said paternally, accepting that I had no plans of forking over my real name. "Take the antibiotics for ten days. If you avoid aggravating the areas, your wrists should heal without any issue."

With the fakest of all smiles, I replied, "Thanks, doc."

13
THE VENOM IN HER BITE

HUNTER GARCIEZ

Friday. 1:00 A.M.

THE FEMALE ASSISTANT WAS GIVING me a scorning look with her drawn on eyebrows. Her hair was as maroon as the cotton pads stained before me. My eyes browsed over her fake face. Behind her mask of makeup, I didn't think she could be much older than I was. This warned me that she hadn't been a doctor for very long. While her unsteady hands erratically sewed stitches throughout the flesh on my cheek, I wasn't sure what kind of monster I would look like after leaving her room.

I sent the woman an amiable smile. I didn't want to conclude she was a terrible doctor without full warrant, but her jerky motions weren't sitting well with me. I needed her anxiety to ease sooner rather than later. I wasn't fond of being sewn up by a doctor who looked more scared than her patient.

I hadn't even wanted the stitches, but I'd known better than to make a big stir about it. Everyone was already curious of me. There would be no benefit in adding to that. Shayla had tried to detour their assumptions by claiming she'd attempted to slit her own wrists, but it was clear her cuts were from wire instead. The doctors knew something was up. If you wore a lab coat and had your name plastered to a hospital door, you probably weren't a complete idiot.

"Some deep gashes you have," the assistant cracked the air with her British accent, leaning to examine her work. I wasn't sure how much a doctor made per year, but the digits in her eyes said her bank account wasn't lacking. "Mind me asking how you got these lacerations?"

I tried to ignore her numbers. I tried not to step into her personal life, but that was much easier said than done. Trying to pretend I couldn't see any numbers in her eyes was like trying to bypass the reality of gravity.

The holograms weren't in black and white in my head; they were always in red. As I dove into her pupils, I dug onto her personal information. I clung onto every digit she knew. Being who she was, she had just unknowingly given me the code to every privatized wing on this level in the hospital.

That's how simple it was for me; *too simple*. It was too easy to use my abilities on things that were the opposite of holy. Most hackers needed a computer to pull of their fancy stunts. As for me, I was the fucking computer.

"The barrel of a pistol," I answered dryly, knowing she wouldn't believe me. "As it turns out, a life in the mafia isn't what it's cracked up to be in the movies. Eventually, times of war and times of peace become one in the same. All else withers away. Before you know it, you view a day where a gun doesn't get pointed at your forehead as a surprisingly good form of day. *The Godfather* made this shit look way cooler than it really is."

The doctor looked down at me with confusion, snipping at the end of the black thread near my eye socket. I was good at holding a gaze of steel, making it difficult to pinpoint the level of truth behind my words. I knew I shouldn't be messing with her head, but I thought reverse psychology might be of some value in this particular instance.

Shayla entered from the opposing room, wearing one of the dresses I had picked out for her. The color of navy looked better on her than I had imagined it would in the store. It wasn't surprising that she stole my concentration upon arrival. She held an envelope in her hands, but I couldn't read her expression well enough to decide whether she'd received good news or bad.

It had obviously been risky to bring her to the hospital. It wasn't hard to see she was suffering from malnourishment, but worse were the judgments from people who assumed *I* had caused her the discomfort. They looked at me like I was the bad guy. And maybe I was. After all, total hell was surrounding me. My sister was being held captive somewhere. Shayla's father had allegedly killed my parents. As if the situation wasn't already fucked up enough, I couldn't deny that the blonde fascinated me.

Her presence pixelated the doctor into total darkness. Her face had been contoured with diligence. Her cheekbones were error-less in architecture. Despite the cut above her upper lip, her smile was nothing less than electrocuting. These things were the physical aspects; things anyone could see. Beneath her beauty, there was a damaged soul; a soul as wrecked as mine. It was easy for me to make out the sadness roaming behind the numbers in her eyes.

I didn't know her background. I wasn't sure how she'd been raised, but she looked like a goodhearted American girl. She had long legs and textbook perfect looks, aside from being too thin, but nothing about her was overdone. Since she'd been held captive for weeks, there was no makeup destroying her complexion. Many girls were beautiful, but few were beautiful naturally.

Divergent from Shayla's wholesome looks, she knew how to use her soft voice to speak with assertion and intent. She wasn't as dumb as her ashy hair insinuated, nor as sweet as her blue eyes had led me to believe. Although many things stuck out about her, the sauce in her attitude was the most intriguing by far.

"Take good care of your boyfriend," the Brit said, sighing as my attention shifted toward Shayla. "If he hadn't received these stitches, infection would have surely settled in. I'm sure we can agree that his face is too pretty to ruin, yeah?"

Shayla's eyes grew globular at the improper referral of me. Her body stiffened, but she didn't legitimatize the doctor's assumptions. Instead, in her velvety sweet voice, she replied, "I can't be held responsible for keeping a man like that in line."

She walked over to me, smiling that perfect smile of hers. I ran my hand over the chest of my black t-shirt, a smirk gracing my freshly stitched face. When I had gone out to buy Shayla a few things, I had picked up some fresh clothes for myself too. I had thought it best to familiarize myself with the color black.

Black hid blood the best.

Although my body was much larger than Shayla's petite form, she managed to pull me out of the medical chair with one good thrust. My cheek felt strange, and I knew I would talk sideways for a good hour now. As I doubted the Frankenstein look was doing anything good for me, we said a quick goodbye to the doctor before exiting the room.

"How long have you known for?" Shayla broke the silence, refusing to face me. I continued to stalk behind her, breathing down her neck. "When did you find out?"

"Find out what?" I asked, purposely acting like a dick. "Might you be referring to the way your dad left me and my sister without any parents?"

At the sound of those words, she spun around like a ballerina. If it weren't for the sour expression lining her face, the motion might have been delightful.

"Drop the bullshit," she tried to put me in my place. "Did you know who my dad was before you drove away from the hotel earlier? The one you left me to shower in?"

"Ah, so that's what this is about," I smirked, piecing her motives together. "Don't beat around the bush, blondie. What you really want to know is when I bought you a box of tampons; before or after I had learned the news about who your old man was."

"Why would that matter?"

"Because you're attempting to decipher which side I'm on; good or evil." I didn't ask it like a question, because it wasn't one. "If I had spent three hundred bucks on a dress while knowing who you were in relation to the man who killed my parents, that would mean I have a soft side. If I had bought those things beforehand, it wouldn't mean as much."

"That's not why I asked," she lied.

"It was," I reaffirmed. "Whenever you get the bright idea to try and outsmart me, you'll be pained to find that manipulation doesn't work on a mind like mine. I can always keep up. Besides, you're spending too much time focusing on the wrong thing. Rather than my former moves, you should be more concerned with what I plan to do next."

I played it off like she didn't deserve to know the activity in my brain, but I didn't want to confess anything either. I didn't want to admit that I had found out the truth about her dad *before* buying her tampons. I didn't want her to know that I'd still cared enough to do those things for her. Knowledge was power. I wasn't giving her that.

"I'm sorry," she croaked.

"Are you really?" I doubted.

"Yes. I should have told you, but it's not like I've known about this for years. I didn't find out until just before you had arrived at the warehouse. I didn't even know if I should believe Grimsaw or not. I still don't. My dad isn't a criminal." Aside from my face, her eyes searched every square inch of the hospital hallway. "I thought you might kill me if I told you. I thought it would be in my best interest to stay on your good side."

"Is that what you've been doing this whole time?" The muscles in my face lost tension at the notice of her fear, but I barked at her just the same. "Catching a free ride on my nicety train? All your cute ass girly shit has been fake? A ploy to keep yourself on my good side?"

"My cute ass girly shit?"

"You heard me, blondie."

"You're crazy…" Her face gave way to a shady burn. "I thought you were kind of boring and robotic at first. I didn't think you had character, but I was wrong. Not only do you have a personality, you have fourteen of the fucking things."

I smiled, sickly satisfied by the venom in her bite. She contended my grin with a throw of her middle finger, sparking me to life a little more. The blue in her eyes began to darken, making her desire to slap me evident. If I was being honest, nothing had ever been sexier.

Straightening out the front of her dress like a prude, she asked, "If you hate me so much, why did you bring me toothpaste and salve? Why am I wearing such expensive clothes?"

"Only fancy places are open late."

"Even so, you didn't buy me the first dress you saw."

"You're wrong."

"Am I?" she countered. "Because everything you purchased was conservative and unrevealing, as if you had seriously considered my comfort while picking it out. Whether you are a piece of shit or not, I really don't care. All I'm asking is that you quit trying to straddle both sides of the fence."

Like a bell, she reminded me of what I hated most about her. She rubbed me the wrong way. The problem was, as much as I loathed her, I was also beginning to think she might be the coolest chick on the planet. Everything she'd just called me out on had been spot-on. The girl had guts. I respected that.

Instant heat warmed my skin as we stepped out through the glass doors of the hospital. Shayla continued to tread ahead of me toward the truck, as if she couldn't stand the look of my face. It made me laugh, because I knew she would grow to hate it even more with time. As for me, if she kept slinging out sarcasm the way she was good at, I would only grow to like the look of hers more.

Once we had arrived at the truck, my eyes trailed across her worried face. The moonlight was powerful above us, shining light on her as I opened the passenger door. Like she had been born for the spotlight, her hair twinkled beneath the glow. As I watched it glint, I deemed it a pity that she would never know just how beautiful I thought she was.

"If my father really did what Grimsaw is claiming, I'm sorry," she apologized, placing her hand on my forearm. My veins began to gyrate when she kept her touch connected. "I find it difficult to believe that he would be capable of murdering anyone, but I also have a hard time rallying in his defense. You all seem so convinced that he ruined your family, but my dad isn't a killer. He's a marketing executive."

"Likely story—" I tried to argue, but she held up her hand to silence me. For some reason, the beast found himself submitting to the wave of the beauty's palm.

"Let a girl speak," she glared. "We've concluded that my father isn't a good man in your eyes, but I've never known him to hurt people. On top of that, I haven't been playing any games with you. If ever I've done any *cute ass girly shit*, it wasn't with dishonest intentions."

My eyes flashed over her face, unknowing of just how much more I could take. Every fiber of me wanted to hate her, but I couldn't bring myself to. When I looked at her, I saw more than what her father had done. I saw a girl who needed my help; a girl I needed to protect.

Her feet were shifting, but she didn't slip her eyes away from mine. My blood lapped in my body like surges of warning, but it didn't keep me from hovering close to her. Footsteps were walking around us in the parking lot, but I didn't notice if any of their gazes flickered our way. Only one thing held my attention; a blonde standing at about 5'7".

It wasn't normal for people to learn who their soulmate was for certain. Every man will call his current wife the love of his life. Most women will say the same thing about the jackass they're married to too. The thing is, how does one really know for sure? The thought of something greener being on the opposite side always causes us to consider the what-ifs.

What if there is more out there? What if this isn't where I'm supposed to be? What if I'm missing out on something great? What if this is all for nothing? What if I'm not destined to be with the person I stand beside?

As I've heard, people have these thoughts. I'd never been in a relationship that had lasted past a week-long stand, so I couldn't say much from personal experience, but my dad's theory stated it was going to be different for me. His theory speculated I would know the girl who was meant to be my wife without any doubt.

I had never felt the need to try what I was about to before, but there was something different about Shayla. There was something unique. The way her smile melted my skin; the way my smile made her nervous; the way each of our hearts rocked the earth when a moment of silence existed between us. For these reasons alone, I found myself experimenting with my dad's hypothesis.

Plunging into her pupils, I tried to squeeze myself beyond her barrier of numbers. I tried to push around all the meaningless trash I could see, like the code to her car and her social security number. I prayed that nothing would happen. Luckily, for quite a while, nothing did.

It wasn't until I began to snap myself out of my daze that something shifted. An endless ocean began to spread out in the azure of her eyes. The digits of her life triggered sideways, melting her personal information away into something like sand. Once I realized what was happening, I didn't blink. It was unlike anything I had ever experienced before. Seeing no passcodes in the eyes of another was unfamiliar. I might have even described it as peaceful...

Until I realized it was fucking horrifying.

In one split second, everything changed for the worse. I backed away from her like she was infected, startling her as I did. I had thought things couldn't possibly magnify, but I had been very wrong.

Every part of me wished her eyes would refill with codes. I had allowed my curiosity to get the best of me, and the knowledge of who she was would eat at me now. I had just fucked up.

I had just manipulated the variables.

"Are you going to stare at me all night?" Shayla asked, pushing against my chest to get my attention. "Whatever you were just doing was weird as hell. I could swear your eyes changed to yellow, maybe even gold. It was like—"

"Get in the truck," I ordered her, unenthused by my new realization. "From here on out, just sit back and look pretty. Don't speak and don't move. Do nothing but exist."

If Shayla knew what had just been unveiled to me, she would understand my animosity. It wasn't like she would be happy about being fated to a guy like me either, so I saw no point in telling her. Anyone with eyes could see she was thirty times too good for me

"Why don't you make me?" she replied deviously, smiling like this was a game to her. "Show me how menacing you can be. If you're as bad as you like to portray, give me a reason to fear you."

Blood rushed to my head.

The wrong head.

"Putting me through another test, are you?" I detected. If there was one girl who knew how to activate irritation to flood through me on command, it seemed to be this one.

"I don't need to test you. I already know you don't have enough balls to make a move on me," she assumed, still feeding me a torturous smile. "You act tough on the exterior, but you cart around a guilty conscience inside. It's kind of pathetic. I mean, what kind of gangster can't prey on vulnerability? I can almost see your clitoris from here."

What a little bitch.

As she called me a pussy in her own unique form, her face tilted in an artfully skilled manner. I had never met a girl quite as courageous as her. I tried to search her eyes for weakness, but there was nothing in her blue irises; not even numbers anymore.

"For being a girl, it's impressive how well you define cocky." I took an intimidating step toward her. She tried to act like my incoming body didn't fathom her, but the way her chest lifted as I approached told a different story. "What if I did make a move on you?"

"I don't kiss strangers."

"Doesn't matter. If I wanted to kiss you, I would do it without your consent. There would be nothing you could do to stop me. It isn't like you could fight me off. I'm triple your size."

I wrapped my arms around her waist, brushing my belt buckle against the front of her fragile figure. I kept myself calm, but there was a part of me that would have enjoyed fucking her right here and now. The deranged side of me wanted to do some terrible things to that brave mouth of hers.

When I caught her gulping, I knew I had successfully terrified her. She looked up at me with widened eyes, but she couldn't bring herself to say a word. It was only then that I backed away from her warm body, proving my point with perfection.

"Unlike you, I don't bluff," I gave her an arrogant smirk. "If you want to play dirty, I'm familiar with the sport. I can be your opponent, but I think your odds might be better if we're riding on the same team. If you want my help after we get to Vegas, quit putting me through tests now. If you keep pissing me off, you'll find yourself blowing on a pair of dice for Barnes in no time."

14
LINK OF MAYHEM

SHAYLA STONE

Friday. 2:00 A.M.

HUNTER'S EYES WERE ADHERED TO the darkened high-way in front of us. Every word I'd once kept tucked in my mental dictionary had now vacated me through the dead of the night.

I had tested the man with my very best. I had pinched at his every level of masculinity. I had compared him to a vagina just to deconstruct his shield. I had been aiming to get a rise out of him, but my efforts had gone wasted. Hunter hadn't latched onto any of it.

He wasn't a filthy animal. In my most defenseless of moments, he couldn't bring himself to make a pass at me. This proved he respected a woman's worth. This proved there was more to him than met the eye. This proved my tests weren't all for nothing.

I was a virgin, but that didn't mean I didn't know how good sex might feel. It didn't mean I had never let a guy put his fingers in places that my guardian angel wouldn't be too pleased to witness, or maybe he would; *the creepy bastard.* It just meant that I had never liked a guy enough to take it all the way.

But something was different about Garciez. No matter how sick it was for me to think of him in that way, which it unquestionably was, I couldn't ignore his presence. From his deep voice to his tall standing, I had already memorized everything about the man seated beside me.

I had suffered over the past few weeks. There was no doubt about that, but it wasn't like I had been locked in Grimsaw's holding for the past five years. I was a little messed up over being kidnapped, as I probably would be for life, but I wasn't delirious. I knew exactly what I was doing.

"Just open them already," Hunter commanded, watching me cling onto my health documents. "Pass the folder my way when you're done."

I didn't know why he wanted my outcomes, but I didn't announce my curiosity. I was scared to peel the backing open, shaking while I held the manila folder in my hands. I wasn't prepared to read what the envelope might contain, so I stalled by asking, "Did you know Grimsaw did this to girls?"

"Stop talking, Shayla."

I glanced at the speedometer. Hunter was surpassing the speed limit by thirty miles, but it wasn't hard to figure out why. We had under five hours to make it to Vegas; five hours until his sister would pay the ultimate price for our straggling.

"You will get yourself killed if you stay linked to these guys," I persevered with fire. "You don't seem stupid. I don't see why you've tied yourself to the mafia. Did you *need* to become best friends with Grimsaw?"

"Do you think I didn't consider other pathways?" Hunter's jaw began to clench. "I had just graduated from high school. I didn't even have a job yet. I was supposed to be heading off to college in a month, but things changed once my folks were murdered. I'm only involved with the gang because of your dad, so don't sit there and judge me on my morals. As far as I'm concerned, you don't come from a great line of attributes either."

"Maybe you're right," I frowned.

"When I first teamed up with Grim, all I knew was that he had a warehouse. I thought he might hire me as a legitimate mechanic. I'd seen a lot of Mexicans coming and going from the place. I knew my dad associated with some people who worked there, but I didn't know I was walking into a union of bloodthirst. I just wanted a job so I could adopt my sister. The government wanted to take her away from me until I could prove I was stable enough to take care of her. Before thinking it through, I had told the agencies I was a mechanic at Grimsaw's shop. I had no choice but to ask him for a position after that. I knew about cars, so I figured he would let me turn some wrenches. I explained my story to him. I told him our house had burned down. I told him my parents were dead. I confessed I had lied to the government about working for him. Grimsaw asked me what I needed. I told him a job, a handful of solid references, and a loan to buy a new place to live. He wrote me a check for twenty grand within the hour. When he handed me that check, I didn't hesitate when taking it. I knew he had tricks, but I figured nothing would be worse than allowing my sister to get dropped into a group home. Grimsaw made it look like I was legally employed as a mechanic to the government. He is the reason that I still have Tessa. Unfortunately, in the end, she would have been better off without me."

"How can you say that? You're her brother, and I can see how much you love her. There's nowhere she would be better off than with you."

"I don't even know where she is right now," he grimaced, managing to show emotion while giving me an icy shoulder. "And I want to hate you so badly, but holding your dad's actions against you would be like having my dad's choices held against me. Who we are raised by doesn't define us. It's just, now that I'm aware of these things, we run into some issues."

"What issues?"

"Your dad killed my parents. What kind of son would I be if I didn't seek retaliation? I shouldn't have had to resort to the low level of joining a gang, but your dad tampered with everything. He erased the records for my parent's life insurance policies. He drained their bank accounts. He ensured that Tessa and I would be left with nothing if we did survive the fire. I would have received my parent's property... if your father hadn't burnt it down."

"He burnt down your house?" I whispered, unable to do much more. The feeling of sickness in my stomach was enough to drop me dead.

"Your dad put a pot of food on the stove before he left my mom and sister to burn alive that night," he nodded, focusing on the road. "He strategically started the fire right next to the stove. I know your dad's an intelligent man, because not too many people would have thought of doing that. That pot ensured it all looked like a domestic accident, like someone in the household had been at fault. He tried to kill my little sister. He burned my mom alive. I'm sure he thought I was in the house when he lit that fire too. He shot my dad in the head in our backyard."

"Supposedly."

"How naïve are you?" Hunter glared at me with a bonfire in his eyes. "If I hadn't been financially strapped and homeless, adopting Tessa wouldn't have been as hard as it was. If you're going to sit there and judge me on the things I do, I figured you should at least understand why I do them. It's not because I think I'm hard. It's not because I grew up thinking the mafia was cool. I didn't just wake up one day and decide it was good day to fuck up my entire life. A long link of mayhem has transformed my reality into this. Everything I hate about myself has transpired because of your father."

I wanted to defend my dad, but no words surfaced on my tongue. Like Hunter had said, out of all the girls in the world, there was a reason I was sitting beside him. The more he explained, the more the picture became painted. My dad was good on a computer, but I wouldn't have guessed he was capable of dissolving electronic records and life insurance policies. I wouldn't have suspected he could ruin a family either.

All to try and save me from cancer.

The real kicker was that Hunter didn't know why my dad had gone after his family. He didn't know my dad's reasoning. He didn't know it had to do with the cures and a briefcase. He didn't know my dad had been trying to protect his own. Hunter wasn't even aware of my battle with Leukemia. I certainly didn't want to tell him that his parents were dead because of it. I didn't want to confess that their blood was on my hands as much as it was on my father's. I didn't want to engage myself in any of it.

And so... I didn't.

15
THERE'S NO PLACE LIKE HOME

SHAYLA STONE

Friday. 2:30 A.M.

HUNTER WORE HIS STITCHES LIKE stars. The dried blood on his face only added to his mystery. If it meant defending someone he cared about, he wasn't afraid to take an ass-kicking. I had a loyal soul too, but I had never taken a beating as bad as he seemed to be accustomed to.

I could faintly recall a day back in the fifth grade when I'd stolen a chocolate pudding from Lucy Romero's lunch kit. After realizing I was the culprit, Lucy had slung her fist back and introduced it to my face. I would describe her punch as a sour gummy worm; a little acidic to eat at first, but the effects wore off quickly.

Her outbreak hadn't lessened my desire for chocolate pudding any, but it had made me reconsider living a life of crime at the age of nine. Once she'd told me that her father, a prestigious lawyer with elite standing, was going to charge me with theft under five grand, I had asked my parents to stock more pudding on our shelves. Lucy had become best friends with Bree and I after that, right up until she had been obligated to move to Iowa with her family in grade ten.

By far, Grimsaw's strikes had been the worst I'd ever received. The man had taken full leave of his senses. His lights were on when you looked at him, but a terrible soul sat inside his housing.

It was because of his maddened mind that Hunter and I were each black and blue.

I pretended not to watch as Hunter swallowed a few pills; the pills that Grimsaw had instructed him to kill me with. I wasn't sure if Hunter knew what they were, but it didn't keep him from testing out their effects.

I could tell he wished things were different. I could tell he didn't like how his life had turned out. Part of me thought he was a fool for signing on with a gang, regardless of his motives. The other part of me respected the hell out of him for giving up his own wellbeing to protect his orphaned sister's.

I didn't like that I was being magnetized to a man who intended to murder my father. This should have been more than enough to make me hate everything about Hunter. I shouldn't have wanted to help save his little sister, just like he shouldn't want to shield me from his acquaintances. We were tangled in a desolate web; a web we were both bound to die in.

"The thing about addiction, when you need your drug, you don't care who sees you get your fix," Hunter met my stare, keeping the steering wheel aligned with his left hand. "I used to want to be a helicopter pilot in the Air Force, but I won't get anything but a coffin now. That'll be when all the suffering ends. It won't matter that I'm dead. It won't matter if my body is never recovered. What matters is that I'll be free."

Grief washed over me. I knew Hunter had problems, but he sounded one move away from jumping off a cliff. He was depressed, just like my mom had been before fading to death from breast cancer; just like I had been while rotting in a hospital bed for months with Leukemia, waiting to die in a similar manner next.

"Things can still change for you. You don't have to stay tied to Grimsaw forever. Once you get your sister back, you can disappear. You—"

"Let me guess, you want to be a psychologist?" Hunter cut me off. Even though his following chuckle was mocking me, it was still nice to hear him laugh. "You might think you can fix everything with a few sessions of emotional revelation, but I don't believe the same. Being optimistic brings nothing but disappointment."

"Actually, I'm interested in psychiatry. Most people don't know this, but there is a difference between psychology and psychiatry.

Psychologists are the shrinks. Psychiatrists are legitimate medical doctors who can write prescriptions. I'm not saying a psychologist isn't a doctor, but all they really do is counsel. A psychiatrist studies chemical imbalances and—" I stopped myself, catching sight of the bored expression on his face. "What...?"

"That was truly fascinating," he said, sarcasm evident. "But I think going to school for six years is foolish, especially if all you're hoping to acquire is the ability to explain why people are so fucked in the head. There's no good explanation for society. You don't need to waste half a decade to figure that out. Take everyone else out of the picture. Take away the stress of holding a job title with a respectable social status. If you knew you could become anything without failure, what would you choose to do? Would you really want to be a psychiatrist? Do you dream of having a closet full of pantsuits, four cats in your living room, and no good memories to look back on?"

"You're an asshole."

"I really am," he acknowledged. "But I thought a girl like you would have a cool story. You said you surf. Why aren't you planning to do that for a living?"

"That's a pipe dream."

"Because you suck?"

"I would annihilate you on a board," I guaranteed with full confidence. "But making a living from it isn't realistic. Only the best in the world can do that. For me, it's just a hobby. The Banzai pipeline is fierce and lethal, but it's always been a dream of mine to ride the Hawaiian coast..." I envisioned myself on my surfboard, lost in wonderment while staring deep into the blackness outside. "In Hawaiian waters, I think death would be worth it."

"To die so young would be a pity, even if your last breath was taken doing something you love. You just turned eighteen three weeks ago. If I manage to keep you safe, I'd like for you to at least see twenty-five. I don't want my efforts to be for nothing."

With shivers roaming down my spine, I cautiously averted my gaze from the full moon and faced Hunter.

"How do you know my age?"

"You told me," he shrugged.

"I didn't," I held my ground. "Even if I had, I didn't tell you my exact birthdate. I gave the doctor a fake birthday too, so I know you didn't just overhear that conversation."

Every red flag in my mind was warning me that Hunter was lying, but his body language didn't shine toward his dishonesty at all. His fingers weren't apprehensively fidgeting. His breathing wasn't shallow. His lips didn't tighten. His temples weren't sweating...

As if he had trained himself to lie well.

"How else would I know how old you are?" He squinted into my eyes, deliberately trying to keep me from dissecting him. "It isn't like I have magical powers."

I could feel my eyebrows narrow as I struggled to make sense of him. I didn't believe in mythical heresy. I bought into magic even less. I challenged all paranormal beliefs, but I could tell there was something strange about him. Something *different.*

I played with the stitches crisscrossing my wrists, stroking the thread like I would somehow be transferred home after the third caress.

There's no place like home.

There's no place like home.

There's no place like—

"Stop it." Hunter's hand left the steering wheel to link his fingers through mine. The electricity in his touch demanded instant recognition. "You'll make the scars more noticeable if you keep picking at your wrists."

"Don't pretend like you care," I scowled, brushing his hand away. "Instead, why don't you tell me how you plan to murder the last family member I have? If you kill my dad, you may as well put a bullet in my head too. Without him, I'll have no one."

"And who the fuck do I have? When I'm having a shitty day, what sympathetic shoulder do I have to lean on? Aside from Tessa and a few burns on my back, I've got shit all too. Why should I let you keep your dad when I have to live without mine?"

Anger took hold of his face. There was no doubt we brought out the combustive compositions in one another; like fire and gasoline. Having the two of us alone in one vehicle was the definition of hell on wheels.

"I'm sorry," I apologized.

"I'm sure you are," he retorted with attitude. "I know you've been cooped up for a few weeks, but did you watch the news much before that?"

"Why are you asking me that?" I shifted in my seat, continuing to stroke my wrists against his better advisements. "Why are you so weird?"

"Just answer the question."

"I follow the news," I succumbed.

"So, if I said I knew how to rob a bank, would you piece it together? If I said I knew how to steal passcodes and memorize pin numbers, would you understand what I do for Grimsaw?"

Although neither of us felt it necessary to look at the other, I thought about what he was saying. The moon glinted against the dark roadway before us, leaving the center line easy to pinpoint despite nighttime obscurity. Hunter's words, however, were much more unnerving than the pitch black surrounding us.

The news had been flooded with bank heists in the state over the past few years. It was somewhat of a marvel in California. No matter what the authorities did, they couldn't catch the criminals behind the acts. The offenders didn't walk into the facilities with ski masks and guns drawn. They casually walked in pretending to be the owners of the accounts they were robbing instead. They walked in with false identification. They walked in with stolen identities. For the most part, the frauds weren't even realized until the actual owners tried to withdraw cash from their accounts and found them drained.

It was clear the criminals were hackers, because the camera systems were always shut down unnoticeably before the robberies even took place. The media had been referring to the crooks as the most advanced offenders of the century. Much to my terror, I was quite certain I was seated next to one of those wrongdoers right now.

"What am I, blondie?"

For the first time, Hunter was testing me. He wanted to know just how much I could handle before crumbling apart. He wanted to know how much I could take before trying to escape from him again. Little did he know, I'd been through worse than anything a human could ever condemn upon me. He wasn't nearly as scary as Leukemia.

As much as Hunter's headlining profession horrified me, it also made him a little sexier. I knew it shouldn't. If I were equipped with a sane mind, the thought of being seated beside a felon would have made my skin curl. If I weren't so far gone, I would have never smiled while saying, "You, Mr. Garciez, are one hell of a thief."

16
THE MARK OF THE DEVIL

HUNTER GARCIEZ

Friday. 3:30 A.M.

WE HAD ENTERED NEVADA A while back, inching toward Sin City. Despite my slip up regarding her birthday, I still hadn't explained anything to Shayla. The less she knew about the things I could do, the safer she would stay.

I knew what I had to do. I needed to find a way to stall Grimsaw. I needed to buy Shayla back from Ray Barnes. Barnes wouldn't be out any money that way, while Grimsaw wouldn't know the difference. When I considered the situation, this was the only deal that held any hope of success.

If Barnes had paid two and a half million to have Shayla delivered, he would want at least double that from me. Although I had an expendable five million spread throughout my accounts, I would need my laptop to transfer the funds unnoticeably. Five million dollars wasn't pocket change, and I knew Barnes would want to deal in cash. Unfortunately, since my laptop was still in San Francisco, this was where a bank robbery would need to tie in.

I had also stewed on what my options were with Grimsaw. I could pay the two and a half million to him instead, playing it off like I had slaughtered Shayla for revenge against her dad. This had started out as my original plan, but there were faults throughout it.

Firstly, Grimsaw still had my sister. Until I had Tessa back in my arms, I couldn't be certain of anything. Secondly, if I were to take the latter path and pretend Shayla was dead, Grimsaw would want to see a murdered body. At minimum, he would want pictures of her; pictures I didn't have time to fake.

This left Barnes as my strongest option. I would take his slave to him. If my plan worked, Barnes would tell Grimsaw he'd received her. Grimsaw would then think I had done what he'd asked of me. The hard part would be convincing Barnes that I was good for my word when it came to paying him. I would get him the cash, but it would need to wait until civilization began to move in a few hours. It would need to wait until I could do what I did best.

Robbing the *Citibank* was the only choice I had. It was the only way I could retrieve that kind of coin without leaving a paper trail. Doing a robbery of such a magnitude alone was completely moronic. Failure rates were as high as 98%, while arrest was basically guaranteed. But if I could get the money to Barnes before any of that happened, my plan would be solid gold. I didn't care what happened to me in the end. I could take the hit of rotting away for twenty-five to life, but only after Shayla and Tessa had been hidden away from danger.

If all else failed, Plan C would have to come out to play. I would blackmail Grimsaw with many detailed images and recordings; recordings that would be enough to put him on trial for multiple crimes. I had already been able to prove his involvement in many illegal activities, but this included the sex trade now too.

The thing Grimsaw hadn't realized in the past few years? I had never entered his warehouse without bugging myself first. In fact, alongside my neck right now, there was a camera clipped to my black t-shirt. It wasn't for the law. It wasn't for intentional disloyalty. It was for personal protection instead. Cameras could be engineered to look invisible to the naked eye. I knew this, because I made them myself.

I could tell Shayla's nerves were shot, but mine were no better off. I tried to ignore what we might be walking into at Barnes' suite, but it was unmanageable. My whole life could be contorted within a matter of minutes; Shayla and Tessa's too.

Russ would be keeling over if he knew who sat beside me right now. If he knew that our conversation in my living room only days ago would morph into reality, especially with a twist like this, he would be in his fucking glory.

Shayla began to slide her medical reports from the manila envelope. She stared at the results for a few moments, scanning her eyes over the printed words before saying, "I have a staph infection. Everything else was negative."

"Did you get a prescription?"

I tried not to recoil as I looked at her, but it was difficult. Every black spot on her body was flaunting Grimsaw's mishandling. All I could see was his face; the mark of the devil. I had a feeling that had been his goal too. He knew I wouldn't like seeing her suffer, but Shayla was just a small sliver in a much larger punishment I had coming my way. In the end, my bones would break.

"Antibiotics," she nodded, pushing the sheets back into the folder before passing them my way. Her gaze lingered as I threw the stack onto the dash. "Speaking of pills, if you keep abusing narcotics—"

"Quit trying to shrink me," I struck her with a shearing look, annoyed that she was still pushing the subject of my drug addiction. "I'm growing tired of your incessant need to save the damaged dog. You might want to be a psychiatrist, but I don't want to be your patient. If the only way to shut you up is to throw eight inches of dick down your throat, I'm okay with it."

"Oh, please," Shayla ridiculed me with a laugh. "Of all the monsters I've encountered in the past few weeks, you're the least scary. There might be a side of you that wants to murder me, but touching me… you wouldn't dare. You're too soft for that."

I smiled to myself.

She had me nailed down as a good guy, but to hell if I was one. When it came to me, nothing was in black and white. Shayla was entering the gray now. One way or another, I would be introducing myself to her father. When I ripped out his heart, she would learn she had me all wrong. I wasn't as evil as Grimsaw, but I was just as far from holy.

Then, as if I couldn't wait for that day to come, the tweak went off in my head. If being nice to her was giving the impression she could talk to me like I was a little bitch, I figured being a prick might convince her to comply instead. I wasn't above using scare tactics to command respect out of her. I needed her to stay in line. I couldn't have her doing something I wouldn't want, especially once Barnes was standing in front of us. Every move in this had to follow my outline with precision. If she decided to cast her scorpion tongue onto the wrong person, it would be game over for the both of us.

My hand cranked on the steering wheel, abruptly detouring the truck onto an off-road approach. We came to a dead halt under the midnight sky, leaving dust to cloak us outside. In a rage, I angrily shifted the vehicle into park.

I would have been fine with taking a few minutes to cool down, but Shayla insisted to toss more gas onto an already raging fire.

"You're crazy! You drive like a—"

I didn't let her finish her sentence. I dove over the center console and latched my hand around her bruised throat. I didn't disrupt her breathing rituals, but she knew I could if I wanted to. I deemed this necessary, because she needed to remember who held the power between us; it wasn't her. I needed her to understand my rules. I couldn't have her running scared to the Feds once I found a way to free her.

"I'm capable of treating you like a whore. I just thought you deserved more..." I threw her neck back with force, digging my thumb deep into her chin. "I think you've been mistaking my previous kindness for weakness. I might have shown you a glimpse of my good side. I might have fed you, but I can be relentless when I want to be."

I coiled a section of her blonde hair around my fist, tugging on it to gain access to her vanilla throat. My tongue ran up the length of her neck, consuming the taste of her creamy flesh; whether she wanted it to or not.

"I'm not sure which of your personalities I like more." She shivered beneath me, but it didn't seem to be due to fear. "The good Garciez... or the bad."

The way she rolled the R in my name made my dick lurch. The girl didn't have a caving point. No matter what I dished out, she dished it back to me twofold. I knew she didn't like having me as close to her as I was. I knew she was playing a game with me, but it was a sport I didn't mind having her challenge me to. Without a doubt, I knew I could win this round.

"Those are only two of my personalities. You haven't met the other twelve," I smirked against her jawline.

"Maybe you should introduce me?"

A dangerous laugh rose from my throat at the sound of her seductive words. Beneath a thick cloud of turmoil, there was something intoxicating in the air; a magnetism I couldn't define. I wasn't sure if she felt it too, but her willingness to provoke me suggested she could.

I couldn't help but wonder what she would be like if hell wasn't consuming us. Rather than connecting in the middle of a gang initiation, I wondered how things might have been if the two of us had intertwined differently; like if she didn't know I was involved with the mafia; like if she had accidently dumped her coffee on me in a café one day instead. You know... the way that normal people meet.

Instead, she had met me while blood was dripping down my face. She had met me while bleeding herself. She had met me while being curled in the fetal position on a cold, cement floor. She had met me in her very worst moment. For that, it didn't matter that she was the girl with no digits in her eyes. It didn't matter that my dad had warned me about this girl specifically. It didn't matter... because I would never stand a chance with her.

Still, I played her choice of sport.

"Careful," I spoke directly into her ear. "If I didn't know any better, I would say the sick side of you enjoys having my hands on your body. I would say it gets you off to know that I'm a notorious bank robber. Since you're a good girl, you should probably tell me I'm wrong. Tell me you don't like having a criminal this close to you."

"I would be lying," she whispered.

As I leaned back to meet her stare, I had nothing left within me. The slave was good at pretending to be promiscuous, but the fact that she was a virgin told me she really wasn't. She thought she could outsmart me, but the odds would never be in her favor.

"Nobody can identify me, but you know who I am now," I glared at her, watching her chest rise and collapse. "You know what I've done. If I save you from Barnes, how do I know you won't run your mouth to the cops?"

"I can't remember anything."

"Good, *hermosa*," I referred to her as beautiful, grazing my fingertips over her knee. It was wrong of me to touch her on so many levels, but it didn't keep me from doing it. "But will you be able to say the same when a pig is as close to you as I am? When a man in a suit is interrogating you, do you think you'll still manage to keep a straight face?"

"I know I will."

"If you make one wrong slipup, my sister will end up at a cabin in the woods. If I go to jail because of something you've said, Tessa will go to foster care. If she goes to foster care, your throat will meet a knife. I will make sure of that."

"I don't know who they were, *officer…*" She grabbed onto the front of my t-shirt, yanking my body closer to hers in the truck. "I didn't see their faces. They were always wearing black masks. They rarely even spoke around me."

I glanced down at the black fabric in her hand, finding it odd that she was touching me at all. Even if this was a game to her, she was pushing it to the extreme. Part of me thought she might not be messing with me at all. Part of me thought she might actually be attracted to me, but I told myself I was wrong before I went too far.

"If you were in the mafia's possession for three weeks, you must have witnessed something of value," I persevered, much the same as any good investigator would. "Tell me something."

"I saw nothing," she repeated, loudening her roleplay. "You can grill me for the next seventy-two hours, but my answers aren't going to change. If you want me to lie, I can detail some fake profiles for your artists to inefficiently waste their time sketching. Aside from that, I have nothing else to offer you."

Teardrops showed just how well she could act on cue. I would have sworn she was really crying… until a cryptic smile began to trot over her lips.

"If you could control your shaking, I might believe you," I said, positioning myself back into my seat. I removed my hand from her lower thigh, but it wasn't something I wanted to do. "You're a little messed in the head, blondie."

"And what exactly are you?"

After taking a moment to think about it, I answered, "Bound to die."

Keeping my eyes deadlocked through the front windshield, I slid the truck's tranny back into gear. I didn't turn to look at her.

I didn't want to see her; the girl I was becoming infatuated by; the girl whose father had murdered my parents; the girl I felt the need to safeguard when I shouldn't. Protecting this girl wasn't in my best interest.

Protecting this girl...

It was going to get me killed.

17
PSYCHOMETRIC FATE

HUNTER GARCIEZ

Friday. 4:30 A.M.

"WHY DID YOU BRING MY results?" Shayla wondered, referring to the envelope hanging from the back pocket of my jeans. Her health documents would play a role soon enough, but I wasn't about to give her the details.

We stood in the elevator of the *Forum Tower* at *Caesars Palace*, taking the long ride up to the very top. People seemed to enter and exit on every floor, lagging our time even more than I already had.

There were ten other bodies in the mechanical box, but Shayla was the only one I took notice of. We stayed in the very back, making it relatively simple for me to slip my hand around her right hip without anyone noticing. They might have heard the change in her breathing pattern as her chest hitched in surprise, but no one turned around to see what had caused her malfunction.

I pulled the back of her body into the front of mine, telling myself that I was only doing it so she could hear my whispered words more clearly. I wasn't a fan of the sad cowboy tune playing through the radio above us, but it helped to conceal my voice from the others.

"We're on our way to Barnes' room. This is the guy who has directions to my sister. This is the guy who bought you. I don't owe you anything, but I'm about to walk in there and try to swing a deal for your life. In one form or another, you better make this risk worth my while."

I straightened as an older woman left the metal cart, even more so when she turned to say goodbye to the hag she'd been chatting with on the ride up. We had 27 flights left to go before hell would unveil itself in one shape or another. Grimsaw hadn't called my cellphone again, so I knew he was busy setting something up along the horizon.

He might have managed to rig the Camaro up with tricks, but I knew he hadn't bugged my phone. I had the security set with too many anti-hacking mechanisms to count. I had implicated barriers that the most technologically advanced minds would struggle to break through. Grimsaw was nothing close to the sort. He could barely figure out how to change his own banking password without having his hand held. Not to mention, his beady eyes ratted him out to me every time he did.

Floor 61.

A group of people left the elevator. I watched as Shayla stole a glance at the ascending digits. Her body vibrated against the front of mine, but my hold around her hip ensured she couldn't slip.

"Do you trust me?" I asked.

"Not in the least," she whispered back.

I smiled as the final couple exited on the 64th floor. I took a step to the side, releasing Shayla's hip as the box climbed higher. I slanted my neck to catch a glimpse of her appearance, unsure which of our hearts were pounding louder. There was something unusual in her eyes, but nothing was easy to identify when it came to the workings of her. I was learning that rather quickly.

Floor 69.

We left the cart and entered a red hallway. Only one door stared back at us on the level, and neither of us approached it. I crossed my arms over my chest, glaring at the door like it might burst into flames if I thought about it hard enough. Shayla kept her hands wrung against her stomach, picking at her fingernails like we were only minutes away from death.

"You know what I think, Hunter?"

"What do you think, blondie?"

"I think your drug addiction is something you garnish yourself with on the surface." The glands in her throat tightened as she swallowed. "I think it's a defense mechanism. I think you can get off the drugs. I also think you should avoid acting like a macho ass once we're inside this room. I know being a dick is a habit of yours, but your sister needs you to survive this."

Had she really just said that?

"I might be a dick, but you're a snarky little bitch. You can go from kitten to tiger in 1.9 seconds, so forgive me for finding your advice unprofitable."

"Coming from a thief, imagine how much that hurt," Shayla tried to act tough, but all I could see was a Chihuahua taking a nip at my socks. "Your words can't cut me."

"And yours can't fix me," I told her, rubbing at my eyes. "Look, you're going to hate what you hear in there…" I nodded toward the entrance of the penthouse. "But I've made up my mind. The only way you'll be getting thrown into the sex trade is if I'm dead. To get to you, they'll have to go through me."

As her annoyance subsided, fear took its place. Since I was refusing to inform her of my plans, she was being left to rot with whatever conclusions she could scrounge up on her own.

She'd probably considered that I was lying to her. Maybe she thought I was making her feel safe for my own benefit, so she wouldn't see it coming when I threw her bones to the wolves. And she could think that, but it was the last thing I intended to do.

"What's your plan?"

Since I knew she wouldn't like the truth, I didn't reply. No matter how smart a girl seemed to be, she always asked stupid questions just the same; questions she wouldn't like the answers to.

I reached into the front pocket of my jeans and pulled out a bankcard. When Shayla refused to take it, I slipped it into the pocket of her cardigan forcefully.

"Should my methods fail, you'll need to save my sister for me. You'll need to get in touch with my best friend; Russ Delaney. How well can you remember phone numbers?" As her chest began to heave, I gathered, "Not well?"

"I don't want to remember anyone's phone number," the Chihuahua roared, giving a glimpse of her pearl-white fangs. "I want us to leave this suite together."

"His number is stored under *Delaney* in my cell," I ignored her pointless jabber. "The pin to my cellphone is F094R50—"

"Are you kidding me?" Shayla disbelieved. "Who the hell does that? Why not use something simple like 8100? How do *you* even remember that password?"

"I would change it for you, but I can't do it locally. If you're unable to remember the code, Tessa should know Russ' number by heart. Use a payphone to call him."

"I'm not leaving—"

"The pin to the bankcard in your pocket is 3836. The funds are under checking. For whatever reason, if I can't leave with you, take the truck and head to the bank. Pull out a grand for a safety net. There's a few hundred grand in there, but you won't get more than a thousand from an instant teller per day. You can't physically go into a bank with that card either. The account is registered to a dead man. Since you're not a man…"

I scrambled toward the long wooden cabinet sitting just outside the elevator doors. I quickly emptied my pockets into a vase full of plastic flowers. Shayla watched in confusion as I dumped out a fake passport for Tessa, my cellphone, another debit card, and the keys to the truck we'd been driving. Only two items were left in my jeans when I was done; Shayla's test results and my dick.

"I'll get the directions to Tessa while I'm talking to Barnes. When he gives them to me, make sure you memorize them. Call Russ and have him meet you. Wherever my sister is, find her. I'll go out on a limb for you. I'll do everything I can to protect you, but you need to make sure Tessa stays safe if things go wrong. Russ will have everything necessary to help you both. There is another debit card in the vase with a million dollars attached to it. It's registered to a young girl. Tessa can go into a bank and withdraw money from the account, but she needs to use her fake passport when she does. Now, do you remember the pin number to the card in your pocket?"

"3638."

"It's 3836," I growled.

"I'm not a felon like you! You're barking eighty orders at me, as if I stand a shot at remembering any of them. I can barely remember where you parked the damn truck." Tears began to form along her lower eyelids. "I'm an impediment."

There was no arguing that.

"Do something for me?" I cradled her neck, placing my hands below each of her ears. Her hair draped over my fingers, glinting beneath the fluorescent lighting above us. "Close your eyes."

"Why?"

"Just fucking do it."

"Fine," she obliged.

"Imagine you're in Hawaii. It's day one of the Banzai Pipeline. There is a crowd of people cheering for you onshore, but all you can hear is the pound of your heart. You're sitting on your surfboard, preparing for a perfect wave to come your way... what do you feel?"

"The neoprene of my wetsuit is tight upon my skin. The sun is fierce. I can taste the salt of the ocean. The teal water is lapping against the bottom of my board," she played along. "I can see a wave coming. Should I take it?"

"You score a perfect ten," I smiled as her eyes remained shut. "The paparazzi swarms you, begging for autographs and interviews. Your name will be all over the headlines now. Surfing representatives will be banging on your front door."

She opened the slits of her eyes, stirring up a tropical storm when her blue irises collided with the green of mine.

"What are you doing?"

"Showing you the reasons for my upcoming choices," I shrugged. "I don't want this life to be yours. I don't want a life in the sex trade to be reality for any girl. If I can help you, I will."

If Shayla was my destiny, it was my duty to protect her. Based on notion, it wasn't Barnes who was meant to fuck her for the rest of her life. Given our psychometric fate, it was me who was supposed to gain the prize of her virginity. She just didn't know it yet.

"Follow my lead," I directed her, giving a disgruntled shake of my head. "Hold yourself together, but be sure to look frightened. Act as though I've tossed you around a little. Can you do that?"

"I will," she agreed.

Judging by the glitter in her eyes, I thought she might try to kiss me. It was a stupid thought; one that was confirmed when she didn't complete the movement.

Since I had scolded myself into remaining somewhat respectful, I didn't move in for the kill either. Keeping myself in line, I gave a loud pound against hell's door instead.

18
AN ALPHABET OF DISEASE

SHAYLA STONE

Friday. 5:00 A.M.

A HATCHET-FACED MALE IN HIS MID-FIFTIES opened the door. His facial features resembled an olden day Elvis. He had a Cuban cigar hanging from his lips, which I assumed was against hotel bylaws.

Then again… this was Vegas.

His skin was crinkly, his aged body was hunched, and the ridges of dehydration along his face told me that he'd been a binge drinker in his younger years. His pinstriped dress shirt was unbuttoned at the top, revealing frizzy salt and pepper chest hair.

He scoped me from head to toe, spinning his liquor-filled glass in circles, causing ice cubes to tap against the crystal in an audible rhythm. Though his hair was graying around the temples, his Elvis hairline didn't seem to be in any imminent danger of receding during the days he had left. Which, by the way he coughed as he stole the next draw from his lit cigar, were assumingly limited.

I toyed with the hem of my dress. It was a challenge to get a good glimpse into the man's eyes. Purple sunglasses were obstructing my ease of access. I wasn't sure why he was wearing them indoors, but I knew just who he was; the man who had purchased me like a rug. He was a shopper with a serious case of demented desires. He was a man with no soul.

He was Ray Barnes.

"Cazador Garciez?"

"No shit," Hunter sassed.

"You look just like your dad used to," Barnes said, taking a quick drink of what smelled to be the good stuff. "It's like I'm staring at Emiliano himself."

The wrinkled pervert opened the door and allowed us to enter the extravagant room. I followed through the threshold behind Hunter, praying to myself that he was trustworthy. I had never relied on a criminal before, but there was a first for everything.

Three sectional couches filled the room, each cream in color, while pieces of gray artwork were accessorizing the walls. To my right was a staircase winding upward. To my left was a generously-sized kitchen, hickory oak spread throughout. Since the suite was two levels of pure swank, I knew there were bedrooms somewhere. I assumed them to be closed off by some magical button that released a revolving bookcase, or something equally dramatic.

Hunter stared out the glass windows, his form relaxed while taking in the glow of the Vegas view below. The suite was undoubtedly incredible, but I didn't get the opportunity to be captivated by the grand view. It was hard to focus while Barnes was breathing down my neck like a thirsty vampire.

It became even more impossible when he began to slide my cardigan down from my shoulders. Every voice in my mind was telling me to backhand the creep, but I doubted that would be the appropriate response in Hunter's eyes.

"Do you like all of your girls that skeletal, Barnes?" Hunter's deep voice cut through the vast room. I could tell he was watching my reflection through the floor-to-ceiling windows. "Do you like seeing every thrust you push into their gaunt bodies?"

"If they know I can kill them, they don't step out of line," Barnes chuckled, coughing a gross phlegm from his throat. He swallowed it back down not long after, taking another drag from his girthed cigar to follow. "But this girl looks especially weak. Grimsaw does good work."

"Grimsaw is educated," Hunter's tone was flavorless. He turned around, but he didn't allow himself to look affected as Barnes curled his arm around my waist. "It's been a long drive. I could use a beer."

"Go grab us men some drinks," Barnes ordered me, smacking

at my ass belligerently. "When you get back, you better not be so fucking frigid. I own you now."

I scooted into the kitchen at a hurried speed, leaving their chatter as faint mumbles in the distance. I took my time grabbing their drinks. I carefully removed the lids from two *Coronas*, dropping a slice of lime into each of them like an obedient slave. I thought of smearing Ray's lime along the garbage can before plopping it down the neck of his beer, but I figured that would only ensure I saw a smack across the face sooner rather than later.

I made my way back into the living room at a turtle-like pace. Hunter didn't smile as I passed him his drink, but his emerald eyes comforted me just the same. I took a seat beside Barnes after delivering his beer next.

"You want a Cuban, kid?"

"A cigarette," Hunter requested.

Barnes pulled a cigarette pack from the depths of his chest pocket. Along with a lighter, he tossed the chemical canes to Hunter.

"They'll put you in an early grave."

"Every step I take leads me closer to my coffin," Hunter gave a scathing smirk. I tried not to judge as he lit one of the death sticks to life; a habit I didn't know he had. "Should disease grow beneath my skin, I'm sure I'll find a way to cure myself. Besides, cancer wouldn't be the worst way to die. Many deaths come more violently."

"Tell that to those who've nearly died from it," I gritted, snagging each of their attention immediately. Hunter held a look of confusion at first, but his eyes told me to shut up just as fast.

"Give me a minute." Barnes readjusted his sunglasses. My neck slanted as he stood from the couch we were sharing. "I told Grimsaw I would give him a ring once the blonde met my possession."

He exited the room and headed upstairs. Hunter kept his arm slung over the back of the beige couch, casually smoking his cigarette until Barnes was just out of sight. Once he was, he stood and charged across the room.

Leaving an orange-filtered stick in the corner of his mouth, he used his muscles to pull down a picture frame above the stone fireplace. Gray lilies and water droplets decorated the art, but Hunter wasn't after the picture. As he set the piece aside, a steel safe was revealed behind it.

I didn't know how Hunter had known where it was located. It didn't make sense for his fingers to be fidgeting with the dial. It didn't make sense for him to know the combination code. It didn't make sense for the container to click open upon his command… yet, it did.

He withdrew a pistol from the secret hideaway and checked the safety, throwing it into the waist of his tan jeans once he was certain the trigger was secure. I heard footsteps as they began to approach the top of the stairwell, but Hunter didn't seem to take notice.

I knew he wouldn't have enough time to shut the safe before Barnes began to descend, let alone hang the picture back up, and I knew one other thing too; I couldn't let Hunter go down in this for me. If we were a team, I had to assist in some way.

I did the only thing I could. I ran up the stairs to meet Barnes on his way down. I offered him a sweet smile, placing my hand in the palm of his. Batting my eyelashes like my head was vacant, I said, "Mr. Barnes, I would love a tour of your suite."

"Of course," he smiled, tilting his head to scope over the length of my body. "I should have already offered."

Trying my best not to physically recoil, I laced my arm through the triangle of his. As he flicked on the chandelier lighting in the first upstairs bedroom, I swallowed down the buildup of bile in my throat.

I took in the classy furniture trimming the room. A bed that looked to be bigger than a king-size sat in the corner. The fluffy coverings made the mattress resemble a cloud, giving me a reason to wonder if I would ever manage to sleep again. Judging by my current situation, the answer was no.

I was just about to ask to see the next room, not wanting to spend too much time alone in one place with the old mutt, when glass broke loudly downstairs. I envisioned one thing; *the lily picture.*

Barnes headed back down the stairwell in a hurry, interested in what Hunter was up to below. I followed behind him quickly, one foot after the dreadful other, praying things weren't as bad as I knew they had the potential of being.

Once we'd arrived below, we found Hunter standing in the center of the living room with a blank expression on his face. Nothing looked out of place around the fireplace, which was the first area Ray's eyes darted toward.

"Got a broom?" Hunter asked.

I glanced at the marble flooring. A shattered beer bottle sat oozing by his feet. Golden liquid sprawled out in rolls around the clear glass, a yeasty foam rippling along the surface, and I knew Hunter had broken the glass intentionally. He had broken it to get Barnes to come back downstairs. He had broken it to protect me.

"I didn't choose the Rainman suite so I could clean up after myself," Barnes snickered at the mess, patting Hunter on the back. "I'll get room service on it after you leave."

Hunter glanced my way, but he kept his stare from lingering on me. After clearing his throat, his vision was back on Ray.

"What did Grimsaw say?"

"Esteban!" Barnes shouted.

As predicted, a bookcase on the far side of the room began to slide open. A man exited from one of the stalls, shutting the door before I could catch a glimpse of too much. He was short and Mexican, dressed in a nice suit and bowtie, and he made his way toward Barnes like a servant.

I officially hated everything about Las Vegas.

Like most of Grimsaw's gang, though this didn't include Hunter or Ray, Esteban was missing his front teeth. I assumed Ray's mouth was full of veneers. If the pervert could afford to pay over two million dollars for me, there was no doubt he could afford a set of sixty thousand dollar teeth too.

"Bring her out," Barnes commanded.

"Tessa is here?" Hunter watched Esteban leave in the same direction he'd come. "What has been done to her? I swear to fuck, if anyone touched her—"

"Relax," Barnes smiled as he sat back down. With a point of his finger, he requested I take a seat on the couch beside him. "Nothing happened to your baby sister. I would never hurt Emiliano's only daughter."

A few moments later, though I was sure it felt more like weeks for Hunter, a girl ran out from the passageway as fast as she could. Every step she hustled caused her brown hair to sashay across her back. She had Hunter's shade of unusual eyes, but the fear leaking through hers was heart-splitting.

Clothing her torso was a t-shirt supporting a young boy band. Clothing her legs were purple tights. Green chunks were streamed throughout her hair. I tried to make out the slime, but I could only come up with one possible explanation… *avocado*.

They darted toward each other. She lunged herself into her brother's arms like a gymnast, clutching her wrists around his neck with a death grip. I watched him exhale a deep sigh of relief as he clasped onto her.

"You okay, squirt?"

Hunter allowed emotion to mark his face. Tessa's nose was squished against his t-shirt, her feet dangling in midair, but she didn't seem to mind. As close as siblings could be, despite their age difference, I knew they ranged at the top of the charts.

"I'm fine," she hushed him, barreling down his expansive body like a spider monkey. "But you've clearly seen better days. What happened to you? You look like Frankenstein."

"I know," Hunter smiled, grabbing her hand like he never wanted to let it go again. He whispered something into her ear, inaudible to the rest of us, and then they each took a seat on the couch.

"Let's hear this business deal you were mentioning," Barnes brought my attention back to realities far more important than the green in Tessa's hair. "State your proposal."

"Do it now," Hunter told her.

With a nod, Tessa plugged her ears with her index fingers. She began to hum quietly, blocking out her brother's upcoming words with her eyes slammed shut.

"The slave holds information I require. I want to buy her from you," Hunter stated. "I'm aware she didn't come your way cheap. I have no problem making this transaction worth your time."

Even though they were discussing my fate, it felt as though they were exchanging casual chitchat. If peanuts were sitting on the coffee table beside the ashtray before them, I didn't doubt each of them would start snacking as they bartered over my life. Listening to Hunter haggle was like watching an old lady drive in traffic. I prayed she knew what she was doing, but I wasn't confident she wouldn't slam on her brakes without advanced warning.

"To sell her before I've taken her for a ride would be a sin," Barnes shook his head, comparing me to a bicycle. "You say she has information you want, but I think it's more than that. What's your real motive, kid? Grimsaw told you she was a virgin, is that it?"

"She's not a virgin anymore," Hunter kept up his charade. "And before you get too pissed with me for sliding in on your turf, you should know the slave has AIDS. Check out the tattoo on her right wrist."

Barnes slid up the sleeve of my cardigan, catching sight of my hidden barcode. The disappointment that settled on his face was extremely satisfying to witness.

"Grimsaw used a dirty needle on her?"

"Bingo," Hunter nodded.

"He should have known better."

"Grimsaw should know better than to do a lot of things, but the guy never stops surprising me. Long story short, after I fucked her, I began to rethink my choices. I started to worry she might be infected with something. Out of curiosity, I took a detour to the hospital..." Ray's attention shifted as Hunter threw my test results onto the table before him. "Since she's a walking alphabet of disease, my reasons for wanting her are evident."

With age-spotted hands, Barnes slid my medical records from the envelope. His eyes began to storm over the words angrily, as if I had missed something while analyzing them myself.

When I peeked down at the files, I found black X's across the letter stationary; X's beside numerous infections; X's that hadn't been there before; X's that Hunter must have premeditatively sketched onto the documents when we had separated to use the washroom in the hotel lobby.

The thug was proving to be more than just a pretty face. Not only did his actions impress me, his poker stare wasn't anything to mess around with either.

"How luckless you must be," Barnes muttered, glaring at me like I'd just pushed him straight into dog shit. While his sexual thirst drained from him like an evaporating lake, I was in my glory. The problem was, like anything good...

Glory didn't last.

19
A LEGEND IN THE MAFIA

SHAYLA STONE

Friday. 5:30 A.M.

"WHAT'S THE CATCH, KID?" BARNES wavered, cautious of what Hunter might be up to behind his psychedelic eyes. "With no money in your hands, I strain to see what you have to bargain with."

"Five million," Hunter announced what he was willing to render for me. "Like I said, I will make this transaction worth your while, but I can't withdraw that kind of coin without leaving a paper trail. If you want the money in cash, you're going to have to respect my time restrictions. I can't do anything until society begins to move for the day. You know that."

I moved through Hunter's eyes. Five million dollars was no chump change. I knew he had money, since that tended to be what people robbed banks for, but I wasn't sure why he was willing to dish it out on my behalf. And if he couldn't transfer the cash electronically, how the hell was he planning to pay Barnes?

"Then you leave a girl with me." Barnes slumped forward to rest his arms against his knees, giving Hunter his best mad-dog face. As expected, Hunter didn't faze. "I don't care which one, but I haven't gotten this far up the ladder by being a fool. I don't run by words."

Hunter thought silently for a few moments, his vision browsing through the windows to his left.

"I don't know what to tell you, Barnes. The banks don't open until ten, and I'm not letting either of these girls out of my sight until then. I'm sure we can come to an understanding, can't we?"

"If I allow you to depart with each of them, what leverage will I have against you? There will be nothing motivating you to come back and pay me."

"I plan to rob the west side *Citibank*," Hunter confirmed my suspicions. "What assurance do I have that you won't be calling every police detachment in the state of Nevada to warn them of my upcoming maneuvers?"

"You don't," Barnes said.

"My point exactly."

"You've got yourself a deal." Barnes ripped a corner from my test results, designing the paper with his phone number in blue ink. "Since she's full of transmittable diseases, I have no use for her anymore. Unlike you, I can't heal disease. I see this as an easy opportunity to double my money." Barnes folded the paper and passed it to Hunter. "I'm giving you until noon. If I don't hear from you by then, I'll be sending my men out to find you."

"Don't mistake my age for naivety," Hunter laughed like the threat bored him. "After all, we're a team in this. You'll find that I don't like to burn my bridges."

"If you're anything like your father, I trust your word. He and I used to work in the sky together. Emiliano was the master of flight. While in control of a helicopter, he was a force to be reckoned with."

"Since he's dead now, I find it ironic that you speak as though he was invincible," Hunter replied. "I also found it odd when Grimsaw said you worked with him. My dad wasn't the kind of man who traded girls in the underground."

"Your father ignored many things, but he wouldn't allow schemes like these to slide if he were still alive." Barnes took another pull from his cigar. "Would it be benign to assume you've already raided my safe?"

"I didn't take your money."

"What did you take then?"

"Your pistol. I'll be needing it this morning. It's hard to rob a bank without any leverage. Cracking into a metal safe is much simpler."

"You didn't break into that safe just by listening for clicks in the mechanisms," Barnes doubted. "I want to know how you cracked into it. I know you have a photographic memory, but you've never seen me open it before. I have my theories on how your father's abilities worked, but Emiliano never confirmed them for me."

"There was probably a reason for that."

"While your mother was pregnant with you, your dad was so worried you might wind up like him. For good reason... evidently," Barnes chuckled, a jolly red tint on his cheeks. "I can't help but be curious, have you ran across the girl you're destined to be with yet? I know your parent's love story well."

"We don't need to talk about that," Hunter glanced at me; the sheep on the sidelines. Whatever Barnes was referring to, Hunter didn't want to discuss it in front of me. "I didn't come here to give you my life story. If you knew my dad like you say, you should know your sunglasses aren't protecting you. I can still see everything about you."

Hunter stood and grabbed Tessa's hand. She quit humming, looking confused as she rose to her feet. Hunter snapped his fingers my way next, ordering for me to do the same, but I didn't listen. If I really thought he was going to end my life, I wouldn't walk toward him on the first command. Since we only had one chance at this, I wanted Barnes to believe our performance.

"Go stand in the hall," Hunter instructed Tessa.

With a scoot of her pink sneakers, she did as he directed. Once she had disappeared, her brother turned back toward Barnes and smiled.

"Can we drop the charade now, Barnes? I think you know why I want the slave. I'm sure Grimsaw explained the plotline to you."

"You got me." Barnes allowed an uncanny smile to crimp his lips. "My real motive wasn't the blonde, though I would have made her useful if my plan fell through. I did this because I knew *you* would want to buy her from me once you found out who she was. Grimsaw called me and said he had a plan to introduce the two of us. I didn't argue. Much like your dad, you're turning out to be a legend in the mafia. Everybody wants to meet you."

"I should be flattered to have such dedicated fans. You could have asked for an autograph. I would have given you one," Hunter remarked snidely, commanding for me to move with a second snap of his fingers.

Again, I ignored him.

"Are you deaf, blondie? Stand the fuck up." I obediently stalked toward him this time, using slow feet for the look of added terror. "What would you do, Barnes? If this girl's dad had killed your parents, how would you make her pay?"

"I would bury her alive in a coffin and route air through the dirt to keep her awake with oxygen. I would force her to spend days in the dark knowing she was about to die. Emiliano didn't deserve to go out like he did. Neither did your mother."

"So very true." Hunter lifted his hand to tug at the back of my hair, using his other to travel up the curve of my bent neck. "What do you think, blondie? Is that how you want to die?"

"Please don't hurt me," I faked fear. Although half of it was real, the other half was just a ploy to deceive Barnes. "I'll be a good girl. I'll do whatever you say. Just please... don't hurt me."

"This business transaction is between you and me now," Hunter told Elvis, removing his hand from my neck. "If your purpose is to distinguish just how well-endowed I am in the art of theft, Grimsaw no longer requires involvement. You can double your money by using me, but you let him believe you bought the slave. Are we clear on that?"

"Grimsaw won't be notified unless you don't follow through with the payment. It doesn't matter who you are, I still want my money for the blonde. If you manage to pull this stunt off, I'll have a few other jobs for you to take care of. If you want to make some real money, that is."

"I'll think about it." ·

"Whatever you decide, don't try to screw me around. I was looking forward to a relaxing weekend. It'll be the opposite if I have to track you down."

"Don't ever threaten me," Hunter sneered. "You could never outsmart me, old man. I can be untraceable in a matter of seconds. I can have a new identity even faster. Until I call, grab some popcorn and flick on the news. Just like my dad used to, I always put on a good show."

20
TOXIC AND POISONOUS

HUNTER GARCIEZ

Friday. 6:00 A.M.

THE SUN WAS STARTING TO come out. An orange crest was peeking along the brim of the morning clouds, threatening to overtake the entire sky in just minutes. Dawn was on the rise, so I knew hell was too.

I set Tessa into the backseat of the truck. After buckling her in, I opened the passenger door for Shayla next. I wandered around to the driver's side to follow, but I wasn't quick to hop in. I stayed outside for a few moments, scrambling to devise my next move. I had to get the girls somewhere safe, but would they really be safe anywhere?

Probably not.

Shayla had heard too much in that suite; too much about my dad; too much about me. It was with hesitation that I eventually climbed behind the steering wheel, my pockets full of my belongings again. Shayla stayed silent during my entry, but Tessa would never be so kind.

"What's up with your face?"

I rubbed my palms against my temples to try and work out the charley horses in my mind. Once I realized it was ineffective, I lunged around to encounter my sister.

"What did they do to you? Did they touch you? I'll kill them all,

Tess. I'll rip out their—"

"I would have already told you if they had," she silenced me, cupping my shoulder with her palm. "It really wasn't all that bad. They fed me some ice cream and candy. Esteban let me watch *Comedy Central*, which I knew you would hate, and I drank some posh water that was poured straight from a glass bottle. It even had gold flakes in it. I don't know if it was real gold, but I still felt like an aristocrat. I bet the bottle ran that old guy a hundred bucks."

I unbuckled my sister as fast as I had locked her in, pulling her into the seat separating us. I knew she had to be uncomfortable being pressed against the back of it, but I didn't care. I was so happy to see her… safe and unharmed.

"I'm so sorry, Tess."

"Don't be a wimp."

"I feel like shit."

"Stop it," she scolded me, tightening her eyebrows in disapproval. When she pushed me away, I let her. "Who's the blonde sitting in the passenger seat? Is she deaf and mute?"

"I can hear everything you're saying, so I'm certainly not deaf." Shayla faced the little gremlin, smiling like she got a kick out my sister's rude manners. "I'm Shayla Stone."

"Tessa Garciez."

"I've heard," Shayla nodded, giving my sister an inquisitive look. If I had to guess, I'd say she was wondering about the green gunk in Tessa's hair. My hypothesis was validated when she asked, "Why do you have clumps of avocado in your hair?"

"Because you can't choose your family," Tessa groaned. "Hunter has all sorts of girls calling the house for him. It drives me nuts. Since he refuses to talk to any of them, I took matters into my own hands."

"Tessa," I cut in with a shake of my head. "You're making it sound worse than it is. There are *a few* girls who call the house for me; not all sorts. And if I wanted to talk to them, they would know how to reach my cell."

"Like fifty girls," Tessa insisted.

I revved the truck's motor to life. Like the solid unit it was, the diesel engine purred with the sound of perfection. I hated the thought of giving the truck up, but I would have to eventually. If the cops ran the plates, I was sure it would already be listed as stolen in their directory.

"What did you do to him?" Shayla giggled.

"I answered every phone call and told each of them that Hunter was gay. That took care of one problem, but it created a much bigger one for me…" Tessa pointed at her dirty hair. "If you ask me, I kept those girls from walking into a landmine."

I shot my sister an unenthusiastic stare.

My mom had slapped me across the face a few times as a kid. Whenever Tessa did her best to gnaw at me, I understood the motivation. I would never actually hit my sister, but I did have my own ways of getting revenge on the little hellraiser. I knew how to spook her. I knew the best places to hide when I wanted to scare the living shit out of her.

It was possible that I had filled her shampoo bottle with guacamole yesterday. I might have dumped some raw eggs into her conditioner bottle too. I was too old for such juvenile pranks, but Tessa had a way of pushing my limits. Since I couldn't exactly smack the kid, I viewed raw eggs and guacamole as a decent replacement. I might have been her sole guardian, but I was still her older brother at heart.

"I was headed to the store to buy more shampoo when your friends kidnapped me." Tessa cuffed me upside the head, inching my baseball cap forward. "They left my bike laying on the sidewalk, so you need to buy me a new one; a better one."

"You shouldn't have left the house," I tried to lecture her, but guilt settled in when I realized I had no right. This was my fault, and all I could picture was the gang rolling up next to her as fear varnished her face.

"¿Ella es la chica sin dígitos?" Tessa asked if Shayla was the girl with no digits in her eyes.

I sighed. Between my sister's comments and the remarks Barnes had made earlier, Shayla had to know something wasn't normal about me by now.

"The blonde speaks Spanish," I revealed.

"Whoa, really?" Tessa considered it for a minute. "Are you two dating? What did I miss? Why do your eyes get sparkly whenever you look at her?"

"Stop talking," I demanded, but the damage had already been done. As I felt the effects of Shayla's gaze singeing through my skin,

I mentally assessed what the best possible way to kill myself would be. In the end, I concluded an overdose would be the least messy.

"We're not dating," Shayla solidified the truth. "For your brother to successfully date anyone, he would need to admit that he isn't a brainwashed fool. I don't foresee that happening anytime soon."

"Why do you sound bitter when you say that?" I grew confused by the melancholy in her words. "No girl deserves the baggage that comes attached to a guy like me. Have the past three weeks been fun for you? Because this is what my reality is like; absolute hell. Grimsaw wanted to test my loyalty, which ultimately makes me the reason you were kidnapped. I'm also the reason Tessa was kidnapped. Do you see the common factor here?"

Before she could reply, I flicked on the radio to drown her out. I had enough going through my mind. I didn't need Shayla adding to my disarray, which was about all she was doing at this point. She was keeping me from what I needed to be focused on most; my upcoming robbery.

When a slow song began to tap out from the speakers, it snagged her attention immediately. Her vision lowered to meet my bloody knuckles, warning me that she would break each of my fingers if I even thought of changing the station. The song wasn't one I would listen to on my own time, but I didn't so much mind it when she began to sing along with the music. I didn't mind... because it kept her from talking to me.

As the song ended, Tessa's snoring began to avalanche through the truck. Along with Shayla's singing, my sister's breathing was somewhat of a lullaby too.

Deep down, I had known Grimsaw wouldn't do anything to Tessa. By kidnapping her, all he'd been trying to do was rattle me up. It had worked too, but the mafia held too much respect for my dead father to kill her. As for me, not only was I male, I was old enough to know better. The bounty hanging over my life was fair game.

I tried to keep my eyes on the road, but it was hard when Shayla was seated beside me. Without considering the repercussions, I reached out to grab her hand in mine. I didn't let go of it either, even though I knew I should. I meshed my fingers with hers, squeezing them, wondering if she knew what I was trying to say through my touch.

As it seemed, I wasn't as cold as I alleged. I did retain the ability to develop emotions, but only at the worst time imaginable. Tessa might not have been wrong either. I probably did look at Shayla with sparkly eyes. I hardly knew the girl, but she was seeding my interest rapidly. Every move she made, every breath she took, every smile she offered had an impact on me.

And I fucking hated it.

21
DRENCHED IN JEALOUSY

SHAYLA STONE

Friday. 6:30 A.M.

THEY SAY THAT ALL GOOD things come with time, but I'm not sure how much I buy into that philosophy. When I think about the greatest derivatives of my life, they happened within the blink of an eye. When you're least expecting it, sometimes the best things in life come quickly... *too quickly*.

The thing about time; you can't slow it. A wave can come your way at any given moment. In that moment, it's up to you to decide if you want to catch it. Cutting out from the swell with a duck dive can be beneficial at times. Others, you'll regret not taking the ride forever.

In regard to the *Bay of Hunter*, I knew I shouldn't want to surf the waves he created. I shouldn't want to be touched by a set of hands that had killed before. I shouldn't want to be kissed by lips that were trained to lie. Yet, there was a sliver of me that wanted to experience each of these things.

"I'm going to take you and Tessa to a safe spot," he spoke in a cracked whisper. "Once you two are secure, I'll head out and take care of my business. If I make it out of the bank safely, I'll come back for you girls. If I don't—"

"I'll take care of Tessa," I pledged my commitment to the beast in the backseat. Although his sister was tiny, the decibel level of her snoring indicated she was a fully-grown man with breathing troubles.

"Tessa isn't your responsibility."

"I'm the only reason you're doing this robbery. If something goes wrong, it will weigh on me forever. If it weren't for you, I'd still be in Barnes' suite acting like his newest toy. The way I see it, I'm indebted to you."

"You're not."

Hunter shifted the black hat on his head. I knew he was wearing it to keep his face concealed from the many cameras of Sin City. If he was as famous in the mafia as Barnes had implied, I imagined he was consistently worried that someone was out to get him. The saddest part was… they were.

"Let me come to the bank with you," I insisted, doing my best to be of use. "I might not know the first thing about committing theft, but can't you use me as a decoy somehow?"

"If shit goes haywire, the last thing I want is for you to be anywhere near me. I know you're a tough little thing and all, but I'm not convinced you could adapt to being hammered with twenty-five to life."

"And you could?"

"I've survived worse than prison."

"I don't want to believe that."

"It's the truth," he shrugged. "Look, I'll get my hands on the cash. If the Feds swarm me at the bank, I'll stash the money for you in a place of hiding. I'll write down the passcode for my cellphone soon, and I will find a way to notify you of where the cash is hoarded. Once you've retrieved the funds, get the money to Barnes in a way that doesn't involve showing him your face. After that, phone Russ. Do whatever it takes to keep yourself and Tessa safe."

"There has to be another—"

"This is our best shot, Shayla. You just need to trust that I'm good at what I do. It's not something I'm proud of, but I'm known for this shit. I've just never had to do it without being properly prepared…" He licked at his lower lip apprehensively. "I'll be walking into this robbery blind."

"And what am I supposed to do? Just lounge around with your sister while you go get yourself arrested?" I shook my head at his foolishness. "Why does your intelligence seem to be lessening as this conversation progresses?"

"You'll do what I instruct."

"Not if it involves leading you to jail."

"Let me worry about that." His gaze challenged mine. "Even if I do manage to pull this robbery off, this is just the first initiation in a newly invented cycle. Once Grimsaw realizes I didn't kill or sell you, he won't stop until I'm six feet under. Even if he's scared to lose me, it's the way the mafia works."

"What is your ranking?"

I had assumed he was just another gangbanger, but too much respect was given to Hunter for that to be true. When Grimsaw had looked at him back at the warehouse, there had been an indication of fear in the leader's eyes. I knew something had caused Grimsaw's fright to develop, but I doubted I wanted to know what.

"I'm a Captain," Hunter forfeited.

"Which means?"

"My hands aren't as dirty as they once were. I give orders to one guy. It's my Lieutenant's job to notify the other soldiers beneath him of my requests. The only rules I adhere to are Grimsaw's. He is my General. Most Captains give instructions to murder. They decide when to retaliate against the gangs who have crossed ours. Me, I don't design hit plans."

"You hack instead."

"Exactly," he nodded, surprised I'd pieced it together. "Grimsaw knew I was good with numbers, so he put me in charge of overseeing the electrical and computerized operations within the brotherhood. My role can be as simple as showing some guys how to hotwire a rare model of car brought in from overseas. On a different day, I might shut down a bank for a week."

"If you're so high up, why do you do these robberies yourself?" I turned to make sure Tessa was still sleeping. "Why do you run the risk of going to jail when you could just send someone else to do it?"

"Because there is nobody else to do it." A spooky look crossed his face. "I shut down the camera systems before I walk into these banks, which is why the Feds haven't managed to catch me. Once I arrive at the establishments, I rob them by improvisation. It's not something I can teach; it's something I do. That's why I've scaled in ranking so quickly. That's why I need to get my sister out of

California as soon as I can, and you need to leave too. You'll be safe from Barnes once I pay him, but Grimsaw likes to play cat and mouse. He will come after you again. You can't stay here either."

My heart dropped like deadweight.

What was I going to do?

I could go back to San Francisco and track down my dad, which was my most logical plan, because it was my only plan, but my house would be the first place Grimsaw would look. On top of that, Hunter was right. While gangsters were trying to toss me into the sex industry, lingering around the area probably wasn't the brightest thing to do.

I was no good at these games. I could lie when necessary, but I wouldn't stand a shot when it came to fighting off the mafia. I didn't think ahead like Hunter. In my current mental state, I could barely survive the next hour placed before me. I gave myself a week before I wound up back in Grimsaw's possession.

Hunter made a right-handed turn. He ambled slowly down the Vegas strip to avoid running over the many pedestrians littering the magical city. Drunks were scattered everywhere I looked, leaving the truck practically floating at about seven miles per hour.

"Look at this guy," Hunter changed the subject, pointing to a man who was walking two steps forward and nine back. "It's only seven in the morning, so you know that guy had a rough night."

I motioned toward a young couple next. The man had his girlfriend pinned to a palm tree, his tongue deep down her throat like he was panning for gold in her tonsils.

"Looks like they've had a better one."

Hunter laughed as he looped up to the front entrance of a hotel shaped like a glass pyramid. The veins in his forearm jostled while he transitioned the truck into park, and he slunk out of the vehicle to exchange words with the valet attendant outside. A flock of glass dolls walked past him in skimpy outfits, but Hunter didn't take notice.

After making his way to the passenger side, he opened the door and greeted me with a coy smile. The group of prissy girls continued to gape at him as he helped me to the ground.

"They're eyeing you up like you're the newest line of *MAC* makeup," I nodded toward their predatory gazes. "The one on the left looks like she might come take a pounce at you. At the very least, she's contemplating it."

Hunter's eyes skimmed their way, settling back on my face a fraction of a second later. Once he realized what I was referring to, a boyish grin bloomed over his lips.

"It's pretty hot to see you drenched in jealousy, but those girls have nothing on *you*." He wrapped his arm around my lower back, drawing me closer into the front of his build. As his grip tightened, I swear I stopped breathing altogether. "I'm not a fan of chicks who use slime and paintbrushes to decorate their faces. As I'm learning, I gravitate more toward surfer girls instead."

I stumbled as he released me. Everything he did added to my instability, and he knew this too. In fact, he seemed to be feeding off the knowledge. For a girl who claimed to be unaffected by the opposite sex, I was sure acting like I didn't know my left foot from my right around him.

He pulled his sister out of the backseat before passing me the bags of necessities he'd previously bought for me. Tessa grumbled as he slipped the valet driver a few bills. She even turned her head against his shoulder to prove she was still alive, but her eyes didn't open in the slightest.

"Smile pretty for the drag-queens," Hunter told me, insulting the thick makeup on the faces of the girls watching him. "If you make them frown, their artwork might split down their chins like cement."

I smiled as we crossed paths with the mannequins, giving the group a pleasant curtsy in a much longer dress than any of them were wearing. Hunter snickered as we entered through the entrance of the hotel. The space that greeted us indoors was even more cosmic than the exterior had been.

"Whoa," I breathed out, fascinated by the lights. I had never been on the inside of a casino before. Where I came from, you needed to be of legal age to see things like this.

"Tessa…" Hunter shook her awake, placing her sleepy feet to the ground. "I need you to stay with Shayla, okay?"

Tessa nodded and turned to lean on me, sleep deprivation taking a serious toll on her. I coiled my bag-less arm around her neck to offer added balance, listening as her brother carried on.

"There's too many cameras pointed at the reception desk. It's best if you both stay back here and just try to blend in. If anything happens, call out my name."

Without waiting for a reply, Hunter barged to the front of the long lineup of waiting bodies. I would have normally found his impatience disrespectful. Considering our current situation, I deemed it vitally necessary instead.

"What's his plan?" Tessa muttered.

Shrugging, I replied, "To hell if I know."

22
SCULPTED TO BECOME EVIL

SHAYLA STONE

Friday. 7:30 A.M.

A LITTLE WHILE LATER, HUNTER WAS back and holding a plastic key. Tessa and I followed him through the overpopulated lobby, and then down a slithering hallway decorated with black and silver carpeting.

Once we had made it away from the crowd, I asked, "How did you get a key before everyone else?"

"I got a room on the first floor," he ignored me; a habit of his which no longer surprised me. "Whatever you do while I'm gone this morning, don't leave this room until you hear from me."

"Got it, boss," Tessa cooed sleepily.

Hunter slid the room key into the pass box of a white door, motioning for his sister to enter the room first. As she did, I caught him glancing behind us like he thought we were being tailed.

Instead of following his sister inside the suite, I sent him a worried look. As if it was becoming a reflex of his whenever he knew I was feeling uncertain, he snaked his thick arms around my waist and enveloped my body with the comfort of his.

With his lips pressed against my earlobe, he whispered, "You're going to be mine, Shayla."

While my heart began to flutter, my mind began to doubt I'd heard him correctly. I pushed back from him slightly, but he kept his palms resting against my hips as I did.

And I liked the feel.

"What did you just say to me?"

"I said you're going to be fine," he replied, confirming I had hallucinated the whole thing. "Are you okay? Your forehead is dumping sweat..."

"You think I don't know that?"

After breaking free of his encirclement, I struggled to work the room key into the pass box. I grew antsier by the second. Once the light turned green, I stormed into the suite faster than Hunter could have said anything else.

I was just about to flick on the light when I noticed Tessa laying in one of the two beds. I set my bags to the side and made my way toward her. I unfolded the woven blanket by her feet, thankful for the sunlight gushing through the windows. I wouldn't have been able to see what I was doing without it.

As I tucked a strip of it beneath the crook of her neck, her brother finally decided to grace the room with his always enjoyable presence. His vision instantly caught sight of my fingers.

"Did you just tuck her in?"

"Is that a problem for you?"

"Okay..." He gave me an unsure look, as if he was stepping into a cage with a tiger. "Why are you being such a bitch?"

"What would you prefer?" I asked innocently, keeping quiet so I wouldn't stir Tessa. "Since you don't like it when I act concerned about your wellbeing, I figured I should act like I hate you instead."

"That isn't what I want."

"What *do* you want then?"

"I want to tell you that it took everything I had not to break Barnes' neck," Hunter declared, keeping his mournful eyes away from mine. He continued to stand in the doorway, scared to approach any closer. "I want to tell you that I considered killing him for touching you, but doing so would have put an even bigger target on your back. Much like Tessa, you would have become pegged as my weakness. They think I hate you, but they're still using you to get to me. Imagine what would happen if they knew the truth."

"What's the truth?"

"I want to protect you," he spoke hollowly, almost like he was ashamed to say the words. "I know I shouldn't. I remind myself of who your dad is. I tell myself we're enemies, but I can't force myself to feel negatively about you. I've tried."

"Why are you even doing this robbery?" I minimized our space with a slow stalk, making sure to keep a few feet between us as a protective barrier. "As it stands, you're safe. Why are you risking your freedom to pay Barnes? Why don't you just disappear with your sister right now?"

"Leaving might solve my problems, but it won't solve yours," he whispered, a gunning determination on his face. "If I don't do this robbery, you will die."

"And that bothers you?"

"Severely," he nodded.

"You're only doing this for me?"

"What better motive is there?"

I felt my cheeks warming. Accepting his decision was like drinking a vile of straight cyanide, but the dark fog in his eyes told me I couldn't change his mind. For whatever reason, he was set on helping me.

As his gaze swiped over the fingerprints along my collarbone, his concern was as clear as his sorrow. He had never inflicted any pain onto me, but he acted like he'd caused every one of my bruises.

He raised the hem of his black t-shirt, offering a glimpse of his molded pelvic bones. His tan jeans sat just below the upper band of his white boxer-briefs, making bad look all too tempting. I did my best to keep from drooling as he removed Barnes' handgun from his waist.

"If we aren't already being followed, they'll be after us soon," he warned me, placing the pistol in the top desk drawer beside the entryway. "If anything goes wrong while I'm gone, don't hesitate to shoot. You do know how to work a gun, right?"

"Of course," I nodded, though I had no fucking clue. The way his eyebrows were prickling told me he didn't believe me either, but he didn't pick me apart about it. "How did you get into Barnes' safe? How did you even know where it was located?"

"Luck," Hunter alleged.

"I don't buy that."

"Of course you don't," he rolled his eyes. "I breathe in my surroundings. Every picture in his suite was completely straight. The only frame that held any sort of slant was the one above the fireplace. It made pinpointing the safe easy."

"Even if I did believe you, that still wouldn't explain how you managed to get inside it. What's your favorite hobby, Hunter? Being full of shit?"

"I wouldn't call it my *favorite*," he smiled, though I had been aiming for the alternative effect. "It was a manual combination lock, as basic as they come. A metal safe consists of a drive cam and a spindle. A driver pin sets the wheels in motion, causing a reverberation in the—"

"Forget it." I held up my hand. "I don't want you to explain the technicalities. I want you to give me the truth. I know something is weird about you. Your eyes do bizarre things. They change color, and I swear your pupils enlarge when you look at me. Why can't you just explain it?"

"Let's say you're right then," Hunter played my game, his fingers rubbing at his eyes like I was giving him a migraine. "Let's say I found the combination just by looking through Barnes' sunglasses. Do you think you'll benefit by knowing?"

"Definitely," I nodded.

"You won't," he disagreed. "The things I can do will flip your entire world. Do you think that's something I want? To freak you out so badly that you'll never be able to look at me the same? I shouldn't even care how you look at me. It pisses me off that I do. I was designed to be a hacker and sculpted to become evil. I wasn't meant to have feelings like this."

"Feelings like what?"

"Like anything."

"How vague," I shook my head like it would somehow dissipate my frustration. "Whether you're a criminal or not, it doesn't matter. I know you want me to fear you, but I don't. The fact that you're a little crooked is what has been keeping me safe. The labels you place on yourself don't define who you are. They define what you've done."

After sending him a red-hot glare, one that he replied to with the bluest of all frowns, I entered the washroom and shut the door quietly. If Tessa hadn't been sleeping, I would have slammed the fucking thing.

23
RUSSIAN ROULETTE

SHAYLA STONE

Friday. 8:00 A.M.

"GET YOUR HEAD TOGETHER," I lectured myself, dabbing a wet washcloth against my forehead. "You might be going insane, but at least act like you aren't."

I stripped myself naked and stepped into the shower. Tessa was the one who really needed to wash her hair, but it didn't seem like she planned to do so anytime soon.

I didn't necessarily need another shower, but I wasn't going to complain about the dual-headed nozzle above me. I slid the glazed door shut and allowed uncountable droplets to spray across my face. A complimentary razor sat wrapped near the soap dish, calling out to me like I should make use of it.

After I had finished taming the hair on my body, although I wasn't sure why I did, I shut off the crystalized tap and twisted my hair dry the best I could. Once the drops had lessened, I reached for the towel I'd set over the ledge of the opaque door and packaged it around my body.

I stepped out from the fancy shower, hearing a throat clear as my feet hit the ceramic floor. I found Hunter sitting next to the sink on the counter, his wrists resting on his knees.

"Hi," I gulped, wondering what he would've done if I had walked out naked. "If you wanted to take a shower, you should have said something. I would have waited."

Offering no eye contact, he shook his head and threw his hat onto the countertop next to him. His untamed hair was poking in every direction, hinting at what it might be like to wake up beside him on a lazy Sunday morning.

While I fantasized, he raised himself from the sink to wash his face and hands. He looked at me through the mirror, using a hand towel to dab off the excess water dripping from his chin.

"Let's say I don't do this robbery…"

"I'm listening," I nodded.

"I have a fake passport for myself with me. I have one for Tessa too, but I don't have one for you. Using anything other than faulty identification to flee would be suicide. Grimsaw will have his crew scanning every flight scheduled to leave the state and country. If they see our names listed as boarded passengers, they'll know exactly where to find us once we land. If we're going to act sloppy, we may as well pull out the gun and start playing Russian Roulette right now."

"Your only option is to leave without me," I said glumly, because we both knew it was true. "As it sits, you have an opening. I'm the only one who can't board a plane without leaving an imprint."

"That's your decision? That I just up and leave you to fend for yourself?" A tangle of emotion flickered through his eyes. "The mafia is after you. Do you understand that?"

"I do, but I'm also a hindrance. I have no identification on me. It's not like we can go back to San Francisco to get my passport. Even if we did, it has my real name on it."

"You really are a burden." His palm curled around the doorknob to make his exit from the washroom. "And I should have just kept my mouth shut."

I pulled his hand away from the sphere, abducting him in my own form. I followed that with a rough shove against his chest, keeping my other hand against the towel encasing my body. Although I knew better than to strike a gang member with violence, the borders between right and wrong meant little to me anymore.

"If leaving me behind isn't your best option, what is then? What the hell are you trying to say to me?"

His fingers folded around my wrist, restraining me from bull-dozing against his chest with another vehement beat. When he gave me a dangerous look that made me want to keel over and die, I began to realize I liked my men how I liked my coffee; tall and fatally strong.

"The next time you hit me like that, you better be riding my dick too," he threatened, a perilous frost in his eyes.

He yanked on my arm to draw me closer to him, but my body didn't respond with waves of terror. His breath hit my cheek from above, and I swore I could hear his heart panging around inside his chest. As nervous as he made me, I seemed to make him the same.

"I swear you're bipolar," I spat recklessly. "You don't want me to act like your shrink, which is fine, but be sure to find one elsewhere. There's no doubt you need one."

"Says the slave," he wisecracked.

"Shut up."

He began to remove his t-shirt from his bronzed body, examining my face as he threw the fabric aside. I didn't look up to mingle with his gaze. His defined stomach wasn't giving me room to concentrate on anything else.

"I need to show you something," he whispered, his breath striking my bare shoulder. "You need to understand why you're like kryptonite to me."

Subtlety, maybe even fearfully, I glanced down at his body. I ran my eyes over the bruises designing his sculpted stomach, recalling the moment when herds of men had been swinging at him with bats and boots. I decided Hunter was somewhat of a gym rat. His muscles weren't overpowering, unlike some guys who lifted weights, but he was perfectly toned and athletic just the same.

On his left arm was a simple black tattoo. Although it was small, I could tell it hadn't healed in a proper fashion. Like mine, the ink was in the form of a number; 13:13. I ran my fingers over the engraving in his skin, peeling my stare away from his body to meet his somber expression.

"What does it mean?"

"Mexican Mafia," he answered, a rasp in his voice. "It pledges allegiance to the brotherhood. M is the thirteenth letter in the alphabet. When you decode 13:13, it translates into M:M. It's a prerequisite when committing obligation to the syndicate, but that isn't the tattoo I'm trying to show you."

My eyes darted toward his reflection in the mirror. Shaded ink caught my attention, halting the trail of my finger on his arm. Introducing itself was a colored portrait of two people; a portrait that took up every inch of the skin on his back.

Nothing about the portrait was lacking in detail. The colors and outlines were too perfect to have been sketched by anyone other than a professional. The two inked faces were smiling at each other, giving the assumption they were a couple. It didn't take me long to piece together who they were.

The date of his parent's harmonized deaths sat just below their permanent pictures. Below Hunter's mother was a row of purple and blue orchids. Below his father was a helicopter, reminding me of what my dad had supposedly done.

"My dad was the getaway artist," Hunter explained. "He helped the members of his faction escape. He waited on skyscraper roofs in a helicopter. He was the one who flew over cities, pinpointing which direction his men on the ground should take to lead the cops on a highspeed goose chase. He hacked like me too, but he was most passionate about flying."

I continued to breathe in the artwork. Flames circled the orchids below his mother's face, symbolic of how she had passed in fire. A pistol sat inside the helicopter beneath his father, indicating his dad had been shot. It was unnerving how much Hunter looked like a younger version of the man on his back.

"His life was much worse than mine. Compared to him, I've had it easy. I was never meant to end up where I am. I was brought up right, but my dad's childhood wasn't as healthy. His parents sold him to a gang connected to Grimsaw's family when he was ten. My dad told us he was a pilot, but I knew he did something illegal. An average pilot wouldn't sit down for dinner with a diamond-plated handgun tucked in his waistband, shutting the curtains around the house to keep outsiders from seeing the looks of his family. I put the pieces together as I aged, but I didn't get a taste of this life for myself until after he died."

"How could his parents sell him?"

"My dad never talked about it much. All I know, my grandparents were addicted to anything they could get their hands on. When the mafia wants to recruit younger soldiers, it's as easy as giving some scabby parents a chunk of rock in trade for their kids. It's a fucked up thing to recognize, but it happens every day."

"You were burned in that fire…"

I trolled my fingers over the scars beneath his ink. I didn't need him to explain the burns to me. I knew exactly what they were from; my father.

"That isn't your problem," he said, camouflaging his own pain to lessen mine. "I'm not seeking sympathy, Shayla. When Grimsaw told me who your dad was, I saw red. There was even a second that I contemplated how I could use you to gain revenge. It didn't last long, but it still existed."

I didn't move. I knew he had just admitted to wanting to hurt me, but my body didn't try to escape the nearness of his. No voices in my head were warning me to run, and his sudden grip around my toweled hips was begging me to stay where I was.

I glanced at myself in the mirror, trying to understand why he wanted to protect me. I wasn't completely upsetting to touch shoulders with, but I wasn't the scandalous type of girl that a guy like Hunter went after either. I didn't know the right things to say, and I understood how to be sexy even less. Next to him, I was shooting high when calling myself average.

"Everything you said was true. I don't need to do this robbery," he admitted. "But if I don't, what am I supposed to do about you? I'm willing to give you money to escape in whatever fashion you want, but I know you'll use it to go find your dad. Not only does that put me in a morally awkward position, your chances of surviving on your own are gravely poor."

"This is so messed up." I backed away from him in a brash motion. Hunter remained seated on the counter, keeping his eyes glued to the stone ceramic beneath my feet. "It isn't right for you to be helping me. I don't deserve this from you."

"I think you do," he disagreed, cracking his knuckles. "I know you probably don't want to talk about it, but I need to know how Grimsaw kidnapped you. I need to know *everything*."

"Why?"

"Because I do."

"I don't see why," I sighed, because I knew I had to give him what he wanted. "It was my birthday. My friends and I were hanging out down by the harbor, watching the ships come and go from the dock. It was all I wanted to do that night. It was late and we were drinking. I might have had too much."

"*You?* White girl wasted?"

"I like Chardonnay," I shrugged.

"I thought you were a prude?"

"I let loose every now and then."

"I'd love to see what that looks like."

"Trust me, you wouldn't," I smiled softly.

"Go on."

"When we decided to separate, my best friend's boyfriend offered to walk me home. Bree was even more drunk than I was, and my house is closer to the marina than hers. I told Rylan not to worry about it. I'd made that walk alone so many times before," I shuddered while reliving the experience, finding it even more excruciating than I'd been anticipating. "I heard footsteps walking behind me. The moment I turned around, two bodies tackled me to the grass. I tried to rip off their ski masks, but they were as strong as you. They were hitting me, and one of them unbuckled his pants. I started to scream. I begged for them to release me. I said I was a virgin. I pleaded that my first time wouldn't be rape. I didn't expect anything would end it, but it did. For a second, I remember thinking they weren't monsters. If they were stopping, maybe they had realized they were making a mistake. The man began to do up his pants while the other laughed. Then, just before it all went black, I heard him say, '*Garciez is going to have fun with this bitch.*'"

I took a seat on the toilet, realizing this was the first time I had spoken of the incident aloud. I tried to forget it all; the images, the sounds, the hits my face had taken, but the thoughts refused to vanish.

"Shayla…" Hunter stood and walked toward me. He knelt on the ceramic before me, meeting my eyes from a dead even level. "You have no idea how badly I wish I could change what you've been through."

"For what my dad did…" I trailed off, knowing an apology would never suffice. I hated that I was human and therefore had emotions. "You should want me dead."

"But I don't. This is all happening because I made a stupid crack about leaving the gang to go work for the government. I made the comment around the same time you were kidnapped. Grimsaw's been planning this. I can't believe it bothered him as much as it has. Evidently, he's frightened to lose me."

"Do you kill people for him?"

"I have," he nodded regretfully. "There was a time when Grimsaw forced me to dissect bodies. It was something I had to do to climb the ladder. His victims weren't always dead when given to me. I have taken many lives by means of asphyxiation, but they were all bound to die regardless. After being tortured by Grimsaw, half of them were begging to die. The other half didn't have any tongues left to plead with. Take that how you will, but I don't consider myself a murderer. I'm a thief. On the other hand, if I knew who thought about raping you, I would slit his throat without hearing his side. I would get away with it too. So, who knows what I really am."

"I wish I could tell you who the men were," I sniveled, ignoring the urge I had to break down completely. "They deserve to know how I feel. They deserve to have their lives fade away into nothing but blackness."

Hunter's enlarged pupils began to glimmer with a layer of evil. I could see the same personal vendetta I had for my abductors through his eyes, oozing with predictable payback.

"The name Cazador isn't very difficult to pronounce, Shayla. They refer to me as Hunter because I can track anything down, including your captors. Do not concern yourself with the distribution of vengeance. In soon time, I will hand deliver it on your behalf."

I registered his words, following the guiding light that was leading me toward the cryptic sections of my brain. I knew I shouldn't gain satisfaction from torture, even when directed toward a rapist… but I so clearly did.

Every fiber of me believed that Hunter would do it too. He was crazy enough to accomplish the task. It wasn't like it would be his first time bringing pain onto another human being. And it wasn't right that something about the idea fascinated me; the idea of having a sexual predator get what he deserved.

With hope, I asked, "Can you promise you will take care of it? I need to hear you say it. I need to know they will get what is owed to them."

"A promise isn't necessary."

"Why do you say that?"

"Because before you even realized you were this hurt, I had already declared your suffering a cause for war…" Hunter reached to brush a strand of loose hair behind my ear. "When a man harms Juliet, he coincidingly crosses Romeo too."

24
WITCHCRAFT

HUNTER GARCIEZ

Friday. 8:30 A.M.

"WHAT DO YOU WANT TO do?" I asked Shayla, rising from the bathroom floor. "If I can manage to wake her, Tessa and I should get going. You need to decide what *your* next move is. You either come with me or I leave you behind. If you choose to tag along, I'll need to make you a fake passport. To do that, I'll need my laptop."

"Where is it?"

"San Francisco. We can head back west to get it, but I have no reason to go that way if you're not coming with me. It's risky to go back there; *real risky*. I don't like it, but I understand if you want to go find your dad instead. I just need you to decide."

I watched her squirm. Two metaphorical doors were waiting to be pushed open in her mind, but she didn't know which to enter. One knob would take her toward her dad. The other knob would bring her directly into my circus. No matter what she chose, with every minute we remained in Vegas, the probability of our death was ascending.

I studied her. Her weary gaze was void of hope, meeting mine with a solid foundation of hesitancy. Her eyes were no longer filled with tears, as if she was too numb to shed another drop. I could tell she was officially crumbling, but I was honestly surprised it hadn't happened sooner.

"What should I do?"

"I can't answer that, Shayla."

"Why not?"

"Because I don't want to be the reason you sway one way or another. This decision is yours to make. It isn't mine," I said, concealing how badly I was hoping she would run with me. Her shot at survival tangoed with whether she was by my side or not. At least, that's how I justified my will to protect her; a girl I didn't even know.

I turned to exit the washroom, but her fingernails ripped through the flesh on my forearm in a beastly manner. I whipped around, startled by the feel of her sharp claws. I opened my mouth to demand she let go, but she stole my thunder before I could.

"Can I ask you something?"

"Not if you plan to shred my face apart next." I shook her off my arm, glancing at the imprints in my skin. "You've got some finger fangs on you."

"Kiss me," she whispered.

Those two words…

They stopped my heart.

I looked down at her in puzzlement, wondering which of us had gone mad. I blamed the pills for distorting her words into something I wanted to hear. I knew she had a habit of testing me, but this didn't seem to be one of those scenarios. If it was, I didn't understand it.

"Can you repeat that?" I asked.

Rather than saying anything, she stepped onto the tips of her toes and began to move in for the kill. Her face inched toward mine, dropping the checkered flag that signaled for evil to speed through my veins. In order for a kiss to ensue, I would have to lean down to meet her invitation. I wanted to, but…

Lightning thrashed against my skull. I knew I shouldn't encourage the chemistry between us, but a good chunk of me wanted to do more than just kiss her. The sick side of me wanted to pin her up against the wall and wind her bare legs around my hips. I envisioned removing the towel concealing her body, tracing my fingers over the treasures buried beneath the cotton.

I pictured sliding my hand down her naked frame, my tongue

slinking up her neck as she quivered with my every touch. In my daydream, my middle finger was widening her with slow drives. My thumb was circling her clit, like an instrument I had been playing for years. She had perfect skin, skin I would feel guilty for releasing on, but I imagined decorating her in my cum just the same.

When I thought about what it might be like to have her claws rip through the flesh on my shoulder blades, I began to picture what it would be like to sink my cock through her slits too. I imagined rattling the door with every thrust I plunged into her small body, fucking her with the hate I had for her father. I pictured her toes clenching as she whimpered for me to feed her more. In my head, I was doing just that. In reality, I did nothing but stare at her instead.

"Shayla…" I stepped aside with a frown, my resistance surprising me as much as it did her. "If you knew me, you wouldn't be asking me to do that."

The hurt that washed over her face was difficult to accept, but I knew I was making a noble choice. I was making it with her best interests in mind. And I was sure the separation between us was a good thing, until she whispered, "You aren't attracted to me like that, are you?"

"If I wasn't attracted to you, my dick wouldn't be digging into my belt buckle," I stared at the floor gutlessly. "I just don't want to complicate things any more than they already are. I mean… you're a virgin."

Her face creased with something illegible. She tried to storm around me, but I wasn't fond of the idea. Rather than letting her open the door to make her dramatic exit, I pressed my palm against the gate to keep it closed. I positioned the front of my body against the back of hers, trapping her with nowhere to go.

Breathing into her left ear from behind, I asked, "What's your favorite scary movie, blondie?"

"Who gives a shit?"

She sent her elbow flying into my ribcage, but the pain was mild in comparison to what I'd already been through over the past sixteen hours.

"Jesus," I laughed as the ache subsided, triggering another bout of agitation to rise within her. "You really are too much fun."

As she began to jangle the doorknob violently, I looped my free arm around her waist from behind. Doing something I never should have done, I began to kiss her bare shoulder. My fingers wanted to brush beneath the towel clothing her, but I respected my boundaries like a good guy instead.

"I like plenty about you, but your quick tongue is ultimately my favorite." I used my other arm to remove her hand from the doorknob, becoming surprised when she didn't put up a grueling battle. "Turn around."

"Why should I?"

"Because I told you to." I pressed my groin into her back, threatening her with the feel of me. "You're impulsively fickle, Shayla. You're snarky, sarcastic, and you're a bit of a know-it-all too."

"Those are my best traits."

"I somehow doubt that…"

I flipped her around to face me, laughing to myself when she tried to resist my strength. It was as if she'd been born without the ability to cooperate, but it didn't faze me in the least.

With a brave face, though bravery was not what I felt around her, I crouched my neck slowly to ensure she wouldn't attack me. Just like in my vision only seconds ago, I raised her from the ground by the thighs. She let out a soft grunt as I targeted her spine against the bathroom door, clenching her legs tightly around my waist.

"You're beautiful," I told her, sketching my tongue over the flesh on her throat. "An undiluted beautiful; a classless beauty that can't be faked. If I kiss you, I fear my veins will begin to crave you."

Her head fell back and struck the door, extending her neck to encourage the interaction of my tongue. I caught her eyes rolling, but something told me it was an outcome of ecstasy rather than sarcasm this time.

"Would it be so wrong?"

"It would be fatal," I whispered. "*She loved me for the dangers I had passed. I loved her that she did pity them…*" My words fell directly into her ear, causing her hips to buck against my body. I smiled at the feel, satisfied to know she was under my spell. "*This is the only witchcraft I have used. Here comes the lady. Let her witness it.*"

"*I kissed thee ere I killed thee,*" Shayla smirked a sexy one, recognizing my recited *Othello* from a mile away. "I have but one request. One kiss from a dirty scoundrel."

I was absorbed by her dry wit. I liked her every facial expression. I liked her giggle. I liked that she didn't take shit from anyone; not even me. I liked that she hated me as much as she seemed to want me. I liked every layer that disguised her core. I liked them so much, I decided to press my lips against hers.

When she parted her mouth to permit the entry of my tongue, allowing me to thieve the taste I'd been so desperately thirsting, the thought of death leaked from my mind and vanished. Her tongue passed over mine in soft waves, activating every hair on my body to rise.

Despite my mental warfare, her tongue was highly efficient when it came to placating me. Her hands were in my hair, on my shoulders, on my chest, back in my hair, and then against my neck. Her thighs were digging into my hips with the tightness of her squeeze. The girl was everywhere, slicing me with her finger-nails, suffocating me, flooding me with her passion. It was like she couldn't handle the moment; like she couldn't handle the way I made her feel; like everything inside of her was breaking; like she couldn't think straight; like no part of her even gave a shit to try.

As she wrapped her hand around my throat, my logic collapsed with my airways. She choked me, feeding me her vanilla tongue as she did. When I told myself to release her, I couldn't bring myself to do it. I tried. *I really fucking tried.* I told myself I wasn't worthy of having my palms cradled beneath her ass... but her hands were in my hair, on my shoulders, on my chest, back in my hair, and then against my neck some more.

Only a fool would end something so cryptically divine. It would be a sin to say no to a princess, and I couldn't have that perched on my conscience. But I also knew what my unwillingness to unravel from her body meant. The slips of her tongue were slating my fate in bold letters; letters that flashed through my mind like beacons of warning.

If I was going to act like her twisted prince...

Thou shalt die for the fair maiden too.

25
THE GATES OF HELL

HUNTER GARCIEZ

Friday. 9:30 A.M.

I HAD BOUGHT SOME MORE CLOTHES from one of the gift stores near the hotel lobby. Through piles of Vegas items, I had managed to find another black t-shirt. A clean pair of blue jeans were strapped over my legs. I even had a fresh pair of socks lining my feet.

I'd had a quick shower too, but the ice water hadn't helped to ease the rage of my dick any. I was struggling to understand what had just taken place. I had never been so anxious to seize a kiss from a girl before; not like I had been with Shayla. I didn't know why I had gotten so turned on. I had barely touched her. I hadn't even removed the towel from her body.

Fucking pathetic.

Even while I had been making a move toward her, I knew I shouldn't have been. I regretted making the jump to an extent, but I had also enjoyed it severely. I had wanted to know what she tasted like. I had wanted to know if she was a sensual kisser or a savage one. In all honestly, since she was a virgin, I had assumed she wouldn't be great at it. I had assumed her tongue would be timid and weak... but I had been very wrong.

I exited the bathroom. The sound of Tessa's snoring greeted me, proclaiming she was still asleep. This wasn't unusual for her. She had the tendency of sleeping through six alarms every morning before school. I was always forced to wake her myself.

Shayla's eyes shot to mine, her body sprawled out like a bruised angel on the opposite bed as my sister. I walked toward her with a blank expression on my face, waiting until I was closer to shake out my wet hair above her dry body. I laughed as she shielded her face from the water droplets.

She searched my eyes slowly, taking her sweet time to outline my pupils. Her smile plummeted me further into temptation. My braincells were bursting like gunpowder, and I wanted to tell her why. I wanted to tell her that she was the one for me. I wanted to tell her that I couldn't see any numbers in her eyes. I wanted to tell her that it didn't work like that when I looked at anyone else, but I knew I would sound straightjacket crazy if I did.

So... I said nothing at all.

"Things are really bad, aren't they?"

"They aren't great," I admitted.

She nodded calmly, but I could see just how frightened she was. Even though she was trying to bury her anxiety, trying to pretend like she could handle the gore my world entailed, I wasn't buying her charade for a minute. When employed against me, her mask was entirely useless.

"I will protect you if you come with me," I told her, knowing I needed to have this conversation with her sooner rather than later. "What happened in the bathroom... I won't do that again. I lost control, and I'm sorry for that, but you need to stop pushing me. I can't think properly when you're asking me to kiss you. I can't think properly when you're purposely antagonizing me. You know that, so stop it. If you can't, you'll need to go your own way."

"Is that what *you* want me to do?"

"Why do you keep asking me that?"

"Because I want to know."

"It doesn't matter," I shook my head, knowing I was bound to upset her with my next sentence. "I'm attracted to you, but that's as far as this will ever go. I don't want you to get it twisted. I'm not inviting you to flee with me so we can get to know each other. This isn't a love story, and you need to understand that. For the time being, I'm inviting you with me because I think it's your best shot at staying above ground."

"I do realize we're standing outside the gates of hell, Hunter. I'm not a complete idiot. I mean… is that what you think of me? That I'm some lovesick girl who's going to fall for you now that we've kissed?"

"It could happen," I shrugged, taking a quick glance at my sleeping sister. "But you need to view this as a business deal. That's all it is."

There was no doubt my words were hurtful, but they were required to be. I could tell they had stung her. Her face fell flat and emotionless, as if shock was inhibiting her from experiencing grief. I knew I had sliced her good, but it would help her in the end.

Hurting her was one of the last things I wanted to do, which was why I had spoken the brutal truth now rather than postponing it. It was why I had done it so bluntly. If Shayla started to think something might progress between us, it would only hurt her more overall. When I took my leap against her father, I would destroy her life too. This girl and me… we didn't come from the same side of the tracks.

Alternatively, if I were to let her get inside my head, I could lose sight of what was important to me; gaining revenge for my parents. I knew I had full intentions on killing her dad eventually, which left the whole situation unavoidably awkward. Shayla was a babe, but it wasn't like I could just forget about what her dad had done because of it. Shit didn't work like that.

"Say it, Shayla."

The only way I knew she was feeling anything was by the way her cheeks were growing rosy. I sensed she was considering the different ways to kill me, but she made me want to do the opposite to her. I would never be able to call a girl like Shayla mine, but she reminded me there was a world outside of mafia hell.

If I really wanted to track her dad down, Shayla would be the best method to use. I could probably follow her right to his doorstep, leeching information about him along the way. I could pretend I was over what he had done, following as she led me straight to him. I could then slit his throat in front of her… but I didn't want to use her like that. Something about it didn't seem right.

I hated that I had a conscience.

As she glanced up at me, her blonde bangs fell over her eyes. The look on her face became perverse, and for a second, I regretted being a dick to her at all… then I remembered I was doing it for her benefit.

"Say it, Shayla," I repeated roughly.

"You and I will never be."

26
THE STAGGER IN HIS SWAGGER

SHAYLA STONE

Friday. 2:30 P.M.

HOURS HAD PASSED. HUNTER HAD been running over our upcoming plans when his eyelashes had begun to flutter. His head rested in my lap now, his lengthy body crammed across the front seat of the truck. He looked calm in mid slumber, drifting in a peaceful paradise; a paradise I saw no reason to wake him from.

I drove the diesel while he and his sister slept like mummies. We were on route back to San Francisco to get his laptop. It was asking for trouble, and it weighed on me that we were only doing it because I was useless in the passport area. If anything were to happen to either of them, it would be nobody's fault but mine. They wouldn't be heading back to California if it weren't for me.

For now, I had decided fleeing with them was my best option. I could try to find my dad instead, but I wasn't sure he was even still alive. Maybe he was already dead, or maybe the mafia wasn't after him at all. Maybe their sights were set exclusively on me. I didn't know, but if my dad was alive and I went to him, I would be doing nothing but bringing hazard his way. Since Hunter was already in danger, I figured I couldn't do much worse to him than he seemed to do to himself. I had to wait for things to settle down. As soon as I could, I would find a way to get in touch with my father.

I could hear Tessa as she began to regain consciousness in the backseat, avocado still outlining her hair. I had been worried she'd somehow slipped straight into a coma, but she stretched her arms and banished my concerns.

"Morning," I offered her a timid smile through the rearview mirror. "We grabbed you a bag of dill pickle chips. I was going to grab you some ice cream too, but it's a good thing I didn't. It would have been long melted. You snore like a leaking muffler."

I passed back the bag of confectionery goods that Hunter and I had picked up at our last pit stop along the highway. He had driven for the first few hours while I had rested on his lap. When I'd woken, his eyes had been bloodshot and his words almost slurred. Rightfully so, I had kicked him out of the driver's seat rather quickly.

"I know," Tessa snickered, rubbing her weary eyes. "After our parents were killed, I found it hard to sleep for months. Hearing Hunter strum the guitar was all that could put me to sleep. He would stay up for hours playing it for me. Whenever I'm tired now, I just picture him plucking a lullaby."

"He plays the guitar?" I glanced at Hunter as he drooled in my lap. There was so much I didn't know about him. There was so much he would never tell me.

"Only since he was six," she nodded, wasting no time to rip into the bag of chips. "He hasn't been the same since we lost them. He made it easy for me to move on, but his nightmares have ruined him. There are days when he seems like his old self; happy and fun to be around. Other days, his guilt wins over and all he does is exist. I can tell he wants to die. He views himself as trash, but what happened to me last night wasn't his fault. It was mine. If Hunter had just cut his losses and shipped me off with social services, he wouldn't be involved with the people he is today. This is all because of me."

Although Tessa was young, she had a wise mentality about her. She'd grown up fast, having no other choice, but Hunter still managed to keep her enthused about life. No matter how unconventional his parenting tactics seemed to be, at the end of it all, wasn't that the most important job of a parent? To keep their kid happy?

"I don't know where you came from, but I saw the way he looked at you before I fell asleep," she continued. "There's something going on between you and my brother."

"He's cute," I admitted.

But also a criminal.

"Cute isn't the word I would use to describe him, but to each their own," Tessa grinned. "His cuteness factor will diminish once your clothes are covered in spaghetti. Just wait until you have guacamole in your hair. Wait until your bed is layered with processed cheddar, or he locks you in your room when you have somewhere important to be."

I didn't doubt Hunter could cause a nasty headache, but the thought of becoming beleaguered by pranks wasn't enough to scare me; neither was the fact that he was a drug addict, a bank robber, a smoker, or that he stole vehicles without concern.

"Tessa," Hunter's voice cut in to silence her, as if he'd been furtively awake for a while now. He rubbed at his swollen eyes, tilting his head to look up at me with fatigue. "I'm hesitant to ask how long she's been awake for."

"Long enough to become acquainted with the blonde." Tessa rested her arms along the rear of the seat to get closer to him. Hunter flinched as he stole a glance at the clock. "Which reminds me, can I ask you something, Shayla?"

"Sure," I okayed her request.

"Do you have AIDS?"

I choked on a breath of air, unprepared for a question like that.

"You have no filter," Hunter scolded her, his forehead creasing in a fatherly sort of way. He raised himself from my lap and sent me an apologetic look. "There are certain types of questions you shouldn't ask. Chances are, if you don't already know the answer, it probably isn't any of your business. Asking another person if they have AIDS is definitely one of those questions."

"You think I don't know that?" Tessa scrunched up her face. "But I saw her medical files on the table when we were leaving that old man's hotel room. There was a black X beside HIV."

"What if she did have a disease? Would you say more ignorant things to her?" Hunter whipped around, looking at his sister like she'd just cut off his finger for trade in the black market. "You could at least pretend to have some respect."

"Why are you getting so defensive?" Tessa snorted, enjoying the finesse she had when it came to tormenting him. "It's so weird to see you catching feelings. I bet you would hold Shayla's purse in public if she asked you to. All while she holds your balls…"

"Thank you for that." Hunter's cheeks sparked with cherry, resembling a bulb on a hooker's porch in the red-light district. I never thought I would see him stagger in his swagger, but that's exactly what was happening. "I'm really sorry. I can't control her mouth."

"She's funny," I shrugged.

Hunter released my hand and began to fuss with his chocolate hair. He let out a swearword when it wouldn't relax in the manner he wanted it to. I couldn't help but laugh at him. For being a crook, it was odd how much he seemed to care about his looks. After giving up helplessly, he reached for the black baseball hat sitting on the truck's dash and threw it over his bedhead.

"Where are we going?" Tessa cut in again. "I can see we're headed toward California, but I know we won't be able to stay there. I don't know what's going on, but I can tell we're in a bad position."

Hunter and I exchanged a woeful look. Since she was his sister, and because I had no idea where we would head after accumulating his laptop to make me a fake passport, it seemed only fitting that he would respond to her.

"Look, squirt…" He spun around to face her. "I'm really sorry, but you won't be able to say goodbye to any of your friends."

"I know that."

"I'll make it up to you."

"I know that too," she smiled, slapping the beak of his hat down over his eyes. "As long as I have my big brother, I'll be just fine."

During the following pause of silence, there was enough time for me to pass three vehicles on the freeway. I found myself laughing when I realized how much power the engine had.

"This truck has no governor," I decided, watching our speed incline. "A stock engine would have maxed out at around 105 miles per hour. We're going 120. The speed limiter was raised at some point."

"It wasn't hard to do," Hunter smirked, gripping onto the *oh-shit* handle along the passenger doorframe while I floored it. It became clear that he knew his way around an engine too. "I sense you like speed?"

"Adrenaline in general," I answered.

"Like surfing in Hawaii?" he asked, watching me like there was something he wished he could say; something he *needed* to say. I wanted to burrow through his skull, wriggling my way through his logic, quenching myself with the knowledge of who he was and how he thought.

Trying to break apart the flicker in his green gaze, a mission that was never attached to an easy victory, I replied, "Exactly like I imagine surfing in Hawaii would be."

27
A MEXICAN IN THE CLOSET

HUNTER GARCIEZ

Friday. 5:00 P.M.

I HAD ALREADY STOPPED AT MY place downtown for my laptop. The house was paid off, so I wasn't sure what would happen to it in the end. I just knew I couldn't sell it. Once we made it to Hawaii, trying to play real estate games over the phone would be detrimental to my goal of disappearing without a trace. If I left the house abandoned long enough, I figured it would become government property eventually.

I walked up to another two-story home, ducking as I passed under the giant apple tree sprouting from the soil on Shayla's front lawn. She'd warned me that there would be a security system linked to her house, but I had silenced her when she'd tried to give me the code. I didn't need the digits. I already knew them. I had learnt them through her eyes long before her numbers had dissolved, as well as every other code she'd ever needed to know throughout her eighteen years of life. I even knew the combination to her locker at school. Like she'd caught onto, her birthday too.

I should have already told her the truth, but it wasn't a conversation I wanted to have. There were many ways it could go, but I imagined the likeliest would be something like this:

"Hey, so I've been meaning to tell you something. When I stare into the

eyes of the people I meet, I can see their most valuable information. I can see things they wouldn't want me to. I can detect their bank account pins, along with everything else in code format that is needed to verify their identity. I know their driver's license numbers, even their social security digits. Committing identity theft is as simple as buttering toast for me. It's how I've been robbing banks."

This would be the part where she would stare at me blankly, as if I had grown tentacles on my face and called myself pretty. She would spend a few minutes trying to devise her own theories, none of which would be good. So, I would carry on uncomfortably:

"I don't read minds, but I involuntarily read digits. I don't have an explanation for why it happens to me, but it was the same for my father. I can't keep myself from reading the figures, but it's different with you. There are no numbers in your eyes anymore, so I think … I think this means we're soulmates."

I shook my head at myself, entering through the front door of her dad's house. I ignored the dragon-shaped doorknocker on the outside, weighted with the lushness of the dual-stacked home, and pressed the wooden slab open with my palm instead. The security system didn't bleep upon my entry, indicative that her dad might be home.

I took a deep breath in, unsure of what I might be walking into. This wasn't one of my most logical plans, but I wasn't sure my brain had the ability to formulate an intelligent strategy at all anymore.

There was only one reason I was standing in Shayla's house; I needed a picture of her to put on a fake passport. Since her face was currently cut and bruised, I couldn't take one of the way she looked right now without being required to edit it. The photo would look too skeptical in print if I did, and I didn't have enough time to fumble with software anyway. Since we were already in San Francisco, it made the most sense to copy the picture from her real passport.

Grimsaw's men wouldn't be scanning the airport systems for passport pictures. All they would be able to obtain were the passenger names on outgoing flights. I knew this, because I had created their system. I could do more than that on my own if ever necessary, but I hadn't rigged up the computer structure at the warehouse with too much power. I was too smart for that. Instead, I had manipulated all electronical diaphragms to a position where *I* was the stipulation that needed to be applied to get the job done.

In everything I chose to do, I did it in a way that marked me as a requirement; a necessity to complete the task. Just like that, if Shayla wasn't careful, I would make her fall in love with me. I would do it effortlessly too. The ability to do these things came naturally to me. In everything I did, manipulation played a role. It was an instinct I'd been given at birth; like the act of breathing. Stripping myself of this characteristic was impossible. It was something that could only be done by burning my soul, and in order to burn my soul… one would have to find it first.

The dark hardwood creaked beneath my feet. Shayla's house was fancy, rich like her father. I crept through the kitchen, my thoughts like packets of pressure against my temples. I tried to remember why this had seemed like a good idea. I couldn't think of a reason at first, but then it dawned on me; I was beginning to dig the blonde.

So, there was that.

The stairs to the second story were without carpet. So, not that I would have anyway, I didn't remove the black skater shoes on my feet. Shayla had informed me that her bedroom would be the third door to my left. I pushed into her living quarters, hearing no voices to indicate the presence of anyone else on the inside of the house.

Her blinds, bedspread, and lampshade were all purple. Just about everything else was baby blue. Lights in the shape of stars were strung around the canopy above her bed, giving the room an ultra-feminine vibe.

This was her home.

This was her life.

This was what she was leaving behind.

I sighed with regret, reaching into her closet to clench onto the straps of a pinkish bag. I didn't have time to waste. I had left Shayla with Barnes' gun at a hotel near the airport, just in case any disreputable visitors decided to pay the girls a visit, but I wasn't convinced she would use it if necessary.

I glanced at her desk. On one end of the refined oak sat a picture of a young Shayla with a white woman; a woman I assumed to be her mom. On the other end was a picture of Shayla and her Mexican dad; the dad she seemed to believe was biologically hers. I tossed both frames into the bag. Even though I hated her so-called dad, he was important to her. I had to remember that. Just because I wanted to kill him, the bitter facts weren't going to change.

While seizing some of her clothes next, I took a longer than necessary stare at the purple surfboard tucked in the corner of her room. I wandered over to her bedside table, removing her passport from a drawer she'd previously described. I smiled when I caught sight of the sour expression ornamenting her face in the picture. I wondered if the mugshot on her driver's license would be any better. The girl was beautiful in person. In print, however, she looked like she'd been incarcerated for chopping off her cheating boyfriend's dick.

While picking her room apart, I began to have second thoughts about everything. *Maybe this was a bad idea. Maybe I shouldn't have invited her to flee with me. If her dad was still alive, maybe she belonged with him...*

Shayla obviously hadn't taken her purse out on the night she'd been kidnapped, because it laid on the bench at the end of her bed before me. After tucking her passport into the back pocket of my jeans for ultra-safe keeping, dropping her purse and wallet into the deep bag next, I treaded back down the stairwell. My feet had just reached the last step when I was forced to a dead halt.

"Peach ain't really your color," Grimsaw growled from the living room, referring to the girlish bag dangling from my left shoulder. "I had you pegged for liking the color red more."

"Why is that?" I wondered.

"Because it was a blonde in a red dress that led you to disobey me."

"Among other things."

Grimsaw's eyebrows were flexing with hatred. I could practically taste the bitterness I had left in his mouth on the tongue in my own. He wasn't messing around anymore. He had tracked me down, knowing I would come back to San Francisco for something before fleeing. Now...

I was fucked in a very bad way.

"It's really too bad that I like you as much as I do, G. It pains me to slaughter you, but you're the one who chose to act like an idiot.

I can't be held liable for your stupidity. I told you I would wipe the streets with your blood if you fucked with my plans. Regardless, what'd you go do?"

I took a glimpse at the decor speckled throughout the living room. Shayla's school pictures lined the walls from kindergarten until what looked to be recent, and her school bag was hanging on a rack near the front door. Not only did the flowers on the backpack give it away as being hers, the advanced psychology book hanging from the front pocket was even more suggestive.

"We're gonna have a little talk, because I can't figure out why you've destroyed your life for the slave's." The outline of a pistol sat in the waistband of Grimsaw's slacks. "Do you want to die? Is that it?"

Dying would be easier.

"I'm hoping not to."

"I bet you are," he smiled an ice-cold one, running his fingers through his buzzed hair. "I was hoping you were gonna do what I asked you to, but I received a phone call at noon today. Barnes said you owe him five million? Something about you purchasing the Barbie from him?"

"I have no recollection," I attempted to stall more than I was trying to hide the obvious truth. Lying would get me nowhere in the end, but it might keep me alive for a few minutes longer.

"Did you think you would be out of the country before I caught wind you were trying to fuck me over?" He took a seat on the corner of the micro-suede couch in the living room. He pulled the steel weapon from his pants, setting it onto the polished coffee table before him. "I said it was the slave or your sister. Why would you risk everything for the Barbie?"

"How do you know I didn't buy her from Barnes so I could kill her myself? Maybe I wanted to torture her for what her dad did to my parents? Maybe I wanted to make the bastard pay for his actions by using her?"

"I might have believed that..." Grimsaw chewed at the side of his cheek, stewing over my shit-lathered words. "If you weren't carrying the broad's purse on your arm like a whipped cracker. All I can see is the Caucasian in you. The Hispanic is what keeps you quick. The white blood does nothing but weaken you down."

"That's a little racist."

"You can't be racist toward a white man. White supremacy; ain't you heard of it? When the day comes that a Mexican is running the country from a prestigious suite in the white office, that's when we'll discuss rights and freedoms."

"You need to be American to be the President, dumbass," I stared at him like he was a two-headed fish. "Even if an immigrant could be accepted as a contender, most of the Mexicans I know don't have the time it takes to campaign. They're too busy walking around with a gun in their pants. You're living proof of that."

I didn't know where Grimsaw stirred up his rationality, but I knew it wasn't in the same dimension as the rest of society. If we were talking fact, white people weren't even the majority anymore. Upon entering a gas station in California, it was full of people just like me; the mixed race.

I didn't care to banter about discrimination either. It had just been a good way to distract Grimsaw. It had granted me time to wonder where his sidekick was hiding. Wherever Santiago was, Raphael was never far behind.

"What's your point, G?"

"What's yours?"

"Stop trying to distract me," he hissed, his face contorting like a vampire forced into sunlight. He folded his arms behind his head in a triangular fashion, shaking the loafer on his foot with impatience. "Now that you've come to grab your girlfriend's shit, why don't you tell me what you were hoping to do next?"

I dropped Shayla's bag to the side, taking a casual seat on one of the stools at the kitchen island about twenty feet away from him.

"If I was going to say anything, I would tell you what a piece of shit you are," I smiled.

At the sound of those words, he grabbed his gun and raised himself. He marched toward me with speed, gripping the trigger of his pistol in the curve of his pointer finger. I expected nothing good to come from his quick movements, and my reservations were validated as he smashed the weapon against my face.

I clutched onto the island for stabilization. Something crunched on the inside of my construction, but I didn't fall from my stool. I couldn't deny that Grimsaw packed a mean hit, just like I couldn't deny I had a habit of being a cocky prick. Together... we didn't always see eye to eye.

"I probably deserved that," I confessed, feeling a new round of pain as it discharged around my face. Blood began to slide down my cheek through my stitches, but I didn't worry about it much.

"I don't know why you can't just be solid with me. I gave you a job. I gave you everything you needed to keep your sister by your side. You failed to do what I requested of you. I told you hell was gonna rise."

"Jesus," I gritted. "I'm growing bored of this shit. Decide what you're going to do about it already. It's one thing to rob a bank, but it's a whole different playing field when we're talking about selling girls into the sex industry. If the girl I was given is branded with the number 40347, where are all the others you captured before her?"

"You didn't think I had it in me to do, did you? I like money. I'll do just about anything to drop a million into my account. You know that."

"Everyone likes money, but you don't see the rest of us selling girls to the sex trade to gain it. It isn't like you don't have more than enough cash to get yourself by already. I brought you in three million with our last robbery alone."

"I'm not here to discuss morals."

"Being that you have none, I imagine it would be a difficult conversation for you to upkeep," I criticized his soul.

"Fuck you, ése."

"If you're not going to blow my brains out, but you don't want to chitchat either, why don't you tell me what you do want then, Grim?"

"I want the Barbie."

"I'm sure you do," I recognized, a condescending edge to the key of my voice. "But even if I did know where the blonde was, I wouldn't give up her location. You can spend all night torturing me. You can cut off my fingers. You can cut off my ears too, but I'll take everything I know to my grave."

Grimsaw tugged me from the stool by the collar of my t-shirt. Since I didn't have any leverage to bargain with, I obligingly cooperated. He hurled my body into the entertainment unit in the living room, leaving a nice gash across my forearm as the TV squished me like a bug. I removed the glass from my body, watching Grimsaw make his way over to a set of closet doors. When he yanked them open, only one thing was revealed.

One living thing.

There a longhaired Mexican sat; his mouth sealed by duct tape, his wrists tied with manila rope. His face looked familiar from a picture I'd seen in Shayla's room, and it wasn't long before I had an arrogant grin plastered on my face.

"Crazy, ain't it?"

I barely heard Grimsaw's laugh at all. Rage and sadism took over my mentality. Everything else diminished into inaudible background noise. The man glanced my way, but he was careful not to hold my gaze for more than three second intervals.

I bolted to my feet and charged toward the closet like a bull. Rather than stopping me, Grimsaw graciously stepped aside without conflict. He folded his arms across his chest, still laughing as I grabbed Shayla's father by the dress shirt he wore.

I ripped his helpless body from the closet, noticing a purple windbreaker hanging above him. I knew who it belonged to, but it didn't matter. Nothing could keep me from my revenge. Nothing could save him now.

Not even his daughter.

28
SURROUNDED BY WHITE CHALK

HUNTER GARCIEZ

Friday. 6:00 P.M.

HIS HEAD CAUGHT THE CORNER of the pine coffee table centering his living room, rocking with a jolt as it bounced off the wood like a rubber ball. Red drops began to fall from his divided eyebrow, puddling onto the hardwood floor. Seconds later, as indignation took over me again, I began to boot him in the ribs repeatedly.

I didn't count how many times I struck Shayla's dad. I could only see the images of two people, and their dead faces were giving way for violent tendencies to consume me. No charitable voice tried to calm my feet into slowing their attacks. Bowing at their side-by-side gravesites, I had promised my parents I would kill this man once I found him. I had waited for this moment for three long years.

I crouched and shook his body like he was made of plastic. He continued to do everything he could to keep me from seeing his eyes, as if he knew what mine could do. Grimsaw sneered on the sidelines, proud to see my heartless side surface. Shayla's father, the man who had lifted my glass world in his hands and threw it against a brick wall…

He would get no sympathy from me.

"By the way you're avoiding my gaze, you must know who I am," I said, seeking no real response. "The tables have turned now.

Unfortunately for you, they don't look to be in your favor any-more."

I tore the duct tape from his mouth, making sure to remove the gray as torturously as possible. His eyes remained padlocked while a cocky smile sheeted across his cracked lips.

"It's been a long time coming, Cazador."

I sent the bottom of my shoe into his chest, laying him flat out onto his back. He had no air left in his windpipes, but that didn't keep me from landing another four shots to his head.

Shayla looked nothing like him. She was a blonde-haired, blue-eyed beauty. This man was a Mexican with shit-filled eyes. I had half the mind to suggest her mom had been banging the mailman behind his back, but I had more important topics to discuss currently.

"Where is my daughter?" The murderer had the Spanish accent to fit his part. It croaked with every syllable he spoke. "What did you do to her?"

"I bet you would love to see her one last time," I taunted, having fun with the cruelty. "I know that feeling all too well. I'll always wish I could see my parents again."

"What have you done?"

"Maybe I slit your daughter's throat. Maybe she pleaded as I inched the knife deep into her neck. Maybe she's at the bottom of the ocean as we speak. It wouldn't take long for her lifeless body to sink ten thousand feet. Do you have enough men to send out a diving party?" I grinned as his lower lip quivered. "Then again, I suppose it doesn't really matter. I left your little girl in such brutal conditioning, even if the retrieval of her disposed body was manageable, you would never be able to identify her. She was completely unrecognizable when I was done with her."

"I'll fucking kill you!"

"Careful," I cautioned, displeased by his raised tone. "We're in the middle of suburbia. You wouldn't want your neighbors to hear your screams, would you? Because it wouldn't save you. All it would do is ensure I kill you sooner rather than later."

"Garciez…" Grimsaw tossed me his pistol. "Blow his brains out. I'll get my boys to clean up the evidence. For everything else you've gone and fucked up, I'll take his death as repayment."

"If I kill him, you'll leave me and Tessa alone?" I contemplated

Grimsaw's words. The deal sounded more than just sweet. "I don't believe you. Nothing is ever that simple when dealing with a demented fuck like you."

"Go to hell," Grimsaw scowled, mentally slitting me with his eyes. "I just wanna know you can slaughter when necessary. If ever you've had the guts to kill anyone, it should be this fucking guy. He shot your *padre* and burned your *madre* alive."

I stared at the gun in my hands, wondering what the best choice was. I needed to keep Tessa safe at all costs. If it meant killing Shayla's dad along the way, I should do it. I knew I should take the shot, but something was holding me back.

"Looking at you, I know your last name isn't Stone," I predicted, bidding myself more time. "I don't know how you've managed to convince Shayla she is your blood daughter, but I know your dick didn't throw out the load that was used to create her. Who are you?"

He surrendered and met my stare, scribing numbers out to me instantly. For reasons I was unaware, his pupils were filled with more complexities than most. I spent my time memorizing everything I could about him.

"Diego Alvaro," he introduced himself.

I slashed the pistol across his face. I didn't know who I was right now, but I was far from my old self. Grimsaw was right. The man before me did deserve to feel agony. In this moment, I had it in me to deliver it too.

"You're a smart man, Diego. The way you left that pot on my parent's stove was good. I'll give you that win. Another good one? Wiping their bank accounts. There's one thing you didn't do a good job of, though..."

"And what's that?"

"Keeping *me* away from your daughter."

A tear fell from his eye and mingled with the blood on his face. He was fearing the absolute worst, which pleased me, but my defiance withered as he whispered, "Is my baby dead?"

"The code to your Escalade is 7542."

"How do you know that?"

"You know how," I answered.

"There's no way you can see that just by meeting my eyes with yours. I don't believe the rumors I've heard. If they were true, that would make you quite the act," he sneered, attempting to look strong while bloody. "Where the fuck is she, Cazador?"

"301960," I listed the code to his household security system next, observing the crumple that formed on his forehead. Disbelief looked odd on the face of a murderer. "Every person I meet gets their own little box in my head. Think about how flooded my mind must be. As much as you wish it weren't true, imagine how I feel."

"What else can you see?"

"That is the question, isn't it?" I smirked maliciously. "Every storage unit you have, every stock you've ever invested into, every padlock that protects anything of yours; I know them." I hovered before him, pressing a cold barrel of steel to his temple. "Let me ask you something, Diego. Does it sicken you worse to think that I may have murdered your daughter? Or is it worse to know that my hands have been on her body?"

"I would prefer Shayla to be murdered than forcibly touched by you!" he shouted again, disobeying me. If his ribs had been properly arranged before, my vengeful stomps had snapped at least half by now.

"Don't get it misconstrued. If ever my hands were on your daughter, it was only because she begged me to put them there."

"She wouldn't beg you for a goddamn thing," Diego assumed, unaware of what had circulated over the past twenty-four hours. I knew the details had gone down a little differently with his baby girl, but I let him believe what he wanted to.

"Are you really that stupid?" I kicked a crystalized lamp from the top of a nearby side-table. "If your daughter was still alive, it would only be because of me. That would mean nothing to you?"

"It would mean little."

"Why did you kill my parents?" My veins turned to ice. Every emotion I had was shifting into rage. "What did my dad do to cross you? What gang do you belong to?"

"I'm not a mobster," he scoffed self-righteously. "What happened to your parents wasn't mafia related. Many years ago, *you* just about cost me a lot. You stole a briefcase that didn't belong to you, getting filth all over your hands. Your family paid the price for your foolery. That is all. The files inside that briefcase were mine. I shouldn't have let my driver transport it. I should have warned him of how valuable the contents were, but you had no right to intercept it like you did."

The fucking briefcase?

What the fuck?

I winced, feeling the weight of two deaths on my shoulders. I remained a rock on the external, but a piece of me died a little more on the inside. Dealing with the loss of my parents had been difficult enough while thinking it had been my dad's fault. This new bomb didn't sit well with me at all.

Screw killing Diego.

Place the gun in your own mouth.

Do it ever so calmly.

Take away the guilt.

Save everyone from your poison.

"I jacked that briefcase six years ago," I said, ignoring the voices in my head. "If what you're saying is true, you waited three years before destroying my family. Why did it take you so long to track me down?"

When he didn't reply, my hands curled around his neck destructively. I squeezed as hard as I could, coming close to collapsing his trachea. I waited until his oxygen levels had depleted into critical territory before I allowed him to breathe again. I treated him how I wanted to treat Grimsaw for abusing Shayla. For leaving the marks he had on her skin, part of me wanted to swing around and shoot my boss in the head instead.

"You never completed the transaction," Diego choked as he regained consciousness. "You found the hard drive inside the briefcase. You ran the files, decoding things I made sure nobody could decrypt. I don't know how you did it, but once you realized what you possessed, you never sold it to whoever tipped you off about it."

"That hard drive was worth more than any amount of money those men could have offered me, wouldn't you say? Thanks to you, I have the cures for every strain of cancer known to mankind. I know why I kept them, but I can't figure out why you needed them back so badly... so badly that you killed my parents."

"My daughter had Leukemia," Diego dropped another bomb, like the true terrorist he was. "I knew the government had the cure, so I copied their medical database. I planned to mix it myself.

You may see numbers, but I'm unequivocally versed with technology. When you work at a marketing agency, you need to be good on a computer."

I took a step back from him as I soaked in his words. He hadn't struck me as the type of man who could hack compound databases, but I gave him the benefit of the doubt.

"How many daughters do you have?"

"Ask me, Cazador," he smirked, comparatively cocky on the scale beside me. "Was it Shayla who had Leukemia? Was she the one you nearly killed by stealing that briefcase? Was she the reason I needed the cures back? Was she the reason I killed your parents?"

"Was she?" I complied.

"She was." Diego's eyes were as dark as midnight during January. "Whether she shares my DNA or not is inconsequential. Shayla is my only daughter."

29
THE SOUND OF DEATH

HUNTER GARCIEZ

Friday. 6:30 P.M.

"I HAD HELD HOPE THAT AVERAGE medicine would pull her through, which is why it took me three years to track you down. Shayla was diagnosed when she was twelve, but she didn't hit her deathbed until the age of fifteen. After you stole the cure from me, which had taken me months to properly salvage from the government, Shayla deteriorated for three years. The day I killed your parents was the same day she had asked to be put out of her misery."

This couldn't be real.

"You never got the cures back!" I ran my palm down my face, flinching as my thumbnail snagged my stitches. "But she lived anyway, so did you really have to off my parents? I mean, what'd you think? That the hard drive would just be sitting around my room three years later? It doesn't even exist anymore. All the cures are in my head. They are nowhere else."

"I didn't go to your house in search of the hard drive. I knew you would have destroyed it after memorizing the transcripts. I know you're not stupid either. I showed up at your doorstep with the intention of taking those you love away from you. After all, you just about did the same to me."

"*Just about!*" I picked his words apart, punching him in the face harder than I had yet. "Shayla survived, but where the fuck are my parents? Right where you put them; buried six feet under for the mice to eat."

It took Diego awhile to regain his composure. Once he did, his expression was half as arrogant as it had been before. I liked it too. It meant he was finally understanding me.

"I don't know how Shayla survived, but she was as good as dead when I killed your parents. If I had known she was going to beat cancer, I wouldn't have done what I did to your family. I regret it to this day, but my state of mind wasn't well. My daughter was dying. The doctors had given her only days left to live. By stealing the cure, you nearly took her from me. As payback, I took those closest to you."

"I didn't know—" I cut myself short, halting the regret before it had even pitched residency on the inside of my chest. "You should have approached me. You should have told me her situation. You didn't have to go after my family like you did. I would have given you the cure for Leukemia. I would have made it for you too."

Apparently, while Shayla had been fifteen, she'd been begging for her dad to suffocate her in a hospital bed. While I had been fifteen, I'd been out stealing files that her dad would later murder my parents for. I had gambled with not only Shayla's life, but my mom's and dad's too; all without even knowing it. Shayla had clearly survived her battle with Leukemia, but absolutely no thanks were owed in my direction for that.

It kept getting worse. I couldn't murder her dad. I couldn't take him away from her, even after everything he'd stolen from me and Tessa. Shayla would never forgive me if I did, just like I would never forgive Diego.

Grimsaw muttered a few curse words. My face already stung, but I could tell he was on the verge of teaching me another lesson. The problem was, I still had a gun in my hand. The only thing that kept me from making a move against Grim was the knowing that he had another gold-plated pistol stashed somewhere close to him. He wouldn't have given me the one I was holding if he didn't.

"I can't understand what I'm hearing," Grimsaw's disbelief was genuine. "I've known you for three years, G. In those years, you ain't never brought a wench around. Then, when I give you the daughter of the man who murdered your parents, you not only disobey me, you start falling for the bitch too? Get your mind together. I like you, but I don't trust any part of you. You've gone and taught me one thing in the past twenty-four hours; I fucking can't."

"You've never trusted me," I recognized.

"For good reason."

"That's true, because I have it all recorded, Grim. Things you couldn't even imagine. I have enough to lock you away for life. Anytime I've ever stood before you, I've been bugged. I haven't decided if I should kill you like you killed Antonio, or if I should force you to rot in prison instead."

"You robbed those banks with me." Grimsaw's feet grew toasty; a look I liked on him. "There's nothing you can pin on me without going down for yourself, *hermano*."

"*Hermano*," I used his lingo back on him; a term for brothers, which we weren't. "I have an ingenious mind. Do you think I don't know how to remove myself from the equation? It doesn't take brilliance to edit a stream of footage."

I caught a smile on Diego's lips as Grimsaw climbed off the couch and stalked my way. While he approached, I considered blasting his head clean off with one bullet. Not only had he put me through hell, he'd damaged Shayla worse than Leukemia already had; worse than *I* already had. And Antonio deserved revenge from beyond the grave too. I knew no better time would come than now.

"Kill Diego or I kill you," Grimsaw offered me another ultimatum; something I didn't do too well with. I wasn't surprised when he removed another pistol from the back of his waistband. I didn't get shivers as he pointed it at me either.

I'd imagined being placed in this position so many times. I had considered what I would do after finally getting my hands on Diego, but nothing seemed clear anymore. Shayla had dug beneath my skin like a tick. Because of this, I was one decision away from death.

"This is what you and I come down to?" I dove deep into Grimsaw's fuming eyes. He stood only feet away, his finger trigger-ready. "You blow my brains out in *his* house? The man who assassinated my parents?"

"It doesn't have to. If you kill Diego and return the blonde to me, I'll forgive your mistakes. Once you forget about the Barbie, we can go back to being the dream team. You should also rethink making any more jokes about going to work for the government behind my back. I'm sure you've learned that by now."

"I don't know where the girl is. I let her run off in Vegas. She could be anywhere by now. She said something about having family in Arizona—"

"If you're at her house, you must know where the little bitch is!" Grimsaw bellowed, stabbing the air with his gun. "You ain't getting it, Garciez. The Barbie knew all about it. I told her everything before you met her. Since she didn't tell you jack shit, how much do you think she really cares about you? It ain't like you to get all warped in the head over a broad. She played you fucking good."

While I processed his words, I wondered if death would hurt. Would I even feel a bullet entering my skull? Very rarely did one survive taking ammunition to the brain. By the scarce chance I might, it was likely I would later wish I hadn't.

"Shoot me," Diego demanded, stealing my focus. "I deserve this for what I've done to your family. If you have the ways to protect my daughter, which I know you do, shoot me. I'm begging you to keep her safe."

"Your daughter is as good as dead," Grimsaw spoke to Diego, but his eyes were threatening me. "I'm gonna find her eventually. When I do, I'll make sure the Barbie lives one hell of a life."

At the sound of his threats against Shayla, I made a snap decision. I tilted my entire body toward Grimsaw. Adrenaline took over. My common sense had long deteriorated, which I knew to be true by the way Diego was still breathing by my feet. My finger tugged back on the trigger with the speed of light. I didn't contemplate the penalties that blowing Grimsaw's brains out would bring to me. Reluctance didn't sweep through the cells of my logic. My index finger decided to activate a fucking war.

But no bullet shot through his flesh. The sound of an empty clip was the only clamor to be heard. I swear the silence was worse than the reverberation of murder would have been. I had just proven my disloyalty… *whole-fucking-heartedly.*

I threw the empty gun against the far wall of Diego's living room. I stared down the barrel of Grimsaw's weapon, knowing it was my time to die. With no fear, I slipped my hands into the front pockets of my gory jeans.

"You're a pussy, G."

"Nah," I opposed. "I'm just not as masochistic as you are, despite your best efforts to turn me that way. It'll only be a matter of time before the FBI shuts you down. You and your posse will wind up in jail. If not that, surrounded by white chalk."

Russ would know where to find the blackmail I had accumulated against the mafia. I had prepared everything in case this were to ever happen. All he had to do was head down to the local police station and drop off one perfectly prepared box. The Feds would take care of everything else from there.

Tessa would be financially set. I had jotted Russ down as her godfather upon adopting her, because I knew he would make sure she grew up at least half decent. All the girls trapped within Grimsaw's system would be freed eventually, including Shayla and Tessa. If I had to die for that to come true, I didn't view it as a terrible way to go out. I could rest easy knowing I had done something of value before getting myself offed.

My death would not be in vain.

"The whore doesn't give a flying fuck about you." Grimsaw's lip curled like a rabid dog. "What happened? You ate her pussy and now you're hooked?"

Hadn't even gotten that far yet.

"Blow my head off, Grim," I smiled, unwilling to die afraid. "Just be advised of what'll happen once you do. I have people too. Killing me won't fade my presence. Even after I'm dead, I will still exist to you."

And those were the last words I got the chance to say. That was the last threat I managed to spit out before one sound resonated throughout the whole house, lining Diego's walls with the red of blood.

One sound.

The sound of death.

30
A TICKET TO PRISON

SHAYLA STONE

Friday. 7:00 P.M.

I TREMBLED WITH FEAR, UNABLE TO comprehend what had just happened. I had never seen someone get killed before. I had watched movies, but I had never seen *this*. I had never smelled the sourness that a mass quantity of blood could create, but the pungent rust was polluting the air around me now. I had never heard the echo of a fired bullet. I had never witnessed a body drop. Everyone else here… *they had*.

I heard Hunter say my name, but I couldn't grasp his voice. I couldn't grasp his face. I couldn't even grasp his touch. My vision went black from shock. All I could feel was fear. Not only had I just killed a man, I had just shattered my own life to bits too.

When I finally came to, my body was in the passenger seat of Hunter's stolen truck. I opened my eyes slowly, catching view of his fist as it sailed through the CD player on the dash. My heart tried to leap out of my throat at the sight of his bloody knuckles, but I didn't expect him to be calm at a moment like this.

Mr. O' Riley's car was parked just down the road, like it had been for years with a blown transmission. Mr. Anderson's motor-cycle sat in the driveway of his million-dollar house, like it always was at this time of day. Once his wife came home, his bike would be blocked in by a sparkling silver Lexus for the night. That was all normal, but…

Mrs. Taylor stood peeping from her second story window. Curi-osity and horror were blending over what I could see of her face, while Mrs. Adams was watching from her springtime lawn. The phone in her hand was warning me that 911 had already been notified of the damage I'd just caused.

I didn't blink. I didn't breathe. All I did was shake with a vio-lent tremor. Despite it being over eighty degrees outside, my teeth were chattering together. Sweat fell from my forehead, cascading down the side of my face like a waterfall. I finally allowed oxygen to meet my lungs, but it descended slowly; so slowly, I felt close to death myself.

"I killed him," I whispered.

Hunter clutched his hands around the steering wheel, rocking his body back and forth in anguish. I could feel every organ shift-ing in my body, and I knew he was feeling the same sensation. It was not only panic and anxiety, but a feeling so gut-wrenching it could put you straight to sleep.

"Blondie, listen to me." He cupped his hands around my jaw, trying to align my rolling eyes. "Keep yourself together. You just saved my life."

I had just saved his life.

"I can't leave my father," I spoke the words, but they didn't feel real. Everything felt faded, distant beneath the repetitive gunshot in my head. "He's in even worse condition than you are. The cops will be on their way soon. They will find him."

"You just shot up suburbia."

"I know!" I cried.

"The pigs are *already* on their way."

Hunter combed his fingers through my sweaty hair. Some of his stitches had been ripped out, but he seemed more concerned about my wellbeing than his own.

"I can't leave," I repeated, forcing my head forward. "I saw the way my dad looked. He will die if I don't help him. Grimsaw's body is dead on the floor next to him. Even if my dad does man-age to survive, the cops will throw him in jail."

"Probably..." Hunter considered my words. "But in my opin-ion, prison is where he deserves to be."

"With as much media time as you've received anonymously over the past few years, don't you think you deserve the same?" I attacked him, my anxiety transferring into fury. "I'm not thrilled with my father either, but we have to—"

"*I* don't have to do anything," he corrected me, a brooding mist in his green eyes. "I don't owe you or your dad shit. I have no reason to put my ass on the line to save him. Your dad didn't blink while destroying my happiness. I won't blink while doing the same to his."

"I know you've already done more than enough for me, but I need you. You're the smart one," I buttered him up, selfishly trying to transition him onto my side. "My chances of success will be much greater if you—"

"Do you hear yourself?" His fingers gripped around the back of his neck, squeezing more blood to drain through the slices on his knuckles. "You're out of your goddamn mind if you think I'll be helping your dad. I like you, but I won't be strapping the man who killed my parents onto my back just to prove that. Give your head a shake."

"Don't talk to me like that!" I punched him in the shoulder, adding to the abuse he'd already taken. "My dad is all I have. Just try to under—"

"I understand very well. I know what option I had in that house ten minutes ago. I know what I turned down like an idiot. You should just be thankful your dad is still breathing. I could have brought an end to that."

"You need to leave without me." I pulled open the passenger door, though no part of me wanted to do what I was about to. "Thank you for everything. I wish I had more time to express my—"

"You're buying a one-way ticket to prison if you stay here," Hunter prophesied, cutting me off for the fourth time in a row. "You'll never see freedom again. There isn't a lawyer your daddy could buy who'd manage to keep you out of prison."

"But he'll die if I leave without him, so what other choice am I left with?" I debated silently for a moment. "He has a vehicle in the garage. I'll take him to the hospital and figure the rest out later."

Hunter didn't know my dad, but the man I knew was someone who routinely brought me home ice cream. The man I knew wanted the best for me. The man I knew had sat by my hospital bed for months while thinking I was going to die. The man I knew had refused to give up hope. The man I knew was all I had left.

"I told you not to come here. I told you to just sit at the hotel until I came back for you. Why can't you do anything I say? You're not braindead. Why do you consistently act like you are?"

I flinched under the burn of his words, recognizing how fair they were. Since I had just shot a bullet through an executive in the mafia, there was no room to argue that I did foolish things.

I took a nervous glance down my childhood street. I was anticipating the moment when a colony of SUVs would drift their way down the strip; SUVs full of bodies ready to throw me in prison without hearing my side.

From Grimsaw's dirty cell straight to the government's.

"I watched the ending of that scene unfold," I growled back, flinging my hands as I spoke. "If I hadn't shown up like I did, you would be dead right now."

"Who fucking cares?"

"I care!"

"But you shouldn't," Hunter clashed my growl with a low whisper. He let his gaze linger on my face for longer than I was sure he meant to. "Screw the Feds. They're the least of your worries after messing with the gang. Whether you get locked up or not, Grimsaw's men will find you. Bars won't keep you safe from these guys."

"You don't get it," I shook my head at both him and myself. I should have saw a criminal while staring at him, but I saw so much more. "I've owed you my life from the very beginning of this. I'll take the legal fall. I'll never mention your name; not to the cops, my lawyer, or the judge. I swear to you, Hunter. It'll be like our lives never intersected."

I hastily hopped out of the red truck. I took a final glance back at him, my heart crushing all the while, but I knew what I had to do. I had to reciprocate what Hunter had attempted to give me; a fair chance at freedom.

I turned to head up the pathway toward my house, hearing shoes pound against the cement behind me within seconds. Clutching his fingers into my elbow with deep stabs, Hunter turned my body around to meet his perilous expression. He towed me back to the truck, ignoring my neighbors as they continued to stare. After yanking the passenger door wide open, he pushed against my spine and forced me inside. I tried to fight him off, but his rhino-strength outweighed the limited fighting power that a girl like me came packaged with.

"Let's get one thing clear…" He shook my shoulders, trying to keep my arms from swatting him. "If your father dies along the way, don't look at me for sympathy. I wouldn't mind watching him take his last breath."

My body gave up struggling as fear displaced my will to fight. The way Hunter was shaking me… I wasn't sure what he might do. The look in his eyes wasn't descriptive. I could tell he was furious. That much was certain, but I wasn't sure whether he wanted to kiss me or kill me for it.

"What are you saying?"

"I'm saying there is a blanket under the backseat," he barely spoke aloud. "Lay it down to keep his blood from seeping into the leather. When we leave the truck behind, your dad's DNA will be evidence of which direction we fled from the state."

While attempting to control the emotional tremble in my lower lip, I asked, "Are you saying that you're going to bring him with us?"

"Shocker, huh?" He slammed his palm against the headrest behind me, merely inches from my face. "I can't fucking believe it either, but I'm doing this to save *your* life. I don't give a shit about your dad's…" He wound his fingers around my throat aggressively, squeezing without choking me. "If I wasn't so pathetically infatuated by you, I would leave you here to die alongside your crippled father. You will be indebted to me for this one. Trust me when I say this, Shayla; I always come to collect."

31
STITCH AND DISINFECT

SHAYLA STONE

Friday. 7:30 P.M.

"ARE YOU OKAY?" I TOOK in my dad's wounds as Hunter pulled away from the curb. Blood soaked his face like he'd been viciously attacked by a stream of flying elbows, while his knee was dislocated for certain. "I can't believe Grimsaw did this to you."

Hunter cleared his throat, almost like he was about to say something, but my dad stopped him in a rush.

"My baby girl, I've been searching for you for weeks. I couldn't find you. I thought you might be…"

"I'm not dead," I tried to smile, though it was difficult to ignore the pain he was in. "If it weren't for Hunter, I probably would be."

"I grabbed some clothes from your room," Hunter said, ignoring the appreciation I had for him. "Wrap something around your dad's knee for a tourniquet. There is a first-aid kit under the backseat. Use it, because we can't take him to a hospital."

"He's right," Dad agreed, discomfort shaping his face. "You two need to leave before it's too late. There is a small window for escape. If you spend it worrying about me, you'll both miss your shot at freedom."

"She can't leave you," Hunter answered before my lips had parted to do the same. "If she could, you wouldn't be here right now."

I watched the two of them exchange an unreadable gaze through the rearview mirror. I had only caught the tail end of whatever had taken place inside our house. I had only caught the part where Grimsaw had been about to kill Hunter, but it wasn't hard to see I had missed something of substantial importance.

"This is a bad situation," I panicked, cloaking my dad's mangled knee with a favorite sweater of mine. "What are we going to do?"

"Is my sister still at the hotel?"

"Yes."

"I told you to stay there too," Hunter roared. "We made an agreement. If I didn't come back to the hotel, you were to take off and keep yourself safe. You weren't supposed to come to your house; the one place I specifically told you not to. What if Grimsaw had noticed your presence? I couldn't have saved you. Does any of this register in your thick head?"

"I knew you would wind up getting yourself killed," I tore back at him, holding myself together with stone rather than honey. "You're too brave for your own good. I knew something was wrong. You were taking too long. Not that *you* give a shit if you live or die, but I think I made a damn good call."

"How did you get to your house?"

"How do you think?"

"You took a cab with the money I left you for an emergency? I left you that gun so you could defend yourself if someone came to the hotel door. By trying to protect you, what I've ultimately done is ruin your fucking life."

The veins in Hunter's neck began to dance as he took a sharp left turn, cutting off a minivan to do so. All three of us ignored the following honk we were blasted with.

"Cazador is right," Dad joined in our squabble, wrapping his bloody fingers around my forearm. "You should have listened to him and stayed away."

Hunter pulled into the seaside hotel that Tessa still sat inside of. His emerald eyes connected with mine as he glanced over his shoulder, but I remained focused and kept pressure against my dad's massacred knee. While I dabbed peroxide against his face with my other hand, Hunter reached into the glove box to pull out a tiny glass clip.

Turning around to tack the object onto the cleavage of my sundress, he said, "I need you to go get Tessa. Security will be all over me if I go in there looking like this."

"Is that a camera?" Dad disbelieved. I caught clouds of amazement swirling across his face beneath the blood. "Where did you get that? I've never seen one so small before."

"Thanks," Hunter took his words as a compliment. "The government is equipped with them, but they're challenging to get your hands on as a regular civilian. I skip the middleman by constructing them myself. There's always more than meets the eye, Diego; unless you're me, of course."

A look of humor washed over my dad's beaten face, but I didn't understand it. Hunter reached into the same glovebox, yanking out a clean t-shirt this time. He wiped the blood from his face with the black fabric, throwing it onto the truck's dash once he was done.

"On second thought, I'll go get my sister. You stay here and resolve what you're going to do. Like I've said, we can't take your dad to the hospital. For now, take care of what lesions you can. Stitch and disinfect him. The needles are in the kit."

"Do I look like *Houdini*? Should I just snap his knee back into place while I'm at it?" I asked nauseously. "I barely passed Home Economics. If I can't sew polyester, I doubt I can thread flesh."

Hunter shrunk in his shoulders, almost like he had something to feel guilty for.

"If you recall, my recommendation was that you *didn't* flag down a taxi and shoot Grimsaw in the head."

"You're not helping," I frowned.

"Once the cops find Grim's body, the Feds will flag your house. They'll flag each of your passports. Your faces will be all over the news. We came back to California to create a passport for you, but we can't even do that anymore. Not only is the mafia wondering what your next move will be, the government will be investigating the same thing soon enough too. Even if I did have time to make you a faulty passport, your face would be flashing across the TVs in every American airport by the time I finished. Do you see the predicament?"

"But *you* could get on a regular plane," I pointed out grimly. "You and Tessa don't have any ties to my house. The Feds won't have a reason to flag your passports. They won't even consider you a suspect. You could leave without me."

"If I wanted things to go down like that, I would have left you hours ago," he laughed like I was annoying him. "If I was looking to take the easy ride out, your dad would be dead, you would be a slave, and instead of spending my time arguing with you right now, I would be at home eating a barbequed steak with a beer in my hand."

On that note, Hunter left the truck and marched toward the front entrance of the hotel. I watched every step he took away from me, as if I suspected he might not come back.

My dad tugged on my arm, breaking my fascination with the edge in Hunter's walk.

"That boy has done enough for me. I need to go my own way now. He doesn't want to be around me, which I'm sure we can both understand. I'm going to need surgeries—"

"Why did you do it, Dad?" I stared at his wrecked face with disappointment. "I know about the briefcase. I know about the cures. How could you kill their parents?"

"Your mother had already died," he grimaced, still haunted by it all. "It was hard to watch you slip away from me too. I would have saved you weeks after your initial diagnosis, but Cazador ruined that. He is the reason you suffered for so long."

"I don't even know who you are," I whispered, close to hating him in this moment. "What do you really do for work?"

"I am a marketing executive, Shayla. I'm the same man I've always been," he reassured me. "I just stole a few cures from the government without you knowing."

"You've ended lives," I glared.

"True, but do you remember how sick you were?" His face fell, reminding me of the price of cancer. "You were thinner than you are now. You were a skeleton. I didn't think you were going to pull through. The doctors didn't either. By the time you did, I had already retaliated against Cazador. I made my leap against his family too soon. I thought you were as good as dead. It led me to make a bad judgement call."

"A bad judgement call?" My heart pinched as he downplayed his actions. "A bad judgement call is locking your keys in the car. A bad judgement call is leaving nachos in the oven for too long. Terminating a family is something entirely different. No matter your motives, what you did was murder."

"Baby girl…" His eyes were begging me to understand, but I couldn't relate to him. "You just killed a man to protect Cazador. No matter your motives, what you did was murder too. Things aren't always so cut and dry."

As I realized I was no better than my father, tears began to simmer in my eyes. He placed his hand on my shoulder, but his words were the opposite of comforting. They were a firm slap to my face, because I knew they held validity.

"What happened in our living room before I arrived?" I searched his cinnamon eyes for an answer. "What was said? What did I miss?"

"You missed the moment in which Cazador realized he was falling for you," Dad struggled to laugh, fighting for his every breath. "If you weren't my daughter, it might have been a touching thing to witness. It was a testimony of his feelings when he swung the gun away from my skull. In that moment, I knew you were still alive. If he didn't care about you, I would be dead."

I measured his words and received one hell of an ominous vibe. My hunches told me that Hunter had been given a prime opportunity to kill my dad back at our house. He had been offered revenge on a silver platter; something he'd been in quest of for years.

As I took a glance at my father's cracked face, it was evident. Hunter's fingers might not have fired a bullet through my dad's skull, but his fists…

His fists had taken their shot.

32
DON'T LOOK IN THE BACKSEAT

HUNTER GARCIEZ

Friday. 8:00 P.M.

I WRAPPED MY ARMS AROUND TESSA as soon as she opened the hotel door. She held her stuffed animals in her hands, kicking at my legs while I squeezed her face into my chest. As I set her back to her feet, her green eyes scanned over the blood staining my face. My eyebrow continued to ooze a tarnished red, but she refrained from asking about my physique while we were in public.

"Shayla is the girl with no digits in her eyes, isn't she?" Tessa wondered, hoofing down the hallway of the generic inn beside me. "The girl Dad warned you about?"

"She is," I gave her the truth. I wasn't sure how I felt about having Shayla as a soulmate, because it hadn't been much fun so far. "Shayla doesn't know anything about that, though, so don't mention it. She's only known me for a day. I don't want to freak her out any more than I have already."

"Because you love her?" Tessa giggled, making a weird kissy face at me. It was then that I decided she wasn't allowed to date until she was twenty-one. "Do you want to marry her?"

"Don't be awkward." I nudged her with my elbow. "There are plenty of things I want to do with Shayla, but marrying her isn't the first that comes to mind."

"What is then?"

Fucking her unconscious.

"Taking her to dinner," I said, laughing to myself as we entered the evening heat. Tessa smiled toward the sun, as if today was as glorious as any other day. As for me, I stared hesitantly at the red truck ahead of us. "Tess, what you're about to see is seriously messed up."

"What will I see?"

"Buckets of blood," I cringed.

"More than what is on your face?"

"I'm really sorry," I confirmed it. Before placing her in the front seat and shutting the door, I advised, "Whatever you do, don't look in the backseat."

After making my way toward the driver's side, I opened the rear door to see what kind of progress Shayla had made. Her eyes flashed into mine, vividly displaying she was far from okay. Black thread was dangling from the needle in her hand, having yet to meet her father's face. Although she was pretty, she was being absolutely useless in this moment. I wanted to tell her that too, but since I was practically babying her at this point, I bit my tongue and decided against it instead.

"Shayla, can you drive?"

"I... I think so."

"You either need to drive or sew him." I reached into the back of the truck to link my fingers around her needleless hand. "Which will you find easier?"

"Are you offering to stitch him if I drive?" Shayla shook her blonde hair, streaked with the red of blood. She tried to rationalize my motives, but I knew she was suffering when she asked, "Why would you do that for him?"

I glanced to the front seat, nodding her vision toward Tessa's back. My sister didn't know who had killed our parents. As far as she knew, just like I had thought up until a few hours ago, the unfortunate night had been an outcome of our dad's aircraft endeavors with the mafia. She didn't know their deaths were really a fault of mine. I thought it best to remain that way.

"Is he going to die?" Tessa's palm shot over her mouth as she turned around. Her eyes raked over Diego's condition with revulsion. "He's bleeding out, right?"

"I told you not to look," I lectured her, but I should have known she would press the shiny, red button. "If he fights for his life, he might survive."

Shayla placed the needle aside and climbed out of the truck. I slammed the rear door shut behind her, blocking out Diego's vision of us. We each resembled a scene out of a horror movie, but it didn't lessen her beauty any.

"I can't believe you shot him," I smirked at her, though none of it was funny. "When I turned around and saw you standing there holding that gun, I couldn't fucking believe it. You didn't even hesitate."

"You told me not to," Shayla said, pulling my body closer to hers. "Back in Vegas, you told me to never hesitate while shooting."

Shit… I had said that.

"That was the one piece of advice you chose to listen to?" I took a stab at her ribcage with my thumb. "How much did you see in your living room?"

"I saw you try to shoot Grimsaw," she answered, gripping onto my t-shirt like it pained her to visualize the scenario. "When it didn't sound off, I saw you throw the gun across the room. I saw you smile like you knew you were about to die. When Grimsaw raised his gun at you, that was it. I didn't think. I just… I just killed him."

I could see a variety of different emotions filtering over her face; horror, fear, regret, nausea, disgust; courage, valor, heroism, a self-assurance that what she had done was right. She couldn't seem to decide which of these feeling prevailed; a feeling I knew all too well in itself.

In a moment when your morals are forced to blur together, like hers had been when she'd chosen to shoot Grimsaw to protect me, it becomes difficult to tell what side you're really playing for; the good or the evil. People often wonder how others lose their minds. Myself, I wondered how people managed to stay sane at all.

I mixed her lips with the blood sliding down mine, stealing a smell of her lavender scented hair. She drove me buck wild in ways that a female never had before. I had been dabbling with girls since the age of fifteen, but this one was different than the rest. I couldn't explain it…

I could *feel* it.

When her lips parted for the entrance of my tongue, I followed command like an obedient soldier. While her father suffered in the backseat, I thieved a taste of his daughter. Sadistically, the morbidity of the predicament did nothing but turn me on more.

It wasn't until Tessa banged on the front window that I pulled my tongue away from Shayla's tonsils. After transferring a soft smile my way, Shayla scurried behind the steering wheel up front. I took it as my cue to enter the backseat with the murderer she called Dad.

I glared at Diego, shutting the door behind myself. Tessa had begun to yap Shayla's ear off, asking who the old dude in the backseat was. Since I knew neither of them were looking at me, I squished my elbow into Diego's broken knee with force. The pressure caused him to wail out in beautiful agony.

My last hit for now.

Holding a sewing needle an inch away from his eye, dangling the thread vindictively as he staggered on the verge of passing out, I couldn't help but notice the motion resembled the swaying hand of a grandfather clock; the grandfather clock Diego had torched to rubble alongside my mom.

He watched every pass the needle made toward his face, as if he thought I might push the tip directly through his pupil. I smiled at his yelps like they were a musical orchestra. Every laceration on his body was an outcome of my temper. Grimsaw might have tied Diego up, but he hadn't hurt him. I had been the real monster. I had created the bloody masterpiece.

What a lovely form of art it was.

"Maybe one day you will forgive me?" Diego fantasized. Reconciliation wasn't an option listed in the pages of my personal grudge book. "I really am sorry, but I'm still her father. If I'm alive, I hold the right to walk her down the aisle."

"Jesus," I grimaced, gaining a better perspective on how Shayla had managed to stay single for so long. "Is that the speech you give every guy she digs? Marriage isn't something we've discussed in the day we've known each other."

"But we both know she is the one for you," Diego smirked slyly. "I might not be involved with the mafia, but I did my research before coming after your family. I heard your name dropped on the streets a few times. I wish it wasn't my daughter who your eyes were set on, but I appreciate the way you've been protecting her. To show my gratitude, I will never tell her the truth about my injuries. She doesn't need to know *you* did this to me."

"That's not a very diplomatic fathering tactic," I probed at his ethics with a slanted stare. "How do I know you won't tell her behind my back?"

"Because she cares about you," he flinched as the next stitch met his flesh. "What she doesn't know can't hurt her. Grimsaw is dead. It isn't like he can speak the truth. You and I are the only ones who can. Call me crazy, but I think we both know how to keep a secret."

No shit, Alvaro.

I wasn't sure what I would decide to tell Shayla. I wanted to be honest with her. I really did, but would she see her father's wounds for what they were in my head? A fair retribution?

"You should have killed me when you had the chance," he grinned, showing that one of his front teeth had been knocked out within the wrath of my elbows. Diego was one tough bastard. Not only was his knee sideways, his cheek was sunk inward too. There was still a chance he might die, but you wouldn't know it by listening to him. "What if the situation were reversed? What if your sister had cancer? If someone destroyed your only chance to control the situation and save her, wouldn't you have done the same as I did?"

I might have, but I wasn't going to admit it. Diego could try like hell to change it, but I would always hate him. Bygones couldn't be left in the past when it came to the unnecessary deaths of my parents.

The voices in my head were telling me to strangle him, but Shayla's face funneled through my thoughts as I considered it. That was all it took for me to know what I had to do. If admitting her dad into the Honolulu hospital would make her happy, maybe it was the right choice. After all, Shayla had saved my life. I owed her something, and it wasn't like any of this would be permanent for Tessa and me; not Diego, not Hawaii…

Not even Shayla.

I pushed myself over the barrier of the front seat and reached for the dial on the truck's dash, rousing the navigational system to life. Taking a glance toward Tessa, I placed a kiss against her cheek. Like always, she wiped my germs away with a "Yuck!"

I began to type in an address on the touchscreen; a place I was vaguely familiar with; a place I knew we could snag a private plane and medical aid. Thanks to the profession I was now trying to escape, I knew where to find the right people. I knew some men who owed my dad a few favors. They had said I could swing by anytime and collect on his deceased behalf.

Thieving a look at the blonde, I dropped a kiss against her cheek the same way as I had Tessa's. Ignoring how it made my little sister giggle like a hyena, I smiled at my star-crossed Juliet, and said, "You're a crazy bitch."

"Maybe a little," Shayla winked as she drove. "But isn't that why you're so captivated by me? Because you know you shouldn't be? Out of all the girls in the world, I'm the one you shouldn't want to know."

"I'm not *captivated*," I denied.

Tessa snorted. "That's a big bullshit."

33
MAFIA PRINCESS

SHAYLA STONE

Saturday. 2:30 A.M.

A S WE CONTINUED TO ASCEND, I watched the landscape fade to dust below us. The air in my lungs tasted differently. It was musty, which was to be expected on an airplane; even an expensively private plane like this one.

Tessa sat next to the window seat, asleep and wasting the view, while Hunter sat on the opposite side of the aisle. I sent him a curious gaze, watching him flip the pages of a hotrod magazine. One of the paramedics on board had resewn his face, as well as the gash along his forearm. He no longer bled, while my dad was in the back gaining medical attention.

I wasn't sure what the medics were doing. They wouldn't let me stay with him, which was probably for the best. But since his screams had slowly dwindled to silence, I figured the anesthesia had kicked in by now.

I had three pieces of watermelon chewing gum in my mouth, but my ears were still popping as we reached an altitude of thirty thousand feet. Silence draped over Hunter and I like dew, weighing down my shoulders with a fog comparable to the mist on a morning commute across the Golden Gate Bridge. His skater shoe was tapping against the spotless blue carpet on the floor, his thoughts eating him alive.

Trying to be as stealthy as possible while leaving Tessa's side, I stood to make my way toward her brother. As I plopped myself onto the reclining sofa beside him, his hot stare matched mine.

"I'm not in the mood to talk."

"Oh?" I shrugged like I didn't care, because I didn't. "Seeing as though you haven't talked to me once since boarding this plane, I kind of figured as much."

"Then why are you sitting beside me?" He raised himself into a vertical position, as if I was a venomous cobra that needed to be avoided.

"If you ask me, this whole *'playing hard to get'* act is getting old," I buried him with a sweet smile, extending my legs so he couldn't evade me without hassle. "Aren't you getting tired of the monotonous motions? Don't you want to break the rules just a little?"

"The only rules I have are the ones I create for myself now." He lowered his kaleidoscopic eyes to meet the level of mine, placing his hands on either side of my head against the leather couch. "And I have already violated them by bringing your dad."

Before I could respond, he brushed my legs to the side and charged toward the front washroom. I watched his intimidating walk, checking him out with blatant desire. I told myself it would be inappropriate to follow him. It was obvious he didn't want to converse with me, but I wasn't going to let something that trivial stop me.

For the next fifteen minutes, I waited for his tall body to exit from the bathroom stall. When it didn't, I waited another ten more. After twiddling my thumbs for another five, I finally had enough.

I rose from the sofa and made my way toward the same washroom. I gave a loud bang against the door, biting my lip when he didn't answer. Rather than going to reseat myself, which is what I should have done, I twisted the golden knob. To my surprise, the door opened.

I entered the vast room, receiving a smack of hot air against my face. The barreling steam told me Hunter had just taken a scorching shower. Disbelief washed over me as I realized the room was equipped with a jacuzzi tub and an elegant glass shower. Hunter, however, was in neither.

"Lock the door," he commanded, surprising me when he walked through a doorway connected to the bathroom. "I'm washing some of my clothes. Do you want anything thrown in?"

Laundry on an airplane?

He walked toward a pile of his dirty garments next to the shower. A black towel was wrapped around his waistline, low enough to give me views of his grooved muscles. His abs were like caramel, rippling with waves of pure delight. Water was glistening against his tattoo, slithering down his spine and into the crook of his ass. He brushed his chocolate hair away from his face as he stole a glance at me. Like supermodel hair, it stayed where his fingers directed.

"Do you?"

"Do I what?" I puzzled.

"Need anything washed?"

My body with your hands.

"No," I shook my head. "I'm good."

As an unusual look took hold of his face, he retreated through the side room with his bloody clothes in hand. I turned to take a good look at myself in the mirror, realizing I needed another shower. Dried blood was again knotting my hair, but I didn't know if it was Hunter's or my dad's.

When Hunter came back, he walked toward the shower and cranked on the tap. I watched him through the mirror, but he paid as little attention to me as possible. He stuck his wrist into the shower, testing the stream of water with the sensitive area on his skin. After deeming it a satisfying temperature, he shut the crystal door and crossed his arms.

I gulped, wrapping my hair into a messy bun with a hair elastic Tessa had given me. I stared at him through the mirror, wondering, "Why are you looking at me like you want to cut off my face?"

"I would rather cut off your clothes," he replied, his steel gaze on my backside. "Why did you follow me in here?"

"Because you've been avoiding me. Cornering you seemed like the only way to get you to talk to me. Forget talking. You won't even *look* at me."

He ambled my way, keeping his arms folded over his chest. Every step he took caused my heartrate to speed, increasing my erratic arrhythmias by the second. The way he approached was threatening, but I didn't back away in fear. With the guts of a warrior, I turned to face the impending Viking instead.

"You think you want me, but you don't." He took a scratch at his bruised chest. "I refuse to be the reason you regret your first time. You can go to therapy because you killed Grimsaw. You can go because you were kidnapped and beaten, but you won't be crying in a psych office because I took advantage of you."

"It's nice to know I no longer speak for myself," I shot him a vindictive stare. I could tell the psychotic side of him wanted to do terrible things to my body. The guilt-ridden side of him… not so much. "Is it wrong that I want to feel normal for a minute?"

"Of course not."

"What's the problem then?"

"I'm destroying you." His tone was piercing and forceful. "I've only known you for what, thirty some hours? In that time, I've already managed to morph you into a murderer. If you understood what was best for you, you would go back to your seat."

I took a stare at the glass shower, wondering why he had turned on the waterfall. Since Hunter had already bathed, I got the feeling he didn't want me to head out of the washroom at all. Underneath his mask, he wanted the exact opposite instead.

"*Grimsaw* destroyed me," I corrected.

"Who were you protecting when you fired that bullet?"

"That doesn't matter."

"You killed him for me."

"What was I supposed to do?" I turned around angrily. "Should I have just stood there while you took a bullet to the head? Would you have preferred that? I can't even believe we're still arguing about this. I just want to forget it all."

"That won't be possible."

Hunter skulked over to the cabinet near the door, latching his fingers around his cellphone. Every step he took made his pelvic bones shift, invoking a flurry of saliva to drip from my taste buds. After walking back my way, he passed me the phone with a flat expression.

On the screen, there my dad was. A picture I had never seen before, incriminating him beneath a headline that read, '*Wanted for Suspicion of Murder*'. A brief description followed, but it lacked thorough details. The media's failure to explain much about the night prior, other than a gunshot and foul play, proved the cops didn't have a damn clue as to what had gone on at my house.

"Slide left."

I did what Hunter told me to, and there *I* was. The picture from my driver's license lit up his display; wanted for the exactly same suspicion.

I knew Bree would be panicking. She would be trying to blow up my phone; a phone I had lost while being kidnapped. Not only was my face blasting newspaper articles, so was the name of the high school I attended. Everyone I knew was going to see this.

"I guess university is out of the question," I muttered, trying to formulate a straight thought. I was too afraid to meet his glare. "What if I turn myself in? I could tell the Feds the truth. Not about the briefcase, or about you and Tessa, but about how Grimsaw kidnapped me. I've been missing for three weeks. Many people could back me up on that. I'll say I managed to escape and came back home, but Grimsaw found me again, so I shot him."

"Where'd you get the gun?"

"I'll say it was my dad's. He has plenty in his safe upstairs. I'll say I came home and found him tied up. I'll say I crept upstairs to get a weapon. I'll play it off like it was self-defense. It isn't like I'd be lying."

"My blood is painting your house. Chances are slim that your dad has the same brand of customized gun registered to his name like the one you used to kill Grimsaw. With just that one answer, you've already left a trail of lies. Since you can't stitch flesh, I doubt you'll be able to create an entire alibi without leaving holes in the lines; holes that will lead back to my profession. I won't be going to jail because of your mouth. From here on out, you go where I go. It's the only way I can ensure your lips stay sealed. I don't trust you. That's why you're still with me."

I took my medicine silently. As I continued to slide left on his phone, Hunter's bloody face popped up. I knew right away that one of my neighbors had taken the photo. In it, he was walking my dad down our front walkway with a crazed expression on his face.

Mrs. Adams; the nosy bitch.

"Your hat covers most of your face," I tried to remain optimistic. "Nobody will know who you are. They might recognize the truck, though..."

I kept swiping, finding an excessive number of bloody images of us arguing inside the truck. When I swiped left again, just like mine, Hunter's driver's license picture was flashing across the news articles of America.

"Everything I do, I do it to protect my sister," he sighed desolately. "It might not seem like it from an outsider's perspective, but she is my world. You've put her in a bad position. Once the Feds find my blood, the adoption agencies will be notified. They will classify her as abducted in no time. I'm her guardian..." he trailed off, too upset to finish the sentence. "In the last three years, I've gotten away with hiding hundreds of bodies. I've stolen so much shit from the government, you couldn't even imagine. I've manipulated the stock markets in a way that could get me locked up for life, but I've never come close to getting caught. With one bat of your baby blues, you've managed to fucking drown me."

The frown on his face contrasted his natural cockiness, plaguing him with visible affliction. As for his words, they stung like sulfuric acid. They hurt... because they were indisputably true.

"I'm sorry," I whispered.

I spun to set his phone down onto the counter, having seen enough. If those were the newspaper write-ups, I cringed at the thought of what our faces would look like as they flashed across a row of 50" TVs in sequence.

Hunter began to stalk toward me, confidently eliminating the gap between us. Once he met my standing, his steady arms caped around me. His eyes stayed in mine while he began to lift my dress. The next thing I knew, the bloody fabric had met the floor with a flick over his shoulder.

He began to slide off my panties next, allowing them to fall to my ankles, but his eyes didn't once detach from mine. He grabbed my hand with a piercing grip, leading me toward the fancy shower. For a split second, everything was okay. Hunter was close to me; close enough that I could smell the body wash wafting from his body; close enough to feel his chest. In the heat of the moment, the newspaper articles didn't exist. Even Grimsaw Santiago didn't exist.

In my next breath, Hunter was in the shower with me. Employing the restraint of a criminal, his eyes still hadn't shifted downward. Here I was, naked and only inches away from him, and he was wasting his time by shampooing my hair.

It killed me.

"I can control myself," he said.

"What if I don't want you to?" I stretched to grab onto his sudsy hand, keeping him from massaging my scalp. "What if I want you to look at me? Would you still say no?"

"I would."

"Why?"

"Because you're a virgin, Shayla. You've made it this long without giving yourself to anyone. You only want this because everything else around you seems so hopeless. I don't want to be *that* guy."

He shook his hand from mine, shutting his eyes while grabbing a bar of soap. Once he'd unwrapped it, he tried to pass it my way in silence. I sassily brushed him off, letting him know that his words had irritated me. I was fully aware I was a virgin. I certainly didn't need him to point it out to me.

I wanted him to glance down. I wanted him to see what I looked like naked. I wanted to feel his fingers on my body. Hell, I wanted to feel them *inside* my body. I knew I shouldn't. I didn't know why I wanted him to touch me so badly, but I got the feeling it was because he was trying so damn hard not to.

Tribulation adorned his eyes while water passed down his face, but he did his best not to break apart. The only way I knew my proximity was getting to him was by the pained expression on his face. Without exchanging a word, his eyes told me the story of a damned soul; a sad and ruined soul; a soul that wasn't all that different from mine.

Making a bold decision, his hand began to rub the bar against my shoulders. His fingers trolled over my arms with a feebleness I had doubted him to be capable of. His movements were incredibly cautious, as if he thought I was a fragile bird. The lock of his eyes on mine, however... *fierce.*

"Look at me," I begged.

Slowly cracking down, his vision sloped from mine. His chest rose as he took in the sight of my body, but he didn't say a word. His towel fell from his waist as water weighted the cotton, leaving him just as exposed as I was.

"I've pictured you naked a thousand times…" he finally spoke, creeping his palm down the side of my ribcage. "But I never imagined you would be *this* perfect. No matter how much I resent you, I still want you."

My mouth was craving his. His fingers were running over my ass, heating my core with an explosive essence. When his mouth finally made its way up to mine, his kiss started off as soft and sensual. Once my fingers began to scrape down the center of his chest, his tongue picked up pace and crashed into mine with urgency; an urgency I understood all too well in this moment.

He pushed me into the corner of the square shower, using the strength of a machine to do so. Each of us were liquefying with desire, melting into something we couldn't understand. The way he was holding me made it clear he wanted everything I wanted. He wanted to touch me. He probably even wanted to fuck me too. I wasn't quite ready for that, but there were many other things I was willing to do with him.

I knew we wouldn't be a forever type of thing, but for right now… I was taking what I wished could be mine.

I severed his hand from my ass, slipping it toward the front of me with a twist. He knew what I wanted, but he gulped like he was nervous to deliver. It was odd, because I knew he was no stranger to sex. I was sure girls flocked to him, so it didn't make sense for him to be acting jittery around me; *the virgin*.

His breathing was both heavy and short, and he looked me in the eye as his soapy finger met my creases. More than sexual predation, there was a longing in his eyes; a longing I was unable to read.

"Grip on tight." Hunter motioned toward the metal railing built into the shower's stonework. Water fell from his hair and down onto my face, riveting in the corner of my lips. His hands were on my body, his chest pressed against mine, but it wasn't enough to satisfy me.

I did as he told me to, understanding why the added stability was necessary when he dropped to his knees. He flung my right foot over his left shoulder, providing his face with direct access to my most intimate parts. His teeth nipped at my inner thigh, delaying the introduction of his charmed mouth to my lower creases.

As he hooked his tongue around my clit, short gasps crawled from my mouth. It wasn't long before I stopped breathing altogether. I squirmed while my body racked with guilty pleasure, causing Hunter to smile against my slits.

"Why aren't you breathing?"

"I forgot how," I replied brainlessly.

"I need you to remember."

"Why?" I panted.

"Because I'm going to make it worse."

On that note, while watching my face for any indication of pain, he pressurized his middle finger into me slowly. My body responded with fits of temptation, as if the conceited smirk on his face was enough to send me over the edge on its own. The circular motions of his tongue were one thing, but the way he was amusing my insides...

This must be heaven.

My head slammed back against the ceramic tile. The corresponding pain surged throughout my core instantly, but I didn't care to know if I had cracked my skull. I was too fascinated by the way my hips were bucking.

Recognizing that my body was on the verge of convulsing, he pressed a second finger into me. The pain was enough to make me yelp, but I liked the hurt attached to the pleasure. It was almost like Hunter had known I would.

He curved his fingers against the internal me, massaging a space that I could only assume to be my g-spot. The mixture of his methods invoked a violent spasm to tear throughout my soul. I covered my mouth with my arm, attempting to smother my moans, but I wasn't able to safeguard them all.

Hunter continued to smirk while my insides fluttered against his fingertips. He licked up my river like it was the best fluid he'd ever tasted, acting like he wasn't as furious with me as I knew he was.

"Like candy," he whispered.

His lips were glistening with my juice as he rose from his knees. His forefinger continued to work my clit, while his other hand kept a tight grip around my thigh. He thrashed his tongue back into my mouth, and there was nothing sweet about the way he did it. He was angry and hostile, kissing me with the hate he felt for me; kissing me with the taste of myself.

When he pulled away from me, licking the remainder of my fluid from his lips, my body began to ache for him all over again. I reached to grip onto him, but he backed away with a shake of his head. His naked body was calling out to me, athletic in ways that triggered my insides to throb, but I couldn't have him. For some reason, he wouldn't let me.

"Don't touch me," he spoke inflexibly, moving his eyes away from mine. "A princess doesn't get fucked by a peasant. I shouldn't have done what I just did, but I had to taste you... just this once."

Using the same two fingers that had been inside me only seconds before, he pried the glass shield open and stepped both feet from the spacious shower. I instinctively wrapped my hand around his stitched forearm, stopping him before he could take another step away from the stage he'd performed his magic on.

"What does the princess get then?"

"A happily ever after."

"With you?" I tried.

"No," he frowned. "I'm the guy who turns your soul black. I'm the guy who molds you into being a criminal. I'm the guy who's too damaged to even consider being with you. I might play it off like you're the one with issues, but it's me who can't be helped. I'm not the guy you walk down the street with holding hands. I'm the guy who nearly kills you by stealing your only cure. I'm the kind of guy who forces you to suffer in a hospital bed for years. That's who I am; a real piece of shit. I don't deserve your virginity. I deserve your forgiveness even less."

Suddenly, it was clear.

"That's what this is about?" I shook my head, realizing his cold shoulder had never been about me at all. It was due to his own guilt and self-hatred. "You found out I had Leukemia?"

"I found out a lot."

He walked toward the linen shelf and wrapped a dry towel around his waist. I continued to stand naked in the shower, watching him while water blurred my vision.

"And so?" I asked.

"So, I picture what it must have been like for you. I know how Chemo works. You would have lost your hair. The drugs would have made you nauseous. You would have wanted to die, and why? Because of me." The sadness in his eyes was haunting. It was something I would remember forever. "For the despair I've put you through, I could never apologize enough."

"You didn't know." I tried to disguise my sobbing, but even the water dripping down my cheeks couldn't mask my tears. I could tell they bothered Hunter, but he didn't do anything to ease their fall. "You're apologizing for something that happened years ago. What about the despair you're putting me through this very second?"

"Yeah," he shook his head, looking at the ceiling with a stretch of his neck. "I'm sorry for that too. I'm sorry I can't be the man you deserve. I'm sorry I can't look at you without seeing the hell you've suffered. I used to see Grimsaw's marks on you. Now, when I look at you, it's like I created the bruises myself. I did worse than slap you around. I made you feel what it was like to die for three years straight. According to a set of lips that weren't yours, although I would have preferred to hear it from you, cancer nearly killed you. How can I live with that on my conscience?"

"The same way I'm looking at you while knowing my dad killed your parents," I stung back. "There are two sides to the coin."

"What are you trying to say? That we're even?" he scoffed, continuing to fade further away from me. "We're not even. What your dad did to my parents is between me and him. What I did to you is between you and me. Guilt works in mysterious ways. You weren't bred to be a mafia princess. Don't let me turn you into one."

After those words, he stalked out of the bathroom; half-naked and dripping wet. The female paramedics on board were getting paid in more than just money today. If they factored in the free views of Hunter's staggering body, they were making the best wage known to mankind.

34
SILENCING MY DEMONS

HUNTER GARCIEZ

Saturday. 3:00 P.M.

HAVE YOU EVER WONDERED WHAT it would be like to run full speed at a brick wall? Have you ever considered how fast your body might drop? Have you ever thought about what the pressure might do to your organs?

I never had…

Until now.

I was falling flat on my face repeatedly. My mind had become my worst enemy. My feelings were diverging with every beat of my heart. In one breath, I was convinced I shouldn't harm Shayla's father. I couldn't retaliate against him, because his daughter was the only reason I was still breathing.

She could have allowed Grimsaw to shoot me. She could have let me bleed out right then and there, ensuring I didn't go after her dad by taking matters into her own hands. She could have stood by and done nothing. She could have left Tessa alone without me… but she hadn't.

For that, I owed her.

For that, I had brought Diego with us.

In the next moment, I wanted to punish Diego more than I had already. I pictured keeping him as my damaged pet; the only kind of pet I would be willing to strike violently. I imagined plucking his fingernails off one by one, and I liked it too.

But I also liked his daughter.

As I paced outside the door that connected her room to mine in a Hawaiian hotel, what I needed to do seemed so transparent. I had to forget about her father's betrayal. I had to act like he didn't exist. I had to pretend as though I hadn't been the reason Shayla had nearly died from cancer. If I ever wanted to know her, these were my only options standing.

Ever so calmly, I tapped against the wooden slab separating us. I prepared to see her face, and I knew what I wanted...

Until I heard the doorknob twist.

Thoughts vibrated through my mind, cooling the air with ice. Deep down, I knew drowning Diego would be the only thing capable of silencing my demons. I had to even the score against him somehow. I would never be satisfied until he was dead, even if Shayla had saved my life. Not to mention, I didn't deserve his daughter. I would never be okay with the pain I had caused her. I would never be able to forget about it.

This was what it was like in my head. Every second felt like a day; every day, a week. I didn't know what was right anymore. Trying to figure it all out had become suffocating. But then, when she opened the door, something inside of me just clicked.

I knew exactly what I wanted.

I wanted *her*.

35
A BODY WITHOUT A SOUL

SHAYLA STONE

Saturday. 3:00 P.M.

THE PLANE HAD TOUCHED DOWN at about eight this morning. The scenery was even more breathtaking than I'd been anticipating. All I could think about was surfing the coastline. I was officially where I had always wanted to be; Hawaii. I hadn't wanted to come here as a criminal on the run, but things still weren't looking all that bad... *somehow.*

Hunter had rented a chain of rooms at another fancy hotel, just meters away from the teal waters of Waikiki Beach in Honolulu. He had equipped each of us with our own room, all with outdoor balconies attached. Two doors separated the three adjoining cubes, making the wing seem like our own strand of elegant bachelor apartments. My room and Tessa's were on the opposite sides of his, leaving Hunter as the man in between.

As for my dad, he was getting cozy at the Honolulu Hospital. By the looks of his injuries, he would be staying there for quite a while... under a fake name, of course. Since his face looked a little different than it once had, I was hoping he wouldn't get busted for being wanted by the government. The reality was, though... he just might.

All of us might.

I didn't know how many days I would receive with Hunter and

Tessa. I didn't know how many sunrises would come before the two of them would move on with their lives, inevitably leaving me to do the same. That time would arrive. I couldn't allow myself to think otherwise.

Like Hunter had said, this was only a temporary band-aid. He had helped me reach this point of freedom, but he hadn't drawn out a future with me. I couldn't expect more than a few days of safekeeping under his watch. There was nothing I could do or say to convince him not to abandon me. Bad blood existed between our families. The chemistry between us wasn't enough to change that. It never would be.

The three of us had dispersed into our own rooms a few hours ago, but a welcomed knock at my door was ending that division now. After tugging the cherry-stained wood open, I found one hell of a sexy body leaning against the ledge of the contiguous doorway.

Hunter was all man standing at 6'3" tall. He had a frame of solid muscle, and his electrifying green eyes didn't go unnoticed either. I tried not to unravel in his towering presence, but every move he made pushed me closer toward my cracking point. It was pathetic how nervous his presence made me.

He uncrossed his arms as he entered my room. I watched his every step before he took a seat on the edge of my bed. We hadn't spoken more than syllables to each other in hours. Aside from telling me to grab my luggage once the plane had landed at the private airstrip, our communication had ended after the mind-bending orgasm he'd induced upon me. Things were at high levels of awkward.

"Did you catch some sleep?"

"Not really," I shook my head, failing to admit that my lack of shuteye was due to incessant thoughts revolving around him. "I'll get some tonight."

"Me too," he nodded, a weird look in his eyes. "I need to go run a few errands. I'll make sure to pick up a cellphone while I'm out. Once I make it untraceable, you can use it to call your dad. He should be out of surgery soon."

"I really appreciate that."

"Don't mention it," he shrugged, brushing the topic aside. "Since I trashed my old laptop, I need to go buy a new one. Once I pirate a few programs onto it, I'll transfer the cash from my old accounts through a stream of electronic ghost-blockers. The funds won't be linkable to any of us that way, but it's going to take me a few hours to do it properly."

"Okay," I nodded, acting like I knew what he was talking about.

"This is the money we have until I can access the rest. I've already taken out the chunk I need." He reached into the front pocket of his blue jeans. After pulling out a thick stack of cash, he tried to pass it my way. "If you don't mind, will you watch Tessa tonight? I'll be gone for a while, so go buy yourself whatever you need. Maybe you could help her pick out some clothes too? Don't let her get anything that covers less than 85% of her body."

I smiled at his brotherly concern, but I refused to snatch the wad of wrapped bills from his hand. I swiped at the front of my t-shirt instead, giving *Bob Marley's* face a small scratch.

"I'm not taking your money," I argued with a shake of my head. "I can get a job. I don't expect a free pass. Somewhere will be hiring a surfing instructor around here. It's Hawaii."

"Your face is all over the news."

"It's a risk I'll have to take eventually."

"I have money," he reinforced. "While I take care of some business, you and my sister *will* treat yourselves to a shopping spree. Consider this an advanced payment for my first lesson on a surfboard. When I get back, if it's not too late, I'll come bang on your door to say goodnight."

Hunter tossed the bundle my way, but I knew he was already capable of surfing on his own. It was hard to grow up where we had and not become involved with the aquatic sport. On top of that, Tessa had already told me Hunter was rehearsed on the waves.

"I'd like that," I smiled, because the bad girl inside me could think of something better for him to bang on. "You will come back, right? I mean… you don't plan to vanish *yet*?"

"Shayla…" Hunter gave a weary sigh, watching my fingers fidget with the cash. "Don't act like you would be losing something if I didn't return. You'd be gaining something instead."

"What exactly?"

"Freedom."

"Define freedom," I clipped back, agitation burning through my cheeks. "Because the way I see it, none of us are all that safe anyway. We're already on the run, praying that nobody recognizes us, and that's how it'll be forever now. If it's my freedom you're worried about, it's a little late for that. I lost that when I shot Grimsaw in the head. I destroyed yours in the same moment too."

While this bud of truth grew in my mind, my breathing took a race against the speed of light. All the consequences bubbling from the death of Grimsaw were my fault. I was the reason Hunter was officially wanted, but I still couldn't see any substitute for what I had chosen to do. My only other option had been to let him die.

I couldn't have done that.

"Unlike I would have been a week ago, I'm thankful to still be alive today," Hunter whispered, flicking his vision through the window in my room. "But I've ruined you. My resentment isn't directed your way. Although I'm sure it seems the opposite, it's aimed at myself. For the past ten hours, I've thought about how to depart from you. I've considered each of my options."

"And?" I mused.

"In every one of them, I'm left worse than I was before. I'll walk around like a zombie, telling myself this was all just a dream. I'll tell myself you didn't exist. When it doesn't work, I'll go back to the pills. Tessa will grow to hate me eventually, and it won't be long before I'll become a body without a soul again. That's my promising future. It's so fucked up when I think about it, because I hardly know you."

"But what if you didn't leave? What if you gave us a chance to know each other?" I suggested an alternative, holding eye contact like some of the best. "What would you feel then?"

"Agony, because that would mean I'd have to let your father live. I'm not convinced that's what I want yet." He rose from the mattress and took heavy steps toward the exit. "You're asking me to switch sides, Shayla. You're asking me to forget that he murdered my family. You're wrong if you think this is easier on me than it is on you."

"But it is easier for you," I gave him a distasteful look. "Because at the end of it all, you still have Tessa. If you murder my dad, who will I have? If you still plan to kill him, why did you even bring him down here?"

"Foolish men do foolish things."

"Give me a better answer."

"Because I didn't want *you* to end up in jail," he surrendered. "I had seconds to choose what I was going to do. I either had to leave you behind and let you rot in prison, or I had to board you onto a private plane beside me. Since your stubborn ass wouldn't leave your dad, I did the only thing I could to protect you in that moment; I brought the piece of shit with us. I hate him, but I don't regret anything I've done that has kept you safe."

"You care about me," I demanded, begging for him to admit the words. "Why is it so hard for you to accept that?"

"Trust me, I succumbed to that fact long ago." His hand curved around the doorknob to vacate my room. He left his back turned toward me, as if he couldn't face me while saying what he was about to. "In the moment when Grimsaw's gun was pointed at me, it was *you* who I was about to take a bullet for."

"What are you talking about?"

"Grimsaw told me to shoot your dad. He wanted me to give you back to him. If I had agreed to those stipulations, my life would be fine right now. I wouldn't be on the news, the mafia wouldn't want me dead, and my sister wouldn't run the risk of being taken away from me. The issue? I refused to give up your location. I refused to burn your life into ash, and I refused to kill your dad. When I tried to shoot Grimsaw, it was because he was uttering threats over your head; not mine or Tessa's."

"That isn't true," I prayed.

"It is," Hunter solidified, staring at the ceiling. Whenever I was a nervous wreck, my sight dropped to the floor. Whenever he was the same, he looked toward the heavens instead. "If I didn't care about you, I would have followed Grimsaw's instructions."

"You were going to die for *me*?"

"I would do it again."

"But why?" I disbelieved.

"Like you said, I care about you…" He tugged the door open, leaving his backside as my final image of him. "I would kill for you, Shayla. Without a dash of hesitation, if it meant protecting you, I would let anyone slit my throat too. The only thing I can't seem to do is allow myself to poison you."

36
BREAKFAST WITH E.T.

SHAYLA STONE

Sunday. 11:00 A.M.

I FELT THE MATTRESS RUFFLE BENEATH me hours later. I didn't know how long Hunter had been home for, but the smell of his body wash in the air indicated it had been long enough to clean himself up.

I stretched my arms above my head, feeling sunshine against my skin as it streamed through the windows of my suite. I couldn't remember falling asleep, but daylight was suggesting I had been out for quite a while.

"Morning," Hunter whispered, sending the warmth of his breath into my barely conscious eardrum. "I have room service on the way."

He curled his arm around my stomach, drawing the back of my body into the front of his. My guts were still full from the oriental buffet Tessa and I had indulged in late last night, but I wasn't going to complain about the nearness of his body.

While spending yesterday with his sister, I had come to realize that she and I had more in common than we'd known. We both liked simple clothes. We both hated brushing our hair. We both went crazy over a bag of mini doughnuts. After taking a few laps around the local go-kart track, we'd learned that we each retained a similar need for speed too.

"It's morning?" I stirred to life, extending my neck as I detected coffee beans in the air. The aroma was barely perceptible beneath Hunter's intoxicating scent. "Did you just get back?"

"I got in at around midnight last night. You were passed out with your hair sprawling across your face. I didn't have it in me to wake you. I went back to my room instead."

I twisted to face him, draping the bedsheet over my nude body, blushing as I met his gaze. His hair was gelled upward in the front with a laid-back finesse, and his smile was warm and inviting. I could never be sure which side of Hunter might greet me. His personalities had a habit of swapping by the hour, but he seemed pleasant this morning; skeptically pleasant.

"Do you always sleep naked?"

"Sometimes," I said, and it was the truth. "It's hot here in Hawaii."

"That box beneath your window is the air conditioning unit," he smirked sideways. "But since you have eyes, I think you already knew that."

"It's broken," I lied poorly.

As my fingers began to trickle down the center of his shirtless chest, his palm rounded against the bend of my hip. He fastened his grip, bringing my body closer to his with a gentle tug. His eyebrow raised like he was struggling to saturate my naked motives, but he never did speak.

He slid his hand beneath the bedsheet, giving my airways a memorable reason to collapse. The way my body quivered as his fingers glided over my bellybutton made his smile widen, enhancing the palpitations of my heart. He affected me both physically and emotionally. So much so, if my body was the trail he wanted to venture, I welcomed him to take the sinful hike.

"If you keep laying yourself out for me, I'm bound to take what's being offered..." His hand snaked lower, lingering just above my pelvic line. "Not only are you gorgeous, but I only have so much self-restraint. Every time you bat your eyelashes, a little more of it disappears."

"My hope exactly," I flirted.

A knock at the door sounded before he could respond. Hunter climbed from the bed and opened it, allowing a male in a white dress shirt to enter the room with a cart full of food. I yanked up the covers to hide my body before the waiter received too much of an added daily bonus.

"Did you buy out the entire buffet?" I gaped at the food towering atop the silver wagon. "You didn't want to leave some for anyone else?"

"I eat a lot," Hunter grinned.

I made a mental note to learn how to cook something edible, even just a sandwich. My dad had hired a personal chef after my mom had passed away. I'd tried to acquire Maria's ability to master the world's juiciest filet mignon, but things had always gone much smoother for her if I was nowhere near the kitchen.

Hunter slipped a few bills into the hand of the guy in a bowtie, thanking him for the food delivery before he left the room. I waited for him to bring his golden body back to bed, but he continued to stand and eat a piece of buttered toast instead.

"Today is the day," he spoke with a full mouth, winking at me. "I woke up this morning and stumbled over to your room. I thought of waking you by sliding my dick in you, because I knew you were intentionally tormenting me by sleeping naked. The thing is, if I had done that, you would have won the game. So instead, I proceeded to spend the next three hours telling myself I couldn't touch you. Toward the end of that time, I realized; fuck the rules."

My eyes shifted between his through the distance. He was blunt, but I liked that about him. When he wanted someone to know what he was thinking, he wasn't shy about telling them. He was raw and unpolished. He was what could only be described as *Hunter Garciez*.

"When I first met you, I thought I just had some creepy fantasy to taste the toxic apple," he carried on, running his hand over his jawline. "But this morning, I realized the thought of another guy waking to you fucking kills me."

When I opened my mouth to speak, nothing came out.

"I don't just want to taste you, Shayla. I want to spend time with you. I want to learn everything there is to know about you. When you're asleep, I want it to be my arms that wrap around your waist. I want it to be my tongue that explores your body. I want it to be me who protects you, because I can do it better than anyone else ever could. I'm done fighting you on this. It's exhausting to pretend that I don't feel something for you when I do. You don't need to understand it, but I was meant to know you. This was fate."

Hunter seemed so innocent as he spoke. His mouth twitched

like he was losing all logic, while his eyes were publicizing his buried anxiety. Vulnerability was bleeding through his pupils; an expression he didn't wear often.

Tentatively, I asked, "But what about my dad?"

"My current strategy is to forget that he exists..." Hunter swallowed a mouthful, running his vision over my sheeted silhouette on the bed. "This plan has a high chance of crumbling. I'll probably end up shattering his skull eventually, but I vow to make an honest effort to do the opposite." As he held up his hand in a Scout's Honor pledge, I knew I was in no position to barter. "Can we start with that?"

"It's fair," I agreed.

"*Why* are you a virgin?"

I cringed. "Really?"

"I want to know," he nodded.

"Are you striving to make me uncomfortable?" I hated the topic immensely, but I knew he was going to force me to answer. "I've never liked a guy enough to offer myself to him in that way. I've always been more focused on my studies. I'm not waiting for marriage if that's what you're assuming. I'm not Catholic."

"You get so defensive over your virginity, but it's something you should be proud of. If anything, it makes you more attractive. It doesn't make you weak. It does the opposite by proving your strength. I can tell you think I might not want you because of your inexperience, but it's crazy how wrong you are. I think about sleeping with you every ten minutes, but that's not all I want from you. You're more than that. I wish you could see yourself through my eyes."

I was left at a complete fail for words. If I was understanding anything in this moment, it was that Hunter was officially caving and dropping his wall. Other than that, I cared about very little.

"But it's probably a good thing you aren't Catholic," he joked. "I'm a little fucked up, and my father raised me to believe religion is for the weak."

"Is that what *you* believe?"

He took a moment to consider his reply. He reached into the back pocket of his jeans and pulled out a white envelope, staring at it like he wasn't confident in what it contained.

"I believe religion has been fabricated throughout the years. The

Bible has been altered repeatedly. I don't wish to live my life by a book, but I think religion helps many souls get through their times of agony. As a narcotic junkie, I have no right to patronize anyone else's preference of hypnosis. Personally, though, I believe in the elements of science and evolution. I believe in mathematics and numbers. Since I've been to hell, I figure there must be a good side to the world too. Maybe the religious know something I don't." He slunk toward the bed and passed me the envelope. The rectangle jingled as it transferred into my fingers. "I'll leave you alone to change. Take your time."

"What is this?"

"Relax," he smiled, flaunting his heart-stopping dimples my way. "You know what I've realized about you? Other than you don't enjoy surprises, you constantly forget to breathe in my presence too. The whole '*jumbled by Garciez*' expression looks great on you, blondie."

While I conveyed an unconvinced look his way, he grabbed another breakfast plate before disappearing into his connected room.

I hurriedly climbed from my bed and changed into a t-shirt and a pair of jean shorts, curious of what the package contained. After tossing my hair into a messy bun, I picked up the envelope like I was afraid it might melt in my hands. Reaching in, three keys met my touch. I took a deep breath before reading his swirl of hand-written words.

Shayla,

I'm a bad fucking seed, but you know that already. I don't know how to be in a relationship. I don't know what it means to be committed, but I know I feel something for you. Anxiety eats through my flesh, because I have so many fears. Fears I won't be good enough. Fears I might hurt you. Fears I will disappoint you more than I already have. Most of all, I fear I could fall in love with you.

This scares me, because I'm bound to fuck it all up. When I fuck up I fuck up hard. I can't touch anything holy without causing darkness to shatter it. I'm no good for you, but you're no better for me. We fit together in the wrong way... like whiskey and bad decisions... like a victim and a predator... like an angel and the devil.

Yet... I still want you.

Like any good love story, both sides must compromise. I will sacrifice seeking revenge for you. I will fight like hell to reverse my drug addiction. I will forget everything I have known for the past three years, but can you do the same? Can you forget my past? Can you forget yours? Can you forget that we're on the run because the mixture of us is fatal?

Three keys are in your hand. I went to a dealership last night to pick up a new truck. Before you panic, it was legal-ish. I used a fake ID, but I did pay for it. While I was there, I realized I wouldn't be protecting you very well if I left you without your own set of wheels.

The black key is for a Jeep Wrangler I parked downstairs in the lot. I chose a purple paintjob to match the surfboard I strapped to the roof of it for you. You need a way to get around... with or without me. I want it to be clear that I'm not trying to buy your affection. I just want you to feel independent. I would rather slit my own wrists than have you stay beside me because you feel optionless.

Next, the stubby key will unlock the front door of a bungalow. It's sim-ple, but the architecture is wild. The house is built into the side of a cliff that overlooks the ocean. I thought of you when I bought it. I could have waited a few weeks before concerning myself with living arrangements, but I drove by it and something felt right. The hotel we're living in isn't a solid foundation for Tessa. The sooner she can settle, the better. I take possession in a week...

Thirdly, the long key is for a storage unit on the west side of Honolulu. The address is listed on the backside of this note. Inside this space, you will find everything you could ever possibly need to disappear. It's likely that you will be running away from me if you ever decide to use this key, but I never want you to feel restricted. Grimsaw did that to you enough. The opportunity to escape is there. You will always have a way out.

In case you're denying it, this is my unorthodox way of asking you to move into the house with me. I know everything is happening fast. I know we don't know each other, but I want to change that. You feel right to me, but I understand if you think I'm rushing things by a year or two. I will respect whatever decision you make. It doesn't matter if I need to drive to this hotel every day to see you. I'm okay with whatever makes you com-fortable. You're the drug I crave now.

Hunter

I gyrated when a set of hands wreathed around my waist from behind. As Hunter's lips began to drop feathery kisses against my neck, I watched my fairytale flash before me; the fairytale I was about to ruin.

I pulled myself away in a hasty movement, foolishly blurting, "Grimsaw told me everything before I met you. I couldn't bring myself to tell you, but I knew what my dad had done to your parents the whole time. Grimsaw told me about the cures too. I knew my part in this from the very beginning."

"I know that," Hunter replied, his expression unchanged. "Grimsaw tried to get in my head with it. He said you didn't give a shit about me if you could lie to me like that."

"Why didn't you mention it?"

"What good would that have done?" Hunter offered a look that silently told me I was asking a dumb question. "I realize your fight with Leukemia was the root cause behind the dismemberment of my family. I don't need you to point it out to me. Just like that, I shouldn't need to point out that I stole the cure from your dad. Ultimately, this was *my* fault. I had a role to play in your extended clash with cancer. I will always regret taking that briefcase. If not for making you suffer, for getting my parents killed because of it." He stepped toward me again, entangling his hands with my much smaller set. "Besides, it isn't like I've been completely honest with you either. You know there's something weird about me, but I refuse to explain it to you."

"You talk as if you're an alien." I stole a glance at the white socks on his feet, wishing I could get the answers I wanted by shaking him. "Why don't you just tell me what you're hiding from me? I won't judge you."

"That's what you think."

"I won't," I insisted. "After everything we've gone through over the past few days... I care about you, Hunter. I owe you my life."

"You've already paid me back by saving mine," he replied quietly. "Once you know the things I can do, you can't *un-know* them. You'll have so many questions. You'll stop seeing me as a regular person. I'll become a computer to you. Whether you want it to or not, it will change your entire perspective of me."

I considered how everyone else acted around Hunter. While alive, Grimsaw had been unnerved by him. Much the same, my dad was too. Everyone but me seemed to be aware of Hunter's *differences*, including Tessa and Barnes.

I knew he was a hacker. I knew he was good with numbers. I knew he dabbled in the stock markets illegally from time to time too. I knew he robbed banks, which he did exceeding well at. Each of these things related to one thing; mathematics.

"You're a closet genius," I discharged my allegation. "You don't think like the average person does, because you aren't average. Your intelligence is what makes you so dangerous. Every time you take a step, you've already subconsciously mapped out your next ten."

"All true," he agreed.

"You broke into Barnes' safe in a way that wasn't human. You knew the code. It's like you can see things before they happen… like you can read minds."

"I can't read minds."

"Then what?" I glued my hand to my hip. I was officially done biting my tongue. "You expect me to ignore your unearthly qualities? You want me to have breakfast with E.T., but it's against the rules to ask him anything?"

"Shayla," he growled.

"Was it really Grimsaw who hurt my dad?" My eyes dodged his, unable to face him while I accused him of such unholy acts. "You didn't have anything to do with the damage he endured?"

I wasn't sure how, but I knew Hunter was about to lie to me. Deep down, it was like our souls were connected. I could see through his bullshit before he even spat it.

He stared at me like he didn't want to answer my question, which was enough for me to understand the truth. Reluctance was a devilish cue, leaving the unspoken facts to ring out loudly. Bygones were best when laid to rest, but this wasn't something I would get over easily.

I shook my head. Whatever existed between us was pulling me to him with a seemingly supernatural force. The linkage was growing stronger by the day. The currents were unnerving, but if they kept up, I would soon have what every girl wished to have. Which, of course, was the ability to know when her boyfriend was trying to cheat his way out of something.

Hunter gripped onto my t-shirt and pulled me into his chest. He grabbed the keys from my hands, watching me attentively while throwing them onto the bed behind me. Gently raising my chin with his fingers, he forced me to meet the truth in his mossy eyes; the truth I already knew.

"I know you hurt him," I whispered despondently. "I can feel it in my veins. I don't know what *you* are. I don't know what *we* are, but I'm connected to you. Even when you're not in the room, you still exist. You're like a ghost, except you don't breathe down my neck. You reside within me instead, possessing my soul like a demon. I can *feel* you."

"I'm not a demon," he said coldly, holding my stare with conviction. "But there is something weird going on between us. I can feel it augmenting too. You're stepping into my core, and the currents will only worsen with time. I know why it's happening, but I'm not ready to explain it to you. Respect that."

"Then explain my dad."

"To tell you I wished Diego could still walk would be a flat-out lie. Deep down, you know the truth. You don't need to hear me say it. In my world, your dad should be six feet under. I didn't get what I really wanted. I didn't get it because of you, but letting him live will be worth it if I get a chance to know you. I'm sorry for the tears I've caused, but forgetting Diego's injuries is one of *your* sacrifices. All couples are forced to compromise. Our compromises are just a little darker than most. They always will be."

I stewed on whether he had just referred to us as a couple or not, but Hunter didn't let me reply. He slipped his tongue into my mouth, toying with mine flirtatiously. His taste made the situation incredibly difficult to dissect. Once he undid the button on my jean shorts, I stopped trying to analyze it altogether.

My zipper descended, but Hunter didn't tug the denim down from my hips. His finger stepped around my shorts instead, slipping in through the front of my lace panties to massage me in a skilled way. Like a seasoned pro, he didn't fumble with inexperience.

"Do you hear that?" he smirked, making a beat with the fluid dripping from me. "It's like music; a better version of *Beethoven*. Fuck playing the guitar. From here on out, I plan to master the art of playing your clit instead."

He pulled his finger from my shorts, giving it a lick before toss-

ing me to the bed with a bad-boy smile. As he crawled above me
with shirtless shoulders, I knew I had already forgiven the cocky
asshole for everything.

THREE MONTHS LATER

"With love's light winds did I o'erperch these walls;
For stony limits cannot hold love out.
And what love can do, that dares love attempt."

Romeo Montague

37
A PAIN WORTH SUFFERING

HUNTER GARCIEZ

Thursday. 4:00 P.M.

I KNEW I HAD TO BE honest with Shayla. I still hadn't told her the truth about myself. We didn't talk about my oddities. We didn't talk about Diego's injuries. We didn't talk about how she looked nothing like her so-called father. We didn't talk about how she had killed one of California's sketchiest thugs. Instead, we avoided each of these topics like the fucking plague.

Shayla had been waking me up with a blowjob for three months in a row, so I figured I owed her the truth now. I trusted she could handle it too. Time had shown me her true strength. Rather than getting down about the things she had gone through, she was trying to learn to cook. Between me, Tessa, and the guy who owned the burger joint down the street, Shayla's food wasn't all that edible. I didn't tell her that, though… *because she had given me a blow job for three months in a row.*

There was one violent day when I had forced myself to throw up after she had experimented with a tuna casserole recipe. By far, it had been the worst meal I'd ever tasted. I had then thrown up naturally after a chicken fiasco had gone wrong, experiencing what was quite possibly my first collision with food poisoning. Any other time she'd fed me, I had just sort of suffered through the backlashing nausea with a smile on my face. It was sweet of her to try, but Tessa and I were both praying she would stop.

"I don't want to freak you out," I told her, taking a seat across from her on our bed. When her spine straightened, I knew my words had put her on edge. I had intended for the opposite, but there was no good way to approach this conversation. "I'm ready to tell you about myself."

I stood back up to retrieve her wallet, unbuckling the silver clasp on the front. The wallet of a female was always heavy, much like carrying around a five-pound dumbbell. The contents always included useless club cards and unnecessary bullshit.

I drew out the first four bankcards I ran across. The cards were void to Shayla now, since she couldn't use them without leaving a trail to us in Hawaii, but they would do just fine when it came to teaching her about myself.

As I found three expired gift cards in her wallet, proving my point about useless weight, I gave my head a little shake. Taking a deep breath in, I tried to ease my nerves by telling myself Shayla wouldn't judge me. I repeated the notion in my mind while throwing her first debit card onto the blanket beside her.

"3300," I stated the pin number to her every day checking account. "There's a savings bond attached to that card too. It holds a balance of $12, 914.32. The pin to that account is 4239."

She took ten blinks without saying a word. Her nod confirmed I was right, but my mind didn't need the positive reinforcement.

I grabbed one of her credit cards and tossed it down to follow. After listing the sixteen digits off the front, all without looking down at the cheap plastic, I gave her the pin number to it next.

"1174. Your credit limit is fifteen grand."

I followed this procedure a few more times, burning through all the cards she possessed. Each of her accounts had a different security pin attached. This pleased me, because I'd come to learn that most people integrated the same number to every one of their financial accounts.

Absolute morons.

I handed Shayla the last piece of thin plastic I could find. She took a deep breath in, staring down at her driver's license as I stated, "A0360764."

"You know my pin numbers?" Her face muddled, transforming her complexion with confusion. Puzzlement shambled around her blue eyes. "Are you planning to rob me?"

"I'm not allowed to steal money anymore. My girlfriend has me on probation," I grinned, thankful she had a sense of humor. "I'm trying my best not to piss her off."

Lately, Shayla had been trying to get me to say three very forbidden words to her; words I had never said to any girl, aside from my mom and sister. Rather than uttering them, I had been making a habit of bypassing her hints at all costs instead. To say that I loved her would be true. She was everything and it terrified me, but I knew there was no coming back from admitting something like that. Once the truth was unleashed, it couldn't be retracted. With love came heartbreak. I wasn't sure if I was prepared for that.

"I don't need to look at the cards," I said, keeping my distance from her. "I saw your numbers through your eyes. I can do strange things; really *strange* things. I know I sound crazy, but I need you to keep an open mind."

"You're freaking me out."

"I realize that," I winced, scared shitless myself. "But I told you I would change everything you know. I told you it wouldn't be in a good way."

"You're trying to say you saw my passcodes through my eyes, Hunter..." She stood off the bed and began to pace. "Are you swallowing pills again? I'll chop off your fingers if you are."

"That would be highly ineffective," I snickered. "Fingerless or not, I would still find a way into the bottle somehow. Besides, I'm stone-cold sober. I just love it when you get all fired up and try to act tough."

She ran her fingers through her ashy hair, looking as stressed as I'd ever seen her before. Since we were wanted fugitives, this said a lot too.

"You're making no sense."

"I am. You're just not hearing me," I insisted, knowing how difficult this was for her to accept. The things I could do were normal to me. To anyone else, they were insane. "It's like telepathy, but I can't read your mind. I can only read your digits. Numbers spin out at me. I can't keep it from happening, because it's always been this way. It's why stealing identities comes so easily to me. It's how I knew your birthday without you telling me it. It's why I can rob banks without any weapons. It's why the Feds haven't managed to track me down. It's all based around my photographic memory."

"Are you kidding me?"

"I wish I was," I frowned, picking at my fingernails. Fidgeting wasn't a habit I normally possessed, but Shayla had me all sorts of twisted. "The world record for reciting the decimal places of Pi is held at 70,000 digits. I can do better at 90,000. Sometimes, when I stare at you, I count the blinks you take. It isn't something I overly care to know, but my mind does it automatically. I can't control it. You've taken fifty-four blinks in the past three minutes. I can remember every outfit you've dressed yourself in since I met you. The t-shirt you're currently wearing has been worn four times. It would have been five, but you decided to change out of it one day last month. I can remember every sentence you've ever said to me in that t-shirt too. I can remember every tear that has slid down your cheeks. There have only ever been six, but that's because you don't like to show vulnerability. Behind closed doors, I know you've cried more."

She didn't move. Standing in one spot, she continued to stare at me like I was from a different dimension. I tried to put myself in her shoes, but numbers were all I knew.

"I've read about it in my Psychology courses," she finally spoke, allowing me to breathe again. "I know the condition exists, but the cases are so rare. Very few people can do these things. You're like… a prodigy."

I wanted to reach out and touch her, but I wasn't convinced it would be the winning move. So instead, speaking the question I feared the answer to most, I asked, "Can you be okay with it?"

I heard the neediness in my tone, but she didn't seem to recognize it. She swallowed deeply as she sauntered back toward our bed, wiping her fingers over her bankcards like she thought they might vanish. It wasn't like I had been expecting her to respond any better, but having her say anything at all would have been more comforting than the silence she offered.

"It's a lot to process." I headed toward the door to leave. "I'll give you some time to let it sink in, because there's more to it than that. There's more than you're prepared to hear."

"No," she halted me. "Don't go."

I bowed my head and turned around, peeking through the slits of my eyes as she sauntered up to me in a daze. I was expecting her to run directly through me. I waited for it, but it never did happen.

"I get that you're scared," I told her.

"I need time to register it," she agreed quietly. "But even if you do have magical powers, I still think you're adorable." She numbed me by locking her wrists around the back of my neck. "I will continue to think so too, even if I don't understand the way your mind works."

"Well, I should confess one other thing too…" I struggled to keep a straight face. "I had to eat the heart of a care bear to make myself this cute."

Her blue eyes began to shimmer like diamonds, but her smile was the most entrapping of all. When she slapped my chest, treating me like the nimrod I was, I could tell how much I meant to her. As much as I needed her, she needed me too.

"I wasn't expecting that," she giggled.

"Neither was the care bear, but chalk lines had to be drawn," I laughed, raising her so she could wrap her legs around my waist.

As I threw her down onto the bed, which was of course decorated in purple linen, I didn't have a complaint in the world. I crawled above her in my jeans. We still hadn't had sex, but we had done everything else two horny people could think of. Now that I had shown her what it meant to get a tongue lashing, she was always shoving my face between her legs. Subsequently, I had officially found the sweet part in deserting California.

"My dad suffered from the same condition as I do. Tessa didn't inherit it, but there is no logical reason as to why. I was the first born, which is the only conclusion I can come up with. My dad warned me of you. He told me there would be a girl with no digits. He said I would have to force it to happen, but that I could wash her numbers away. I didn't know what he meant then, but I understand everything now. What I see when I look at you is different. I know your numbers, but I saw them when we were first introduced. It took me hours to see if I could brush your digits aside. I figured I was better off not knowing if you were the girl, but curiosity bit me in the ass eventually. There is a reason I stare into your eyes like I do. I can't see your numbers anymore, even when I try. Do you know what that means?"

She shook her head slowly. "No idea."

"We're soulmates, Shay," I turned the air glacial with the truth, doing my best to ignore the way her fingers were skittering over the upper ledge of my boxers. "You define everything I thought didn't exist. You're my destiny and my fate. Unlike most people can ever say for certain, I know this to be a fact. Within hours of meeting you, I knew you were the one for me. That's why I couldn't leave you at your dad's house. That's why I refused to let you wind up in jail. I wouldn't have protected just any girl placed beside me. I did it because you're *you*. People only get one soul-mate. If you had gone to prison, it would have been tricky to get you out. I would have done it, but it wouldn't have been easy."

I tried to read her like a book, staring at her through the glass of my every word. She was struck by shock, which was to be expected, but it didn't seem to change anything. She was still watching me the way she always did.

"I'm going to piss you off at times, probably to the point that you won't want to look at me for days," I predicted, knowing the probabilities were high. "But I'll also be here whenever you need someone. I'll love you like you deserve to be loved. I'll give you everything I have until my lungs fail on me."

"I know you will," she whispered. "Every beating I took was worth it, Hunter. Every hour I went without food, every night I spent sleeping on a dirty floor, every day I tallied into that concrete wall, I wouldn't change any of it. I'm thankful Grimsaw kidnapped me."

"That's ridiculous."

"Is it? If I hadn't been kidnapped, I wouldn't be living this new life now. I wouldn't be in paradise drinking margaritas and surfing for six hours a day. I wouldn't be with you."

"You wouldn't have suffered either," I challenged bitterly. "You wouldn't have starved. You wouldn't have a tattoo you hate. You wouldn't have come so close to being raped. You wouldn't have the memories."

There were still so many girls that needed saving from the system. Just because they weren't Shayla didn't mean I could just forget about them. Just because Grimsaw was dead didn't mean that his system would stop either. I was in this world, and I would be for life. I couldn't turn a blind eye. I didn't know what I would do just yet, but Shayla wouldn't have any part in whatever I decided. She seemed to think we were like Bonnie and Clyde, but I wanted no resemblance to that. She'd been a good girl upon meeting me;

lippy, but still good. I didn't want to mess that up any worse than I already had.

"I will never forget what Grimsaw did to me," she smiled rather than frowned. "I will never forget that I took his life. I will never forget the feeling of helplessness while I rotted in that cell, wondering if my life was over, but I wouldn't change any of it. Look at where we are..." She pointed at Honolulu's best beach through the main window of our bedroom. "I have you. I have Tessa, who is the sister I've always wanted. What more could a girl ask for? I'm as lucky as I'll ever be. Our story might be screwed up. My prince arrived in blood. He was cocky and crude, but he protected me like he was invincible. Even though I'm an outlaw now, I received my fairytale. I had to experience sorrow before being led to you. The punishment I endured was a pain worth suffering."

"I'm a puppet on your string," I admitted, treading kisses over her silky neck. "I haven't touched cigarettes or pills for months. For the first time in years, I feel like I might be okay. You're like novocaine. You saved my life by shooting Grimsaw, but you've been saving me every day since too. You're not the lucky one, blondie. I am."

I listened to the thud of her pulse, stroking her pale hair away from her face. It wasn't easy to leave her thunderstruck, so I knew I had succeeded this time. In our tweaked-out love story, she was my princess. Shayla came with horror stories and no verbal filter. I was her suicidal knight, dressed in scars instead of armor. Ironically, even though we were bound to wind up in handcuffs eventually, our smiles rarely wilted.

Tessa had given me a reason to fight over the past three years. She had given me a reason to continue existing, but I couldn't have called myself happy. Now that I had Shayla, things were different.

"When I first saw you gagged and on the floor, my entire world flipped upside down," I reflected upon the memories. "You started a fire inside me, awakening my soul to something real. I was empty before. Nothing made me happy; not like you do."

She looked up at me bashfully, though I had been staring at her forever. I was an indecisive man, but Shayla was one thing I was certain of. She overwhelmed me just by existing. Very few people could relate to me on a personal level, but she could. We rarely spoke of the bad, but it was a bond we shared silently beneath the surface. I could give her one look, she always knew what I was thinking. She was not only in my heart; she was in my fucking head too.

Nothing about Shayla's life had been easy. She'd been introduced to death at a young age; younger than I had even. There was something so morbid about the way this made me desire her all the more.

I didn't want a girl who had never met struggle. I wanted a damaged female; one who was rehearsed in pain. I wanted a girl who used her tongue as a weapon. I wanted a girl who knew what it was like to dwell in the land of lava. I wanted a girl who showed no fear as she reached out to shake hands with the devil. I wanted... *her*.

Everyone Shayla loved seemed to die on her. I understood the regret that came attached to that. Her grandma and grandpa on her mom's side had been in a car wreck when Shayla had been eight. At eleven, she had watched her mom rot with breast cancer for months before she'd eventually passed on. At twelve, Leukemia had destroyed Shayla's world. As consequence, she had suffered through two years of summer school to catch up on her studies. Since I had stolen the only cure that could have healed her sooner, these things weighed on nobody's shoulders but mine.

I had chalked up the situation between me and her dad as an unfortunate predicament. I hated to admit it, but I understood why Diego had done what he had. I was at fault too. I could go after him, but would I gain any satisfaction from it? As Diego took his last breath, would it be triumph I felt? Or would the heartbreak of watching Shayla storm out of my life be worse than allowing Diego to live? If I killed him, I would be saying goodbye to her too.

Some choices in life are easy to make. Some choices are more challenging. Some will test you in ways that you can't prepare for. While staring down the barrel of a Smith & Wesson, prepared to take a bullet for somebody special to you, that's when you learn who you really are.

Three months ago, I would have sworn I would murder Diego upon finding him. It's funny what time can do. It's funny how things can shift. When it comes to breaking the trust of your soulmate, decisions need to be made responsibly. As long as Shayla was alive, I had no choice but to allow Diego to be the same.

Regardless, tonight would be a special night. It was a night I wanted Shayla to remember forever. She didn't know what I was planning, but she would soon learn. Dinner at a five-star restaurant, a diamond necklace, rose pedals, champagne; I was going all out. I wanted her to remember the night she lost her virginity as one of the best she'd ever had.

I wasn't normally a thoughtful kind of guy, but Shayla was also the only girl I had ever labeled as my girlfriend. She deserved everything I had to give. She'd been waiting months to feel me from the inside, because I wanted her to be certain I was who she wanted her first time to be with. I had even tried to intentionally piss her off, giving her a taste of what I could really be like by cutting up her bras. It was a dick move on my part, but she didn't need to wear them. I gave her rack an A+.

As it turned out, Shayla could handle my shit. The next day, she had handed me an impressively wrapped present. She'd put some serious determination into decorating the box, using a bow and ribbon; the whole nine yards. After unwrapping what I had perceived to be a loving gift, I had instead found every pair of my boxers chopped to bits.

The crazy bitch.

I was mad about her and she was mad about me. If ever there was a girl who could handle dating a mentally unstable ex-drug addict, it was Shayla. She acted like everything was made from candy and marshmallows most of the time, but she also knew how to tell a head in the mafia to get fucked when necessary... even while a gun was pressed to her throat.

Her smile had a melody behind it. The song played every time she looked at me. It was hard to describe the taste of water, but it was even more difficult to explain the love I had for her. It wasn't just what I felt in her presence. It was the way I had never felt it with anyone before her. When I woke up in the morning, she was the first thing I saw. When I went to bed, the same. I breathed in her essence every day. I felt her existence beneath my skin.

"I'm so in love with you," I whispered against her throat, meaning every letter I dropped. She pushed against my chest so she could meet my eyes, smiling when she realized I wasn't shitfaced on Bourbon.

SKYLA MURPHY

"Do you mean it?"

"Why are you questioning me?"

"It seems too good to be true."

It was sad to see that her soul was so wounded, she couldn't accept good things when they progressed her way. It was because I knew the same feeling that I loved her so aggressively. Her arrival had been difficult to accept. She had shaken up everything I'd thought I knew, but she was one asteroid I didn't mind having my world struck by.

"Doubt thou that the stars are fire; doubt that the sun doth move; doubt truth to be a liar; but never doubt that I love." I picked up her hand to kiss it. "I've loved you since the moment I met you. I will love you until I take my dying breath too. Forever and always, I will only want you."

"How can you be so certain?"

I tried to think of the best way to explain my feelings for her, but it was difficult when her essence was unlike anything I'd ever experienced before

"Because every minute I'm around you, I feel like I'm choking. There's a constant pressure inside of me; a contentment I've never felt before. Even though the sun would still shine if you weren't here, I wouldn't feel it on my skin. My food tastes better when you're picking off my plate like a vulture. Movies are more interesting when you won't shut up through them. A song sounds better if I'm singing it with the intention of making you blush. A morning surf is always more fun with you by my side. I always feel better about my haircuts when you notice them…"

"Oh, did you get a haircut?"

"Really, blondie?" I frowned. "I got it done this morning just for you. I even got a shave too. I felt like I was beginning to look like Russ."

"I noticed there was something different about you," she smiled, running her thumb down my clean cheek. "But once you said you were in love with me, next to those three words, your haircut didn't matter."

38
THE HAND THAT FEEDS

HUNTER GARCIEZ

Thursday. 6:30 P.M.

A S I MADE MY WAY down the stairwell and back to the main floor, Diego set his afternoon coffee aside. He stood from the living room couch, greeting me with a casted leg. Doing so had become his routine, displeasing me more every time he made the effort. "Hey, Caz—"

"Go die in a ditch," I silenced him. "I thought your condo deal went through today? Why are you still lingering around my house? I told your daughter you had one week to get out of my face. You're on day seven right now."

He took my words like a man, shoulders squared, but he clearly didn't understand the meaning behind them. This became apparent when his mouth tilted to say, "I'll be gone by nightfall. I just thought you might want to—"

"You know what I want?" I whipped around to glare at him, showing him just how much I hated that he was still alive. "I want you to quit trying to chitchat with me like we go way back and in good spirits. There's nothing you can do to lessen my resentment. I will always hate you, so get the fuck out of my house. If you're still here when I get back, I'll break every other bone in your body; the ones I haven't managed to already."

"I'll be gone," he reassured me, a bleak expression on his face. "But for the record, I will never run from you. If the day comes that you decide to pull the trigger, I will take the bullet without refusal. I have told you before, I deserve any pain you force upon me. What I did to your family was wrong. You don't know how much I regret it. I have plans to make it up to you. When that time arrives, know that I have the best intentions."

Images flashed through my mind; images of my hands around Diego's throat; images of watching his blood drain; images of a knife inching into his esophagus; images of my departed parents; images of Tessa's face crying out for our dead mother; images of the blazing fire.

"You're alive because I love your daughter, Diego. I'm keeping myself under control for her, but you're a fool if you think we'll ever grab a drink and hash out our problems," I purposely belittled him. "When I look at you, all I can imagine is inching a knife across your throat. You know the position I'm stuck in because of Shayla, but don't become too cozy with the illusion of safety. I'm a ticking time bomb. I always snap eventually."

Rather than punching Diego in the head, which was what I really wanted to do, I shot him a flip of the bird as I exited through the front door of *my* house.

Sure, I had cracked six of the man's ribs. I had crushed his nose in three places, and his knee injury had been the worst of it all, but he was lucky to still be breathing. He was lucky I had fallen for his daughter. He was lucky I couldn't bring myself to take away the only family she had left.

Tessa would be at band practice until seven, leaving me with some extra time to kill. Since Shayla was itching to put our new barbeque through a trial run, I was off to purchase ten pounds of perfectly good steak for her to create a charcoaled massacre of. I knew it would be in Tessa and I's best interest to grab a burger while we were out. Feeding us anything appetizing wasn't in Shayla's nature, but I didn't care. Even if she was an awful chef, I loved her with everything I had.

Russ was right…

Love makes people do crazy shit.

While I trotted down the front walkway, reminding myself of why murder wasn't the appropriate response when it came to Diego, my pocket began to vibrate. I pulled out my phone and found my best friend's picture lighting up the screen. It was slightly refreshing to see Russ' face, even if it was covered in mangy fur.

"Delaney," I greeted him, accepting his facetime request. "Have you gotten uglier since the last time I saw you?"

"My ticket is officially booked, bitch!" Russ laughed hysterically. Since the guy made everything funny via facial expression, I couldn't help but laugh too. "Thanks for buying it. It's been twelve weeks since anyone's insulted my beard or dreadlocks. California just doesn't feel like home without you."

"After you move down to Hawaii, I'll throw a handful of insults at you to make up for lost time," I promised. "When you coming?"

"In a week," he answered, rifling a pepperoni stick into his mouth like a slob. "Is your girlfriend prepared to meet me?"

A memory of Russ jumping from his parent's roof into their pool clanged through my mind. Since he couldn't judge distance properly, the incident had ended with his blood on deck. Thirty stitches had gone through the flesh encasing his skull. I could swear he'd received a little brain damage too.

"She'll like you," I lied.

I revved Shayla's Jeep to life. I had removed the doors from the vehicle for her, but I was the one who drove it most. I had my own diesel truck sitting in the garage, but I rarely sat behind the wheel of it. Shayla liked my truck better, and since she looked hot as sin driving it, I'd somehow grown accustomed to cruising around in a purple vehicle instead.

"You're still driving *Barney*?" Russ chuckled, nicknaming the Jeep. "I bet Shayla just loves making you bomb around in that thing. It tells other women that you're already shackled and to back the fuck off. Devil pussy has you right whipped. I can't wait to meet the girl who's turned your gay balls straight."

"Go to hell," I muttered.

"Not before I come to Hawaii."

"Send me a text with your flight info." I set my phone into the cup holder so Russ could still see me, paying little attention to his face as I reversed from the driveway. "A beard like yours is bound to get attention. Be sure to head through airport security extra early. You have '*anal cavity search*' stamped across your forehead."

"How long does a strip search take?" Russ wondered, seeming to have already accepted his fate. "Will I miss my flight if they decide to ribbon me?"

"I think they'll just delay it, but the entire plane will be terrified of you. Babies will be crying. Grandmas will be gossiping about how you're the radical who just got rubber gloved by security. Nothing about it will be easy. Maybe you should just shave off your beard?"

"I'll take the rubber glove over shaving off eight inches of pure perfection, Garciez." I watched him stroke his fur as I approached a red light. "Two men are walking up behind you right now. Are you stopped?"

I turned to see what Russ was talking about. As a man in a black suit entered my vision, and then another on the opposite side of the Jeep, I knew things were about to get ugly.

"Cazador Garciez?" One of the suits asked, a pair of dark shades covering his eyes. There seemed to be some type of protective barrier over the lenses working to block me out. "You're a hard man to track down." As he backed up to steal a look at the purple paintjob surrounding me, a smirk raised his upper lip. "I see the blonde has you eating from the palm of her hand."

"*No hablo inglés. Mi nombre es Michael*," I claimed my name was Michael, and I didn't understand the English language. I knew it was ultimately pointless, but it was a time-killer nonetheless. Pointing at my mind like I was dumb, I claimed, "*No comprende.*"

"Shut up, ése," the other suit growled.

Lacking any sense of humor, he lifted the hem of his black jacket to show the gun he had tucked in the waistline of his slacks; a gold-plated pistol with the syndicate's logo engraved along the frame. This announced they weren't cops, but I would have almost preferred the Feds over the mafia.

"Where's your girl, Garciez?"

"Which girl's that?"

"The one who shot our brother."

I took a good look at the men. Each of them resembled Grimsaw, but the two before me looked like identical twins. Although they were a few years younger than Grimsaw, their suits warned me they were equally trained in the art of killing.

It didn't make sense for them to have found me. Every move I had made after landing in Hawaii had been to conceal our location. None of our real names were placed on anything; not even on the house title. Our computer didn't have an IP address. Our cellphone wasn't attached to a legitimate phone number or carrier. I was good at what I did, which meant someone had ratted me out.

I should have known better.

"How long have you two known Diego?" I asked the suit on my left; the one with the gun. "He spat out his own daughter's location just to have me hunted down?"

"The Barbie ain't really his kid."

"You don't say," I gave a fake gasp, shifting the Jeep into park to get comfortable. "Did you figure that out by noticing she's white?"

"You're a real piece of work," Lefty grew agitated, stepping closer to the vehicle to intimidate me. "When our brother rises again, he won't be pleased with any of you. You dove into some risky waters by letting your bitch kill him. It won't be easy to settle Grimmie down."

"Listen to you," I laughed at the goof. "Your threat game needs a boost. Your older brother was a guy who knew how to make me flinch. Grimsaw was drastic and vulgar. You… you're nothing more than a puppy looking to get his ear scratched."

In a flash, Lefty lunged into the door-less vehicle and coiled his hand around my throat. Without taking a blink, I uncurled his fingertips just as fast. I didn't stop there either. I curled his pointer finger back as far as it could possibly go, and then a little more for good clarity, until I finally heard the snap of bone.

"That's what a real threat sounds like," I smiled like a psychopath, pushing him out of the Jeep and into traffic. Luckily for him, the street wasn't all that occupied. "I dare you to fuck with me again. I have tons of pent up aggression that I've been just dying to release."

"I'm Alexandro," Righty introduced himself, chuckling as his brother stared at his busted finger in shock. I became puzzled when neither of them drew out their weapons, because it meant they had no intentions on using them. Limits meant nothing to me if they didn't truly exist.

I pointed to his bloody brother. "Who's that fuckup?"

"The knob with the broken hand is my twin, Bruno. I told him not to mess with you, but he doesn't listen very well." Alexandro climbed into the Jeep and shouted at his brother, "Go back to the SUV where it's parked! You're a goddamn embarrassment, *hermano!*"

"Fuck that!" Bruno climbed into the backseat of the Jeep at his own discretion. I glared at him through the rearview mirror, to which he replied with, "Relax. I've learned my lesson… for the moment."

"I thought the name Grimsaw was bad, but Bruno is even worse." I put *Barney* back into drive and hauled us out of traffic. After settling into a nearby stall, I added, "Alexandro is the only name that shows your mother might not have resented you all straight from birth."

"Our mother was a crack whore," Bruno clipped back. "Each of us brothers were bred to become mafia men. She didn't love our father. He raped and forced her to deliver us. So yes, she did resent us. Unlike your privileged ass, we weren't raised with love. We were raised with sticks and branding irons instead. You think you've had it bad? You don't fucking know bad. Wait until you meet our father. What you and that little white bitch did was unforgivable."

"I'm rather fond of that little white bitch," I shot daggers at Bruno. "If you talk ill about her again, I'll break your nose into eighteen pieces to go along with your finger."

"You are some cocky," Alexandro noted. His accent was identical to Grimsaw's, but he employed better grammar. "We will not hurt your little Juliet. If you aid us, we will do the opposite instead."

"Elaborate," I invited.

"For starters, I will wipe your recent media fame under the rug with a smooth transition. I will reconcile the damage that is currently troubling your rap sheets. I will send one of my men to jail for the death of Grimsaw. I will line it up so that you, your girl, and your sister, will all come out with clean slates in the eyes of the law. Many men owe me debt. You know I can make this happen. What I say I will do, I do."

"What do you want from me?"

"Resurrect Grimsaw."

"I'll hop right on that," I said sarcastically, catching sight of Russ' disbelieving face as he kept himself linked to my phone. "You want me to help you resuscitate a man who is going to want to torture me when he rises?"

"Let us worry about Grimmie."

"*Grimmie* was a piece of shit during his first life," I reminded them. "He sold girls to the sex trade. I doubt he would act any better if given a round two."

"*Si*, I know how my brother was," Alexandro agreed, grinning. "He acted so drastically, you know? Everything always had to be some sort of big action scene with him. He lived for the blood and the sound effects. I never understood it myself. If you want to kill someone, kill them. It's as simple as that. He always prolonged things with torment. Me, much like your girlfriend, I'm a *one-shot-one-kill* type of soul. I had a good laugh when my monkeys brought Grimsaw's body in. Your little lady hit him dead center of the forehead. You might consider making her a mafia bride. She has the shot of a natural born killer."

"She's not involved."

"Fine, but the operation has already begun," Alexandro persevered. "Grimsaw's revival is in full sway. There are many others too, but their skeletal structures haven't been progressing the way our scientists would like. That's where you come in. We need you to finetune the codes necessary to reboot their immune systems."

"I'm human; not God. What you're suggesting isn't within my range of ability. I can cure disease. I can't fix death," I shook my head at the twins. "Secondly, even if I did believe reviving the dead was conceivable, why would I help you bring back a man I was happy to see die? You guys didn't think this game plan through, did you?"

"We got something you want."

"And what's that, Bruno?"

"Grimsaw would use your girl against you, but we have more extensive tactics," Alexandro answered, reaching into the front pocket of his black slacks.

Goosebumps began to climb up my neck as he passed a photograph my way; a photograph of my father's body in a cube full of fluid; a photograph of my father with wires connected to his chest and ankles; a photograph of my father looking years younger than he had upon dying; a photograph where a bullet hole didn't exist in his forehead.

I froze. "What the fuck is this?"

"In any good partnership, both parties must be left appeased. If you find a way to cure our brother of death, Emiliano will live to see another day too. Your father's revival has been ongoing for thirty-eight months. We have managed to de-age him by fifteen years. For every year a deceased body spends in a watercell, five years are reversed from their physical form. Brain activity suggests your dad can hear us, but he is unable to express it physically. Once *you* find a way to strengthen his systems, that will change."

As I stared at the picture of my dad, my blood began to drain to my toes. I told myself that none of this could be real. I told myself they were related to Grimsaw, making them insane by DNA, but it didn't feel like they were pulling my chain.

"If you have my dad's body, who did I bury alongside my mom?" I tried to sift through their words, remaining skeptical. "Do you have her too?"

"Unfortunately, we were unable to do anything for your mother. Her burns were too severe. The skin grafting would have been too complex. I give my apologies. For standing beside your father through his dedication to our brotherhood, I have no doubts she was a good woman. As for the man you buried, after you decided you didn't want an open casket ceremony, it was easy to throw a John Doe in your father's coffin. We paid the mortician at the funeral parlor to swap out the bodies."

In one instant, everything I knew shattered. Shards of guilt sliced through my organs, leaving behind too many paralyzing cuts to count. The numbness came back with a stab, proving the mafia would always own me.

"If you join us, we will pay you twenty million," Bruno bargained from behind. "If you have anyone on your hitlist, including a man named Diego Alvaro, I will personally take care of it by sunrise. Even though you just broke my finger, you can be sure the task will be followed through appropriately."

"Sweeten the candy," I negotiated.

"I will bring a stop to Grimsaw's sex-trafficking acts," Alexandro offered, as if it would be no sweat to shut down such a large operation. "I don't gain pleasure from that area of business either. I much prefer supplying America with Ak47s and cocaine, but Grimsaw was his own person. Who was I to stop him? But to ease your troubled mind, I will devise a plan to free the girls. Their memories will need to be wiped clean upon release. I'm sure you can understand why."

"You're getting warmer," I smiled, though I didn't know what the crackpot was talking about. He acted like removing memories was as simple as embedding Trojan viruses into the government's electronic infrastructure.

"I will instruct my best men to protect your sister, your Barbie, and anyone else you consider worthy. I will have constant 24-hour watch on them in a way that does not impinge upon their privacy."

I considered the position I was in. Even though I couldn't pull off what they were suggesting, I knew I wouldn't be able to say no to their demands. They would kill me if I didn't agree to try, and I wasn't even sure I wanted to turn down their offer. I didn't believe their story about reviving the dead, but if there was a possibility I could see my dad again, why wouldn't I want that? When I asked myself this question, I had no good reply.

If by some rarity what the brothers were saying was true, I owed my dad the fighting chance. Had it not been for me and Diego's briefcase, he wouldn't have died to begin with. It wasn't macho to admit, but I missed him on the constant. To see him again...

I would do anything.

As I stole another look at my dad's printed face in silence, one of Grimsaw's favorite threats crept into my head; so loudly, it was like the ghost of him was seated next to me.

Never fuck with me, G.

I am the hand that feeds you.

"List your demands," I requested.

"You will move in with our family at the Santiago residence on the outskirts of L.A. Since you will no longer be considered a fugitive, you are welcome to come home to California."

"I like Hawaii," I said.

"*Shayla* likes Hawaii," Bruno corrected me, taking a pinch at my final nerve. I had known the guy for under a half hour, but I already wanted to cut out his voice box.

"If that is the issue, allow her to continue residing here," Alexandro shrugged his suited shoulders, insinuating something I didn't particularly care for. "If you ask me, she would be better off without you. I know you won't leave your sister, but your girlfriend is unnecessary baggage. Once I show you the things I have devised, you will never be the same again. Save the blonde the heartache."

"I can't leave her," I disagreed.

"I am turning you into a made man. After that, all you will bring her are tears and sorrow. You and I are the next generation of genius, Garciez…" Alexandro held out his hands, as if his fingertips could hack as well as mine. "Grimsaw had his threats, but I will literally make hell rise. Every mafia member our family has been sad to see die will live to fight for us again. This is the new world order. My Mexican army will take over every other Latino gang that thinks they know anything about *my* streets. We will all combine into an immortal empire. After that, the Irish, the Asians, the Triads, the Aryans, the Guerrillas, the bodies who wear red, and the bodies who wear blue… they will all go down. Like magic, I will make them vanish. I will place a 13:13 on everyone I destroy, because I've had enough of the bullshit in this world. It's time for everyone to experience what *Méjico* is made of."

"What are my options?"

"Leave the girl or make her your wife," Alexandro smiled at me. "You know how the mafia works. Should you choose to marry her, the syndicate's logo will be placed on her body. She will take cooking classes and learn how to become a woman of the faction. I know you like that burger shack on the corner of your street for a reason…" Chills crept up my spine as I realized they had been following me. "Something tells me your girl can't cook very well. While you work for us, she will help the other wives around the homestead. There is supper waiting on the table for us men when we get home, and lingerie is encouraged. We can sleep with whoever we want, but our women are not free to do the same. No brother shall touch another brother's wife. However, if you bring Shayla around us without marrying her first, she will be considered fair game."

"You two are so far gone," I chuckled, finding the brothers to be more deranged by the second. "If you think my missus will strap on some rubber gloves and clean a toilet just because I tell her to, you don't know her at all. You guys don't have wives. What you have are a set of trophy mannequins. They are slaves who have given their consent because they have an addiction to owning expensive things."

"Indeed," Alexandro acknowledged. "But they do not mind the routine. They let us fuck them, so we let them live in a mansion and buy them fancy designer clothes. My wife spent thirty grand on shoes last week. I do not believe she is complaining."

"As long as they never question our mafia business, we let them live a free life," Bruno chirped in. "This isn't the 1800s. They are welcome to come and go as they please. They have friends and hobbies. They do yoga and normal shit like that. We don't lock them in a cellar and beat them, but they would die if they ever spoke ill of us behind our backs."

"I'm not doing that to the girl I love," I shook my head with a closed mind. "I don't want my wife to only suck my dick because it's a mafia rule. That logic is so degrading. You can say this isn't the 1800s, but your values are vined into a fucking ball. I understand you two were raised improperly, but seriously…?"

"You sound like a feminist," Bruno snickered in the backseat, forgetting about his splintered finger for the time being. "What this really comes down to is your own personal fear, Garciez."

I felt my eyes flicker. "My fear of what?"

"Fear that Shayla wouldn't have you, even if you were willing to corrupt her. You're a shark out of water when it comes to her. You're like shit. She's the flush that pushes you down the drain."

The sound in my head was a replica of a boom. If I were to take a stab at what the noise was, I would say it was my sense of reason bursting into flame with Bruno's last strike of the match.

I whipped around in a flash, lunging over the backseat like it didn't even exist. I fed Bruno the best shot I could to the face. His neck did a rebound against one of the rear headrests, hopefully gyrating some sense into the idiot too.

"You're the stupid brother, aren't you?" I snarled at him, slapping him to follow for good measure. "Quit trying to talk to me like I'm beneath you. If I was, you wouldn't be attempting to bribe me onto your team."

"He's right, Bruno," Alexandro confirmed it for me, although it had already been obvious. He removed his blacked-out sunglasses, but no numbers scrolled out to me as he exposed his brown eyes. "Consider me the smart one."

"Alex told you we could wipe memories," Bruno grinned, showing that his teeth were glazed with red. I fell back into my own seat as the dumb twin removed his broken shades next. Confusingly, his eyes were just as empty as Alexandro's.

"So…" I took my time considering what their vacant eyes could mean, knowing my next question would lead me into dangerous territory. "If you managed to wipe your own minds to protect your codes from me, you could erase me from Shayla's memory too?"

"Now you're getting it," Bruno nodded, patting me on the back with the one good hand he had. "That's exactly what we're saying. We can erase her from yours too. Why should you be a sucker for punishment while she carries out a happy life?"

"How old are you, Bruno?"

"Twenty-five."

"Have you ever been in love?" I asked, but I already knew what his answer was going to be. "I'm not talking about the trophy wife you have sucking your dick at night. I'm talking about real love."

He didn't hesitate before replying, "Never."

"Then shut the fuck up."

"I have a feeling this bickering will be a constant occurrence between the two of you?" Alexandro guessed, taking a glance at the blood dripping from his brother's nose. He shook his head as he noticed how rapidly the swelling was settling in. "Your nose is going to look like Grimsaw's in no time, Bruno."

"It's not my fault Garciez can't handle the truth. The only reason he's so wound up is because he knows what I'm saying is true. You've seen her too, Alex. For being a bleach-skin, his girlfriend is a looker. I don't understand the whole multicultural thing. Why taint good Mexican blood? But I get why this is a hard decision for him to make. I wouldn't mind abusing his girlfriend's mouth either."

"Let it fade, Garciez," Alexandro growled at me, sensing I was seconds away from punching Bruno again. "Don't forget the initiations that lay ahead of you. Bruno will have his fun with you yet. When the syndicate turns you black and blue as punishment for betrayal, do you really want Juliet to see your face? It will be her fault that it is sideways. I advise you to consider your options before dragging her into this."

I knew Alexandro was right. I knew how my face would look in a week's time; the same way it had looked three months ago after Grimsaw's men had taken their boots and bats to me. There was a price to infidelity. The Santiago family wasn't going to kill me, but they would ensure I hurt for weeks. I would be locked in a dark room for anyone to torture. Tools would be provided but not necessitated. Most members with a grudge would choose to use their fists. It was more personal that way; rawer.

And it seemed odd that I would willingly sign myself up for such exploitation, but the rewards were greater than the risks of brain damage. I knew abuse well, but Shayla wouldn't be able to handle taking the beating I could. To protect her, I knew what was headed my way.

"It is not you who we are angry with, but we assume you would rather take the penalties than have your Juliet do the same?"

Alexandro revealed a pack of cigarettes from his inside suit pocket. He tucked a stick between his lips, lighting it to relieve his stresses. I watched him steal a drag, finding something so rejuvenating about the way he was causing himself a premature death.

Maybe it was because I knew I could cure myself of whatever disease a cigarette could attempt to warp my health with. Maybe it was because the realization that life sucked was hastily cuddling back into my mind. Whatever the cause, before I knew what I was doing, I had a stick in my mouth too.

As I took my first taste of cancer in months, the toxins felt heavenly. Pure satisfaction flooded through my bloodstream. For a second, I forgot why I had quit the habit at all.

"Her sins will be taken out on you," Alexandro stated, as if I wasn't keeping up with his implications. I had been, but I didn't see a point in dwelling on something that was already carved into stone. "Many of us resent her actions, including myself and Bruno."

"I will get the shit kicked out of me for what she did to Grimsaw," I said aloud, just so they knew I was following. "But nobody touches Shayla."

"Agreed," Alexandro approved my demand. "As the man who has chosen to protect the lioness, you must accept the consequences that pertain to owning a wild animal. Very rare is it that we offer someone of Caucasian skin to join our clan, even through marriage, but we are extending the proposal to her. You should consider our handouts to be above generous. If she wasn't your girl, she would be headless already. You know this, Garciez."

I exhaled a patch of smoky O's, watching in a daze as they drifted upward toward paradise. The list would be exhaustively long for those who had a personal vendetta against Shayla. Members would line up around the block to beat and brand her for killing Grim-saw. They would treat her like the trash they thought she was. Only, it wouldn't be her taking the abuse. It would be me.

I sent my fist through the navigational system in the Jeep, break-ing my sanity with a loud snap of cheap plastic and emotion. As a piece of the material stayed stuck in my center knuckle, the phys-ical pain was repairable and of little concern to me. Punishment was not what scared me. I would smile while taking every knock-out for Shayla. I would laugh as the chains met my back. I would request to be assaulted again, just to be certain their hate was taken out on my frame and not on hers.

But it was blistering to know that Shayla was better off without me. If I chose to leave her behind, she would be free with a clean record. She wouldn't have to worry about having her life infil-trated by men in black suits; not of the mafia variety, nor of the Federal.

This was her way out.

The only one she would ever receive.

If I brought her back to California alongside the Santiago twins, I would be consenting for her existence to fall into the mafia's hands forever. I would be pressuring her into marrying me at the age of eighteen, all before we'd even had sex. I was three years older than her. I had spent time fucking other women before her. I knew she was the one for me without question, but I doubted Shayla could say the same.

If I married her, I would be forced to brand her with the syn-dicate's logo. The brothers would make me do it myself. It was a mafia tradition, a pledge of loyalty between man and wife, but I wouldn't be capable of completing the task. I could never bring myself to burn a symbol into her perfect skin. Once she was trade-marked with a 13:13, there would be no departure for her. The situation I currently sat in was proof of that. If I loved her like I knew I did, the best thing I could do was disappear.

"I have one more gift for you," Alexandro presented, smiling with a shadiness that told me his next proposition was going to be the best of all. "I tracked down the guy who came close to raping your Juliet on the night of her kidnapping. I have yet to do anything to him. I figured you should decide how his future plays out... how does that worded candy taste?"

As my new leader dangled his flavor in front of me, I abruptly disconnected my phone call with Russ. Rather than issuing a goodbye his way, I thought of the many ways to torture a soul instead.

Vile images flew through my mind like a swarm of bees. I stirred silently, relishing in the thought of destroying a rapist's life. I could just imagine the things I would do to the piece of shit who had thought of touching Shayla three months ago. Not only was the class act on my hitlist, Alexandro was offering reprisal with ease. I needed to accept their contributions; not only for my dad, but for Shayla too.

"Well played, Alex," I laughed, suckered straight into hell by his last donation. I turned toward the Santiago brother I was growing to like most and said, "Tastes like a jawbreaker to me."

THANKS FOR READING

HELL WILL RISE

Book 1
The Bloodthirst Mafia Series

IF YOU ENJOYED THIS NOVEL, please consider leaving an
honest review on relative platforms like Amazon or Goodreads.
The best way to love an author is to leave a review.

TOASTS & DEDICATIONS

FOR SUPPORTING ME THROUGH EVERYTHING I do, the trails we've stumbled down, the mountains we've explored, the roadsides we've slept at, and for the many times you've watched me fall apart; you are the sun to my dark (Little Foot). For saving me from the sting of a bee, the mornings of drifting our shit-bagged cars, the days of hitchhikers, fallen birthday cakes, 8-hour phone calls, and for the crazy nights like Sylvan Lake; I'm glad your mom picked our rhubarb (Ash.V).

For the zombies we've hunted, the bushes we've whacked, the roadies we've taken, the vehicles you've resurrected, and because you were willing to paint my face on the side of your daily driver; I was meant to know you (Josh.B). For falling in love on a trip that gave me my first taste of the Rocky Mountains, for having faith in me, and for being my all-time favorite Newfoundlander; thank you for moving out west (Tash.C).

For taking my mind off things, winning me teddy bears & lighting off sparklers on some brutal nights, and for the times we've watched the sun come up on the lake & dunes; you've become one of my very bests (Mattie.T). For suffering through a mangled first draft, for thinking you were gangster while I was trying to be goth, and for never showing fear in being who you are; you have shaped me more than you know (Ash.L). For blessing me with the ability to call you my blood, providing me with a solid foundation, and for allowing me to fall comfortably; there are no words (Mom & Dad).

To my editors/formatters/designers/beta readers; I appreciate you all. A big shout out to Amy Podejko & Rebecca Swanson for suffering through my distaste of the comma. And to those who have placed this book on their shelves, those who've supported me from the very beginning, and to those who've ever gave a damn about me; this one's for you babes.

Xo,

Skyla

ABOUT THE AUTHOR

SKYLA MURPHY IS A HIGHLAND junkie from West Coast, Canada. When she's not searching the Rocky Mountains for Sasquatch, she can be found researching every other conspiracy theory known to mankind. Her Yorkshire Terrier is usually clung to her side, but he doesn't buy into her philosophies much. Therefore, she writes about them instead.

Want to stalk her?
It's seriously easy.

www.skylamurphy.com
www.twitter.com/skyla_murphy
www.instagram.com/skyla_murphy
www.facebook.com/skylamurphyauthor
www.goodreads.com/skyla_murphy

www.ingramcontent.com/pod-product-compliance
Lightning Source LLC
Chambersburg PA
CBHW072225190626
46809CB00017B/662